Reason
Number
4

Gregory S. Stuyvesant

ISBN:1545007160
ISBN-13:978-1545007167

DEDICATION

This book has been written because of a statement that I made to my daughter Courtney on Spring Break in 2008. Courtney had given me a book to read, and as she handed it to me she said, "Dad, you will really like this."

It was a murder mystery book, and to be honest, I have no idea what the title was or who authored it. I have never been much of a reader, but facing a week of lounging by a pool, I decided to take her up on it. After reading it, I gave the book back to her. When she asked me what I thought of it, I ignorantly commented,

"I could write a better book than that." I had said it in a non-committing tone, but Courtney took that statement to heart, and for the next seven years, whenever I said I needed to do something or get anything done it was always:

"I know, Dad. Right after you write your book."

Countless times I listened to her rub my statement in my face; albeit, she always said it with a big smile. September 18, 2015 changed everything in my family's life when, at twenty-four years old, after being married for only two years and with a beautiful six-month-old baby, Courtney went to be with her Lord. She died unexpectedly from a minor heart condition that is so rarely fatal it is hardly talked about. Since that day, that statement I made has taken a different priority in my life. Though I really didn't believe in my ability to write a "better" book than the one book Courtney and I shared, I did resolve to write one and to finish it. I'm incredibly saddened that Courtney isn't here to read it, but I am thankful for the drive she gave me to finish it. No matter what anyone thinks of my writing, or if no one ever reads it, I know I completed this book, sometimes writing with tears in my eyes as I thought about my motivation, and I take solace in that. Maybe someday I can tell her about it.

Thank you, Courtney Lynn. I love you.

For anyone who has ever made an overwhelming commitment.

1

Friday April 5, 2013. Marcus Deters knew where he was. He could see the oxygen tanks, a heart monitor, some IV equipment, medical supplies, first aid kits, and two EMTs, one of whom was holding a mask to Marcus's face. He could also hear the awful sound of sirens blaring. He was in an ambulance, but he didn't know why. He could see it was night. The street lights were flashing by while the ambulance sped its way through the downtown streets of some unknown city. His mind was racing. What had happened?! Where was Sheila?! Where were the boys?!

He tried to speak and raise his hand but failed. He heard one of the men say, "It's ok, relax. You're going to be fine."

He knew it was not ok and he was not fine! Something was clearly very wrong. He heard someone in the ambulance talking on a radio. "Patient has lacerations on his face and neck, severe trauma to his torso and legs. He has third degree burns to his shoulder and back. He has lost a lot of blood. ETA 3:45 a.m."

Darkness.

2

Friday, April 1, 2016. Having driven this route for eight straight years before the crash, Marcus knew this stretch of highway well. By year four, he needed no map or directions as he knew every junction, merge, and interchange all the way from Grand Rapids, Michigan to Treasure Island, Florida. He and Sheila had started going to Florida on Spring Break when Dustin was six years old and Dillon was four.

They had connected with the parents of two of Dustin's classmates, John and Sandy Wainwright and Nick and Heather Thomas, and often vacationed with them. Marcus and John had known each other a little before going on the trips as John was also an attorney and their paths had crossed a couple of times. Of course, the kids had so much fun, it was quickly determined that this was to be an every-year event.

The trip had become a routine as well known to his family as a Sunday drive to Marcus's parents' home. The three families would meet at 54th Street Meijer, just south of town, so they could form a convoy and follow each other. They always took the same route, always stopping at the same Chick-fil-A along US 31. Sheila loved the place—sure it's good, but every year? To him it didn't matter where they ate as long as it didn't take too long. Chick-fil-A was quick enough, and the kids all loved it. It was a novelty to them as there weren't any in West Michigan. So Chick-fil-A it was.

Every year they seemed to use the same exits for gas stations and restaurants; they even tried—and failed—to schedule the same rest areas along the way. The drive could be made in nineteen to twenty hours alone, but in the vacation convoy, it took a few more; the seven kids always seemed to have to use the bathroom at different times. The families would drive all Friday night and end up at the condo just after their 1:00 p.m. check in time.

Some people would hate travelling this way, but Marcus loved it—

so much bonding time with the family. With Sheila working long hours at the hospital and with him working at the firm sixty hours a week, family time was limited. If you want to learn what's going on in your kids' lives, drive twenty-plus hours in a car with them. Marcus learned more about his boys during the one week of Spring Break than at any other time of the year—how they acted with their friends, with other parents, and even with each other. As routine and tiring as the drive was, he wouldn't have changed it for anything.

Now driving this route, three years after the crash, Marcus was entering Indiana and it still felt familiar. He knew this area well and could remember all the trips they had taken on these highways so many times, except for the last one.

He remembered leaving Meijer three years ago, but that was as much as he could recall of that last drive. He was frustrated by the knowledge that pieces of space and time were just missing from his memory. He could remember everything in his life in full detail before the crash, but his mind chose to block out the horrific details of that night and the trip leading up to it.

Dr. Bryant told him that it was normal for someone who suffered a traumatic event like he had to have their memory affected, even when there were no severe injuries to the head. She had also said that the subconscious mind can choose not to remember some things and that someday he may recover all his lost memories. Knowing it was normal, however, didn't stop it from being infuriating.

Sheila's phone had somehow survived the crash and ensuing fire so he had seen the dozens of pictures she had taken of the trip up to that point, but without the memories to match, he felt as if he was looking at someone else.

So here he was, three years after the crash. He'd left the store parking lot as they had so many times before and was driving the same route they'd always taken in a desperate attempt to jar some memories of that fateful night loose. He knew Dr. Bryant would frown upon it and Allison would probably totally freak out, but it was something he felt compelled to do. He had told his parents he was leaving for a day, but since he couldn't bring himself to tell them where he was really going, he'd lied.

"I'm going up to the cottage for the night to get away," he'd told them.

He knew even that was going to be hard for them to believe since he hadn't been up there since the crash. They knew there were too many memories there, still too painful for him to endure. But they'd just looked at him, as they always do now, with a sympathetic but worried look, and told him to be careful.

All he knew about the 2013 trip was what had been told to him by the other two families they'd been travelling with. It had all been normal road trip stuff, with nothing out of the ordinary, until the crash. And since his family had been driving last in the convoy, the others actually hadn't seen it happen. While the details of that day had been told to him so many times, it never stopped feeling like a dream. Driving now, he mulled over how different his life was, how different he was as a person. A sign for Chick-fil-A—next exit—caught his eye. Marcus turned on his right blinker and left the highway, and, almost simultaneously, began to cry.

3

"What do you mean he's gone?" Allison asked her mom, trying to stay calm. "Where did he go? If this is an April Fool's Day joke, it isn't funny!"

Allison could hear her Mom sigh just slightly over the phone, and that made her even more nervous. "He went for a drive. He said he was going to Pentwater. He told me not to worry and that he would be home Monday."

"And you let him?" Allison asked, somewhat scolding, but she knew there was nothing Mom could have done to stop him. Marcus had been strong-willed and determined as long as she could recall, and if he wanted to leave, he would.

"Now Allie, you know better than that. Your brother has always done what he wants, and he is thirty-eight years old. How was I supposed to stop him?"

Allison sighed herself and replied, "I know, Mom. I'm sorry. I'm coming over. I'll be there in twenty minutes."

"Ok, Allie. See you soon."

Allison left her office, stopping at her assistant's desk on the way. "I'm heading out, Jessica. Have a great weekend. I'll see you Monday."

"Thanks. You, too." Jessica's words trailed off in Allison's wake as Allison had already moved several steps past her.

Allison was in a hurry and her mind was racing. Why was Marcus going to the cottage? He was going to be miserable up there all alone. Allison was getting frantic. Since the accident, she had been so worried that Marcus would do something drastic, and honestly, who could blame him? She knew the pain that she felt from the loss of her nephews and sister-in-law couldn't compare with what Marcus was going through. Dr. Bryant had said Marcus didn't have the traits of a suicidal person, but who ever really knows how someone will react, especially after someone goes through such a traumatic experience?

Allison was four years younger than Marcus. She had graduated salutatorian from high school, top ten in her class at Michigan State University, and then graduated from the University of Michigan's Law School, just like her brother. After law school, she was hired by Marcus's firm - Davis, Hayes, and Deters- as an attorney. It's now one of the most reputable law firms in the area. She has since made a name for herself in the law community as a promising up-and-comer in her own right.

Allison was always driven to be like her older brother. He was so smart and successful. In truth, he was more than smart—he was brilliant, a fact verified when he had made full partner at thirty-two years old, an extremely rare accomplishment in their field.

Allison had strived to measure up to Marcus in college. In fact, she'd put so much pressure on herself that she suffered from anxiety for years, occasionally even experiencing full-blown panic attacks. However, through counseling and her own determination, she had overcome the anxiety, and now she, too, was becoming very successful. Her plan had been to live and work in Grand Rapids for four or five years and then move to a bigger city, preferably Chicago. But that was before the accident changed everything.

Marcus hadn't stepped foot in the office since the accident, and there seemed to be no timetable for his return. The client whose case he had been working on before he left ended up settling, an unfortunate outcome as a win would have brought in millions for both the client and the firm. Now Marcus lived with Mom and Dad again, and, more often than not, Allison felt like the big sister rather than the little sister. And she wouldn't dream of leaving town.

Before the accident, Sheila, Dustin, and Dillon accompanied Marcus when he visited and helped out their parents. They even lived in the same city, ten minutes away from each other. Mom was so close to Marcus's boys. They were her only grandkids. Allison had not gotten married, though a couple of men had tried to tie her down. Mom always joked that she was too picky, and maybe that was true. Before the accident, she may have been too focused on her career to take relationships seriously, but now settling down with someone seemed altogether impossible. She was thirty-two years old, her family had lost three beloved members all at once, and her brother would never be the same. To find a partner in the midst of all that not only seemed challenging, it wasn't even something she remotely considered.

What she did want, most of all, was to be there for Marcus to ensure he got the medical and psychiatric help he needed and that he didn't harm himself or anyone else. Allison pulled into her mom's driveway and could see her peering through the front window. She waved on her way up the path and stepped inside.

4

The tears were flowing freely. It happened so often now, it rarely even fazed him. Marcus always kept a box of tissues near him wherever he went. Before the crash, he never cried, but now he cried every day. As his emotions shifted, the tears of sadness would turn to anger, and occasionally, the anger would turn to rage. While the tears had slowed a little in the last three years, the anger had not. Rather, it grew hotter and higher inside him—a rising flame he didn't know how to extinguish.

He'd been in and out of hospitals for the six months immediately following the accident. The first two months he was unable to move and so had had to stay in Atlanta, at Regency Hospital, until he could be transferred back home. He remembered very little of that time, again counting on what people had told him; with all the surgeries and medications, what he could recall on his own was mostly a blur. He knew he had suffered severe burns, multiple fractures in his legs, broken ribs, a punctured lung, internal bleeding, and the doctors had had to remove his spleen. After enduring those two months in Atlanta, he was finally stable enough to be transferred home to Grand Rapids' St. Mary's Hospital. There, it was an additional four months of recovery and rehabilitation. He suffered through hours upon hours of physical therapy, something that would have been challenging had he had any motivation to begin with, but was darn near impossible when he felt his life had lost all meaning and purpose.

He used to know who and what he was. He was a husband and a father, a hardworking attorney providing for his family, and he made them happy. They were all so happy.

Sitting in the Chick-fil-A parking lot, the same one he had gone to eight Spring Break vacations in a row, he felt anything but happy. He was scared to enter the building. Would it evoke any authentic memories?

Would he start to cry again? As he left his car and entered the restaurant, he felt as if every eye was upon him, believing they could tell that the last time he had been in this place, he'd had his last meal together with his family. Of course, that wasn't the case, but to him it felt like everywhere he went people knew what had happened to him.

As Marcus sat and ate his chicken sandwich, he looked around the restaurant. The place wasn't terribly busy but there were still plenty of customers enjoying their chicken and fries. For a minute a smile came to his face as he thought of Sheila and her fondness for this place. He quickly got up and left the restaurant as the tears welled up again.

Merging back onto the highway, his sadness was replaced with raw anger. He thought of Simon Daniels. Simon Daniels, the man that took away his family and turned his whole life upside down. Simon Daniels, the man that caused so much pain, who caused him to miss his family's burial service. Simon Daniels, the man who was only sentenced to three lousy years in a medium security prison with more activities than a day camp. Simon Daniels, the man who, after killing his family while drinking and driving, was back on the street, living a life. It was that man Marcus intended to see. Soon.

5

"So, he went to the cottage?" Allison asked her mom.

"Well, that's what he said." Her dad answered quickly, not giving her mom a chance to answer. There was the I'm-not-sure-I-believe-it-either tone to his voice. Allison glanced at her dad, reflecting the same worried expression.

Allison's dad, Brian Deters, was the typical middle class American. Every day for the past thirty-five years he got up and went to his job at the courthouse. He was a bailiff and, as such, sat through thousands of trials. Marcus had gotten an interest in law by visiting his dad at work and sitting in on a few of those trials. Though Allison had also visited the courtroom with her dad, her interest in law was more directly inspired by her admiration of her big brother.

Allison's mom, Marcia, had taught at the local elementary school for thirty years and had semi-retired at the age of fifty-four. Now she worked at the school two days a week as a special needs tutor.

"You didn't believe him?" Although Allison had asked her dad this question, she looked at her mom for an indication that she knew more than he did. Allison knew full well that Marcus had always more readily confided in his mother, so she was looking for any little hint that would substantiate her dad's doubt. Her mom looked down—and there it was.

So before her dad could reply, Allison broke in. "What is it, Mom? What do you know?"

Her mom finally met her stare before guiltily pointing toward the adjacent office. Allison made a beeline through the open French doors of the immaculate work space. She went straight to the desk and asked, "What is it? What's in here?"

Her parents followed closely behind. "Open up the laptop. Password's Sheila."

Allison opened Marcus's laptop, typed in the word Sheila, and up popped the screen saver – a beautiful picture of Marcus and his family. So as not to dwell on the sudden sadness this evoked in each of them, her dad quickly instructed that she open the internet.

Allison, so anxious now, hit the Google Chrome button and waited very impatiently the three seconds for it to open. "I assume I should go to history," she asked, looking at her mom. Her mom nodded but didn't say a word. Allison hit the history icon and, right away, her heart sank. The last ten or so line items were all about Simon Daniels: Simon Daniels' Trial, Simon Daniels' Parole, and, the one that really made her numb, Simon Daniels' last known address. She clicked on that last line and read aloud: *Simon J Daniels, 3217 Whiting Dr. Apt 2B, Marietta, Georgia.*

6

Marcus looked down at his phone as it buzzed on the seat next to him. He could see Allison's picture on the screen and contemplated between the red and green buttons that determined whether he would accept or decline the call. I will call her back, he thought. He really didn't want to talk to anyone right now; he didn't want to lie to Allie, and he knew that telling her the truth was probably not the best option either. She would not handle this well at all. He let the phone buzz until it stopped on its own and continued, south, toward Atlanta, where his previous trip had sadly ended.

The route he took today was not going to be the same as all the other ones before—he had a side trip to make. He was nervous. He was going to see Simon Daniels in person for the first time. He wanted to observe Simon in his everyday life and see what he was all about. Marcus felt he could not start to heal until he knew something more about the kid who'd irrevocably changed his life. What he did know about him was mainly what Allie had reluctantly told him and what he had found on the internet.

He was twenty-eight years old, divorced, had a four-year-old daughter, and worked in a distribution warehouse loading trucks. Allie had said that his parents had never come to any of the court hearings. He'd served eleven months of a three-year sentence. It had been his first DUI and he had been just barely over the legal limit.

Allison had shared with Marcus most of the court hearings' evidence, but there were no witnesses close enough to the accident to see what had actually happened.

The Wainwrights were ahead of them and John had said that his wife and kids were asleep. He hadn't seen anything until he heard the van's brakes lock up and the sound of metal scraping the concrete wall. The judge's decision was based almost solely on Simon's testimony and the police report.

The report indicated that Simon merged onto the highway while Marcus was in the right hand lane. Simon's pickup truck swiped the back of their van, causing them to spin out of control. The van careened across the shoulder and slammed into the barrier wall, almost immediately catching on fire. Marcus was the only one that could be pulled out. He had been knocked unconscious but came to for a moment in the ambulance. That was it.

Even though the evidence was such, Marcus couldn't bring himself to call it an accident; after all, Simon had clearly been drinking. He was over the legal limit and that contributed to the crash. It must have. The fact that Marcus couldn't recollect everything from that night was infuriating, and although he hoped seeing the crash site would spark something in his memory, his expectations were low. So far all the memories conjured up on today's drive were from the years prior to the tragedy.

Marcus looked around as he drove through Louisville. He always liked this stretch of highway with the bridge and the downtown scenery. The boys loved driving by the Louisville stadium, every year yelling, "There it is! There it is!"

Marcus glanced over at the stadium and tears filled his eyes. He quickly looked away and wiped them dry. It was starting to get dark now and he needed to concentrate on the road. He was anxious to get to the hotel. Nashville was just over two hours away, and the hotel he booked for the night was in Murfreesboro, Tennessee, another hour past that. He was starting to get tired and hungry. A hot meal and shower sounded good, but the phone call he knew he had to make did not.

7

Allison was on edge. She had about fifteen of the hour and twenty-minute drive to the cottage left. She was hoping Marcus was there and just didn't hear his phone. Marcus and Sheila had bought a cute two-bedroom cottage in the little beach town of Pentwater, Michigan. It was a five minute walk down to the Lake Michigan beach. Allison always loved visiting there. West Michigan beaches, in her opinion, were among the nicest beaches in the country. The sand was soft, and the water a beautiful greenish blue. The sunsets were spectacular, and the fresh water was a joy to swim in. The boys had always been on their bikes. They would bring their poles and go fishing in the channel, go to the state park and climb Old Baldy, the sand dune, or just hang out on the beach all day.

She would visit for a weekend and sleep on the pullout in the sunroom. Life just slowed down up there, and it was just such a relaxing break from the hustle and bustle of her job in the city.

She could understand Marcus wanting to come up here to get away, but he had had such a strong resistance to doing so since the crash, she had her doubts. She tried to convince herself he was watching the sunset right at that moment. She would head directly down to the beach, give him a quiet hug and watch it with him.

He shouldn't be alone. Should he? She started to question whether she was doing the right thing. What am I going to say to him? Should she tell him she didn't trust him to be alone? She might as well as that's what he's going to think anyway. She would just tell him the truth, or at least part of the truth—she just wanted to support him through what would be another tough "first" thing for him to do without his family there anymore.

Life had been filled with firsts for him since the accident. First birthdays, first holidays, the worst of course being Christmas, and now, first time going to the cottage without them.

Allison turned onto Beach Street and her heart sank. No car. No lights in the cottage or on the porch. Where was he? Allison parked her own car and started the short walk to the beach hoping Marcus had just driven straight there to claim a bench and take in the evening sky. She approached the beach and was welcomed with a breathtakingly beautiful display—the setting sun was shining both on the water and through the clouds simultaneously, creating a dance of orange and purple across the whole horizon—but Allison hardly noticed.

She was too busy looking for someone who wasn't there. She knew he wasn't there; in fact, she'd always known, even before she'd left Grand Rapids, but she'd felt it was necessary to check. She had to do *something*; she simply couldn't sit at home feeling helpless with Marcus gone.

In the upcoming summer months, there would be hundreds of people watching the sunset on this beach. Today, in early April, there were less than fifty, so it would have been easy to immediately spot Marcus. Dejected, she sat down on a bench and stared at the amazing spectacle in front of her, lost in her worries.

"Beautiful tonight, isn't it?" Allison heard a voice and jumped a little. She hadn't even noticed anyone sit down beside her.

"Excuse me?" she tried to casually ask, looking over at the man.

"Beautiful tonight, isn't it?" he asked again.

"Oh, why, yes, it is. It's amazing" Allison quickly responded and turned away hoping that was the end of the conversation.

"They really haven't been that good this week. It's been too cloudy. Tonight seems to be just the right amount of clouds."

Allison smiled. He was obviously a tourist to West Michigan and the "third coast." Allison had seen thousands of gorgeous sunsets here and, though still remarkable, she recognized they didn't match the awe of the very first one she'd ever seen there. She was a little curious of this stranger now, wondering where he was from and what he was doing up here this time of year.

"Oh, have you been up here all week"? Allison asked. She couldn't help but notice how handsome he was.

"Yeah, I got a good deal on a rental cottage up the road a little bit. I had never been to the lake, so I came up. I've been blown away at how nice it is up here."

Allison laughed a little. "If you think it's nice up here now, you should come back in the summer!"

For the moment, she had forgotten why she was there. The sun made its final descent into the water and filled the sky with more vibrant streaks of pink and purple. Allison and the tourist looked away from each other toward the western sky and took in the brilliant light show.

"It won't be long now." Allison broke the silence, just as the sun melted completely away into the water. "I should be getting back," she said.

"Where's back?" he questioned her, and Allison was glad he had continued their conversation.

"Back to Grand Rapids. I need to get home. My car is parked at a cottage on Beach Street a couple blocks away."

He looked a little confused. "May I walk with you? My rental is on Beach Street."

"Sure!" She wanted to get to know him a little more and it was nice to have a distraction.

They started walking away from the beach towards the cottages.

Almost simultaneously, they both asked "So, what's your name?" She laughed and said, "You first."

He smiled and stuck out his hand, "I'm Darrin Warner. It's a pleasure to meet you."

She grabbed his hand and shook it. "Allison Deters," she replied. "I'm very happy to meet you as well." She was in fact happy to meet him. She had been immediately drawn to him. He seemed charming, friendly, so good looking, and she loved the way he looked at her.

Maybe she wouldn't be going home tonight. Suddenly the drive seemed unimportant. After all, what could she do there? She instantly decided—she would be staying at Marcus's place tonight. She wanted to get to know this Darrin Warner. Suddenly, like a jolt from a dream into consciousness, her phone rang.

"Hello, Marcus?" Allison asked with anticipation.

"Hi Allie. I saw you called. What's up?" Marcus asked, trying his best to sound surprised that she had called.

"Maybe I should ask you what's up. Or do I already know?" She said accusingly while doing her best to conceal how worried she was. "Hold on just a minute Marcus".

She noticed she and Darrin were already back to the cottage and she would have to tell him goodbye. She turned to Darrin. "I'm sorry,

Darrin, this is me." She pointed to the cottage and started up the walkway, but turned to smile back at him. "Maybe I'll see you tomorrow."

"But I thought you were leaving?" Darrin remarked, his voice disappearing as she unlocked the door and entered the cottage.

Her attention was back on Marcus. "So, are you going to tell me where you really are?" By her tone, Marcus knew she had talked to Mom and Dad and knew he wasn't up north. Of course she knew. She always knew. That's one reason she was so good at her job; she could always seem to read people and see past the lies.

"I'm in Murfreesboro. I'm staying at a hotel tonight and then driving the rest of the way to Tampa tomorrow." He said this as carefree as if he had said he was going to the movies.

Allison was silent for a few seconds before stating the one word Marcus knew was coming: "Why?"

Here it came; here was the lie to the sister who knew him better than anyone else. Trying his best, he answered, "Well, I just thought the trip would help me remember something about the crash." It was not totally untrue. It wasn't the main reason for this road trip, but Allison didn't have to know everything.

Allison didn't know if she should press the issue or not. She knew if she mentioned Simon Daniels, Marcus would know they were snooping. Instead she simply asked, "Is it working?"

"Not yet," he replied, "but I'm going to the crash site tomorrow and maybe that will help."

"Oh Marcus, are you sure you want to do that?" She couldn't bear the thought of the pain Marcus was sure to endure.

There was a long pause before Marcus replied softly, "I have to. Please don't tell Mom and Dad. I don't need them to worry more than I'm sure they already are."

More than anything, Allison wanted to tell him to turn around and come home. Instead she just said, "Ok, Marcus. Be careful. I love you."

"Love you, too, Allie. I will. Goodnight."

Allison looked around the cottage and saw exactly what she had expected. No one had been there in years. Marcus always had the yard maintained by a local company so that looked fine, but the inside was dusty, very dusty, and the moisture of the beach air had seeped into the empty home, making everything smell more than a little musty. She opened the windows to let in some fresh air and dug through the closet until she found some clean sheets for the bed. Sighing at the dust that rose and swirled with each move she made, she wandered back to the kitchen where she grabbed a wine glass from the cupboard and took a cabernet from the small wine rack in the corner of the kitchen cabinets. Pouring a tall glass, she sat down to reflect.

Many times in this very spot she had shared a bottle of wine with Sheila. Marcus was always an early to bed, early to rise type of guy, so she and Sheila would stay up late and enjoy a good red and even better conversation. Allison's heart ached as she glanced at the other, empty end of the couch.

This time as she looked around the cottage, she didn't notice the dust anymore. Instead she focused on all the pictures of Marcus and his family. How beautiful they were: Marcus was turning gray early but it granted him an air of attractive wisdom; Sheila wasn't the out-of-a-magazine, beauty queen type, but rather her round cheeks, gentle build, and bright smile lit up every room she entered. The boys were simply adorable; still growing, but with sparks of both of their parents shining out of each of them.

Allison whispered, "I miss you," finished her wine, and went to bed.

8

On Saturday, Marcus woke up at 5:34 a.m. He never needed an alarm. He was always up before 6:00, never one to sleep in, even on the rare mornings he wanted to. He grabbed a quick shower, gathered his things, and headed out to his car. He was going to see the crash site today. He was strangely excited about it. He couldn't help but hope he would recall something tangible from that night.

Telling Allison he was going to the crash site was the truth, but he had no intention of going all the way to Tampa and Treasure Island afterwards. Why would he? He didn't make it there the last time he was on this journey, so there was nothing for him to recall beyond Atlanta anyway. Instead he planned on going to Marietta to check on Simon Daniels. He knew what he would do. He would go to his apartment, wait until he left, and then follow him. He knew what Simon looked like from the press article of the crash and his social media posts. The thought of spying on him was exciting to Marcus. His firm generally hired investigators to help in certain cases so he imagined doing surveillance himself would be a novelty.

But first he had a three-and-a-half-hour drive to Atlanta to see the site. With a quick stop for breakfast and gas, he would be there around 11:00. He figured he could find it based on the police reports he had read. He knew what entrance ramp Simon had used, and the collision had occurred almost immediately so it would be right there.

Marcus left the gas station, found the on ramp to 75 south, and merged onto the highway for the next leg of this excursion. Trying to preoccupy himself, he reached down below the seat to make sure his gun was still there. Feeling its smooth handle against his skin, he pulled it out and held it for a moment. Sheila had given it to him when he'd made partner at the firm. It was a beautiful stainless steel barrel with a cherry wood handle embossed with the silver letters DHD for Davis, Hayes, and

Deters. He had a few guns—he loved to collect them as well as to target shoot—but this one was his favorite.

9

Allison woke up right around 7:30. She washed out the coffee pot and took the coffee out of the cupboard. She checked the expiration date: Nov. 2014. How bad could it be? she asked herself, already beginning to make a pot.

As she was pouring her cup, there was a knock on the door. Allison had a hopeful feeling it was Darrin—who else could it be on an early morning in the off-season? I must look a mess, she thought, but what the heck. She opened the door and was amused to realize how happy she was it was him.

"Good morning! I hope you don't mind me stopping by so early, but I was hoping for some company at breakfast for a change. Would you be interested?"

Allison smiled and said, "I'd love to, but can you give me some time to get ready?"

"You look fantastic" he said with a big grin.

"Ha ha," she smirked back at him. "Come on in. I made some coffee. I need ten minutes, and please excuse the mess! No one has been here for some time".

Darrin entered the cottage, grabbed a mug off the shelf and poured himself a cup. "I'm sorry, there's no cream, but I think there is sugar on the counter," Allison's voice called out from the bedroom.

"No problem. I drink it black," Darrin answered back.

She grabbed a sweatshirt and some jeans from Sheila's closet and put them on. Luckily, they were pretty close to the same size. She quickly put her long blond hair into a pony tail and brushed her teeth. She looked in the mirror and was satisfied. Not ready for a night on the town but not too shabby for 8:00 a.m. at the cottage, she thought.

"So where are we heading?" Allison asked.

"Well, if it's ok with you, I'd like to make breakfast at my place," he said. "I have bacon and eggs, and we can talk with no interruptions."

"Sounds nice," Allison said with a smile. She was never one to fall for someone quickly, but there was just something about this guy.

"You can bring your coffee with you," she said as he set the mug down on the counter.

"Do I have to?" he asked with a huge grin. They both started to laugh and went out the door.

Darrin cooked the bacon and eggs while Allison sat on his front porch drinking a fresh cup of coffee. She sat in just the right spot to be able to look through the window and watch him work. She couldn't help but notice how comfortable he seemed in the kitchen. She was hungry and was surprised to realize she hadn't eaten since lunch the day before, but she was equally excited to learn more about her new acquaintance as the morning unfolded. Darrin knocked on the window and motioned for her to come in. They sat and ate the meal in silence, but every now and then, they would glance up at each other and smile.

"Well, that was wonderful," Allison said as she wiped her mouth with the paper towel he had given her for a napkin.

"I'm glad you enjoyed it. Would you like more coffee?" Allison nodded, and he brought the pot and filled both their cups.

"Shall we go on the porch?" she asked, already walking toward the door.

Darrin put the coffee pot back and joined her outside. The rental cottage was on the end of Beach Street, four cottages down from Marcus's. It was nestled in some trees, with a small dune on the far side. It was small, very quaint, and private. It had a covered porch that Allison liked very much. With a tree to one side perfectly placed for afternoon shade, a view of the lake to the west, and Old Baldy to the north, it was the perfect spot to spend a relaxing morning.

"So how long do you have this place rented?" she asked.

"I have it for another week until next Saturday. So far, it's been a real nice vacation. Beautiful view." He glanced at the lake, but his smile suggested he was talking about her.

"Tell me about Darrin Warner," she said, anxious to finally learn about this handsome stranger.

"Not much to tell, really. I'm thirty-two years old. Grew up in

Carmel, Indiana, a city outside of Indianapolis. I have a brother and a sister; I'm the youngest. I graduated from Butler University in Indiana with a business degree, and was destined to work at my father's assets management company, but after college I decided to enlist in the Army instead and totally disappointed and pissed off my father. I served in the military for ten years, enjoying almost all of them." He said this last part with a mischievous grin, and Allison couldn't help but smile back.

"After that I came home to visit my parents, and, of course, to finally go to work for my father. But before I started at the company, I thought I would relax and see some of the country." He looked at Allison, smiled and said, "And so here I am! That's pretty much it."

Allison smiled back. "Short and sweet," she replied as she set down her coffee and leaned closer to him. "What else? Criminal record, wife or girlfriend, drug addiction? You can't be this perfect, can you?"

Darrin laughed. "I don't know about perfect, but there is none of the above. What about you? What's your story?"

Allison then told him everything. He was so easy to talk to, and she just felt comfortable with him. She told him about her schooling, her job, her parents, and of course Marcus and his family. He listened to every detail intently as she told him about the accident, the funeral, Marcus's rehab and memory loss, and how it all had affected her and her parents and the effects it has had on the law firm. She talked for almost an hour and Darrin hung on every word. She even told him why she was at the cottage. Allison finally stopped. It felt so good to talk to someone like that, to share her feelings with someone and talk about her life that had been turned upside down.

Darrin stood up and held out his hand to her. She took it and he gently pulled her out of her chair. He looked deep in her eyes and said with a caring smile, "Thanks for sharing." He then pulled her in and hugged her. Allison squeezed him back, her mind racing. Is this really happening? she thought to herself. Lord, let this be real.

10

The closer Marcus got to the crash site, the more uneasy he became. Maybe he hadn't thought this through enough. Will he know or recognize anything? Should he stop his car and look around when he got there? The traffic would be extremely heavy this time of day. It seemed silly to drive all this way only to blow by at sixty-five miles an hour. Suddenly he saw it: the Hudson Bridge Road, with the on ramp just past it. The ramp was long with plenty of visibility and a large shoulder on the right of the highway. Marcus took note of how easily cars were merging from the ramp, even in the midday traffic. He decided to park on the shoulder.

Putting his blinker on, he passed the end of the on ramp, pulled off to the side, and hit his hazard lights. Hopefully nobody stops to help, he thought to himself. As his car came to a rest, suddenly he saw it. Just ahead on the right was the cement wall that their mini-van had struck. He gaped at it in horror. He felt nauseous as there were still, three years later, large paint scrapes on the wall, the same dark green color as their van.

He thought back to that night, and for the first time in three years he actually remembered something concrete. They were asleep! All of them—they were all asleep! An image of Sheila and the boys came to him. He saw them sleeping in the van! The Wainwright's Yukon had been in front of them. They were 100 yards or so further along, and John must have been looking for something because their interior lights were on. He was starting to remember details!

While still parked on the shoulder of the busy highway, Marcus grabbed the wheel of his car with all his might to stop his uncontrollable shaking. After a full fifteen minutes had passed, Marcus finally felt well enough to safely put his car in drive.

He had mixed feelings about what had just occurred. His heart broke at the picture in his mind of his family sleeping peacefully as he was driving. It was his responsibility to keep them safe and he had failed them. The thought of that was devastating, but he was now more convinced that remembering those details may help him figure out what exactly happened that night. And right now, that was what he intended to focus on.

He knew he couldn't change the past. His family was gone. Someday he hoped to see them again. He had been brought up in a religious household and had raised his kids in the same manner. He knew where they were all going after death. He had known they were all children of God. Knowing he could see them again gave him some comfort, yet he had some strong doubts now, too.

He had not been back to church since the crash. He just couldn't bring himself to go. His parents had asked him to go early on but had since stopped asking, and Marcus knew they were hoping he would choose to go on his own. He felt he would go back someday but had no timetable for that. He knew he had the same questions everyone that loses someone too soon has: How could a loving God do this to someone? Why would He? But the thing that concerned Marcus the most was this: if there is a heaven, how would his future actions affect his being reunited with his family? Or must he find it in his heart to turn the other cheek and forgive?

He exited southbound 75 and re-entered going north. He started to think about Simon Daniels. He thought about the gun under his seat. Did he really plan on using it? Was he smart enough to live the rest of his life outside of a prison cell? "Yes, I am!" he said out loud and with conviction.

11

To Allison it seemed the hug ended way too soon; in reality they had stood there in each other's arms for close to ten minutes. She could hear his heart pounding as her head was nestled on his chest and shoulder. He pulled away and looked her in the eyes, all the while keeping her shoulders in his hands. Her eyes had filled with tears when talking about Marcus and his family, but they were dry now, with only the remnants of a few tears remaining on her cheeks.

He bent down and kissed her cheek and quietly said, "Thank you".

"For what?" she asked sheepishly. "Bringing you down?"

Darrin gave her a reassuring smile and said, "No, for letting me in."

Allison was hooked. This was so unlike her character. She had been chased by boys since she was a teenager, but she had never felt this way, and she had only just met him. He was the one! She felt it. Even more than that, she knew it.

"What's your plan for the day?" he asked, but before she could answer he spoke again. "If it's not too forward, I would like to spend the day with you."

Allison couldn't help but smile. "Honestly, I would love that. Do you have something in mind?"

"Well, I'm a tourist here. I was hoping you could help out in the things to do department."

She laughed again. "Well the town is pretty much closed until summer, but let's take a drive north to Ludington, only about twenty-five minutes from here. We could go in a few shops and take a walk on the beach there. It's very nice."

"Sounds great!" he said, holding out his hand to take hers. She could've said, "Let's go pick flowers," and he would have been all in. He

26

was thrilled to get to spend the day with her and couldn't believe he had met this beautiful woman up here in a remote summer town in northwest Michigan, in the month of April no less.

"Hold on," she laughed. "I do want to take a shower and get ready if we are going to town. Give me thirty minutes."

"Ok, but hurry." He winked at her when he said it. She smiled and headed back to the other cottage. "I'll pick you up in thirty!" Darrin yelled. She waved and went inside.

Allison looked out the window and saw Darrin waiting in his vehicle, a newer model Ford pickup, 2014 or '15, she guessed. Dark green with Indiana plates. Very sharp, and it seemed to fit his personality. She grabbed her purse, stopped and locked the door, and headed down the walk to the street where he was waiting.

Darrin got out of the truck and opened the door for her. "You look fantastic. Definitely worth waiting thirty minutes."

"Ha," she said, "that's the same thing you said this morning." She got in the car and he shut the door behind her, and they started on the short drive to Ludington. Allison noticed his key fob sitting in the center console with an Army logo on the strap. "Sporting the colors with pride," she said as she picked it up and looked it over.

Darrin shrugged and said with a grin, "Of course."

For the next twenty minutes, they talked about everything: his family, her job, her home in Grand Rapids. This was all new to both of them. They both felt they needed to find out thirty some years about each other in the thirty-minute drive. It seemed that in an instant, they were there.

Ludington was a much bigger city than Pentwater; it had some chain restaurants, big box stores, a Wal-Mart, and movie theaters, but downtown also had a small-town charm. There were the beautiful beaches and state park, yacht clubs and marinas, plus some neat little shops. The Pier Marquette River ran through Ludington into Lake Michigan, and nestled just within the river's mouth, there were nearly always fishing boats alongside the famous car ferry, the SS Badger, which daily traversed the ninety miles across Lake Michigan to Wisconsin.

They parked the truck and got out. Allison watched as Darrin locked his truck with the key pad on the outside of the driver's door. She looked inside the truck and saw the fob with the Army band still on the console.

Darrin noticed her looking and smiled. "I leave the key in the truck because I'm afraid I will lose it. This way, I always know where it is. We wouldn't want to be stranded here, would we?"

Allison couldn't help but blush a bit; his smile overwhelmed her. There was something about him that made her forget everything else that was going on in her life. "That," she said and then paused for effect, "would be a tragedy." She smiled back at him and then motioned him to follow her.

They walked around downtown and into the shops. Allison hadn't laughed that much in years. Darrin always kept her smiling. It was the best day she could remember having had in a long, long time. After shopping they went down to the beach and went for a walk on the shoreline. It was a nice sunny day, about 60 degrees, which was a gift in early April, but the breeze off the cool water put a little chill in the air. Darrin held out his hand, which Allison readily took, and they walked that way up the beach.

"So, do you feel like taking some time off work this week?" he asked.

She could sense his hopefulness and that made her giddy inside. Allison really wanted to stay. In fact, the way she felt right now, she could stay forever, but she knew that wouldn't do; she had responsibilities at work and with her family—she couldn't just take off at a moment's notice. It seemed they were always under-manned at the firm, especially with Marcus gone, and they certainly needed her there. She turned to Darrin intending to tell him that it would be impossible. But what she heard herself say was, "I think I just might."

Darrin stopped her and pulled her close and then they kissed for the first time. He gently brushed the breeze-blown hair away from her eyes with his thumb. They held each other tight as they kissed on the beach in the afternoon sun, the waves softly crashing on the shore. Perfect, she thought, absolutely perfect.

12

Marcus was in Marietta, Georgia now. The mechanical voice on his phone was directing him to 3217 Whiting Drive. There was a hotel only a couple minutes away from the apartment complex, so he decided to take a quick drive through and find Simon's apartment before he went to check in. He would come back for the stakeout after he was settled in.

"In 200 yards, turn left," said the lady on his phone.

Marcus could see the sign for Green Meadow Apartments. He couldn't help but think what a strange name it was for an apartment complex with virtually no grass in sight.

"Turn right on Whiting Drive. You have reached your destination."

Marcus obeyed, and he saw it—3217—on the front of the building. Marcus parked his car and approached the main door. The building had an intercom system with twelve apartments numbers listed: 1 through 4A, 1 through 4B, and 1 through 4C. He saw the names next to each button. Seeing the name next to 2B sent a chill down Marcus's spine. He couldn't believe he was actually here. He was this close to seeing the man that devastated his life.

Marcus went back to his car and entered his hotel name into his phone. Upon arriving, Marcus wasn't terribly impressed by the Marietta Oasis Hotel, but it had a bar and a restaurant and, most importantly, it was close to Simon. It was a non-smoking hotel, but you could still make out the faint odor of cigarettes in the otherwise clean and well-maintained lobby. A young gal was smiling at him from behind the desk.

"May I help you, sir?" she asked with that Georgia accent.

Marcus always loved the southern accent. "I would like a room for two nights. Do you have any available?"

She immediately answered back. "The only rooms we have are two double beds at $145.00 a night."

"That will be fine." Marcus handed her his credit card. "How late is the restaurant open?" he asked.

"The restaurant is open till 11:00 p.m. and the bar has last call around 2 a.m." She handed him his room key and his credit card as she spoke. "Can you please sign here, Mr. Deters?"

Marcus smiled and signed his name. "Thank you." Marcus said as he walked away.

"Down the hall, past the elevators, make a left, and your room will be on the right," she called out from behind.

The room was clean, even nice; it was a typical hotel room with two beds, a bathroom, and a little desk. Marcus threw his bag on one bed and turned the air conditioning up. He liked it cool when he slept. He used the bathroom, washed his hands and face, and threw on a clean shirt.

He looked at himself in the mirror. His dusty brown hair had always been cut short: number 3 on the sides and an inch on the top. It was a little long now, and his gray was a little more apparent; he was a couple weeks overdue for a haircut, but it was still manageable. He liked the ease of short hair. He could get out of the shower, throw some gel in it, and go. He wet his hair with some water before heading out, anxious to see what the evening would bring.

He drove over to the apartments and parked his car. It was 5:34 on a Saturday night, so Marcus had to admit it was a crap shoot that Simon would be around, because, after all, he was what? Twenty-eight years old? Marcus was positive he would recognize Simon as he had glowered at his picture hundreds of times. Marcus just sat in his car and waited. He thought about calling Allison but didn't want any distractions. What if Simon showed up while he was talking? No, he was just going to sit and wait, as long as it took. It turned out not to take long at all.

As he was sitting in his car, a red Ford pickup pulled up to his right and parked two spaces over, leaving an empty space between them. Marcus looked over and he saw Simon Daniels in the truck.

It was at that exact moment, 6:13 p.m. on Saturday April 2, 2016, that Marcus's memory came flooding back.

His mind instantly flashed back to the crash. He could see it perfectly. The red pickup was coming down the on ramp. Marcus knew he had plenty of room to get past the merging lane before the truck, but he had changed lanes anyway. Strangely, the pickup sped up until it was almost even with them before falling back a bit. It then turned sharply into his passenger side rear quarter panel. The collision turned Marcus's car sideways, and it sped into the wall.

Marcus was horrified at the memory. Simon had collided with them on purpose! Marcus felt his world crash down again. He had wanted some closure. He had wanted to forgive Simon. He had hoped that his family's deaths had been an accident, though in his mind he must have already known otherwise. His mind was racing and he was in a panic, but he knew what to do.

Simon was already through the main door of the apartment building. Marcus grabbed his gun from under the seat and got out of his car. He walked the fifty or so feet to the main door and pushed the buzzer for 2B and waited.

"Yeah?" the voice came from the speaker. Marcus couldn't talk. He pushed the buzzer again. "Who is it?"

"It's Marcus," he answered, not knowing what to say and still in a daze.

"Who?" the voice from the speaker asked again.

"It's Marcus," he repeated.

There was a pause and then the door buzzed. Marcus pushed through and headed up the stairs to 2B. When he got there, Simon was standing outside his open doorway. Marcus raised the gun and pointed it at him.

"Whoa! Whoa!" Simon yelled out.

"Get inside." Marcus said evenly. He was inappropriately calm considering the situation. Simon backed into the apartment and Marcus followed, shutting the door behind them.

"What do you want?" Simon asked with a whimper.

"You killed my family," Marcus replied, again with an eerie sense of calm.

Simon's eyes got bigger as he understood, and he looked at Marcus in absolute fear. The kind of fear one feels minutes, if not seconds, before they die. Simon was on his knees and Marcus had the gun less than two feet from his head.

"Why?" Marcus asked, still calm.

"I had to." Simon was crying. "I'm so sorry—I didn't want anyone to die."

Marcus was taken aback; he didn't expect that answer. "Why!" Marcus yelled, suddenly shaking with rage.

"I had to," was all Simon would say. "Kill me! Go ahead and kill me!" Simon wailed. Marcus's hand was shaking violently. He grabbed the gun with two hands and pointed it at Simon's head.

13

Marcus sat at the hotel bar drinking a whiskey and water. He felt beaten. He didn't know where this left him. His family was murdered and he still didn't know why. All he knew was, right now, he was going to get drunk. Calling the police would have been pointless, he knew that. Simon had served his time and no one would believe him about what Simon had admitted to, especially when he'd had a gun pointed to his head. And after so much time had passed, they probably would find it hard to believe Marcus now remembered the crash in so much vivid detail that he saw Simon do it on purpose. He would be the one in jail. He had pulled a loaded gun on someone.

It had been so hard to walk out of that apartment with Simon still breathing, but he could not kill him. He didn't know if he was more upset to realize it had not been an accident or the fact he couldn't carry out his vengeance.

He had heard Sheila's voice in his head when he was standing over Simon pointing the pistol at him. She was saying, "I love you, Marcus. Be strong for us and walk away." He just kept thinking about seeing his family again. Would that revenge jeopardize his chances? He figured so. But he was struggling with his faith anyway. Maybe heaven wasn't real. Maybe he just blew his only opportunity for justice.

Marcus called the bartender over. "Can I get a double?"

"Tough night, pal?" the bartender asked as he poured another drink for Marcus.

"Tough life," Marcus answered back. Then he raised his glass and said quietly, "Here's to you, Simon, you fuck."

The bartender had all his attention on Marcus now. He was worried he would become belligerent like a lot of other drunks, and he couldn't have that on his shift. He was always catching heat from management for not cutting them off or asking them to leave. With his focus already on him, he couldn't help but overhear Marcus's sarcastic toast. He knew he should keep his mouth shut but he had to ask. "Simon Daniels?" The bartender looked intensely at Marcus.

Marcus looked up quite surprised and asked, "Do you know him?"

"Yes," he replied a little uneasily. "He comes in here a lot. I got to know who he was really well because the police questioned me a few times about him. He almost got me fired. He was drinking in here the night he was in an accident. He was drunk and killed some people. The district attorney tried to hold us liable for serving him."

Marcus's interest was piqued now. "Was he drunk?" Marcus asked.

"He didn't seem to be. He'd had three beers—I know that for sure because the police checked his tab after the accident. I don't know what he drank before that, but he seemed more nervous than drunk. He got put away for two or three years, I don't remember exactly how long, but he's out now. He was in here last night."

"You were here the night of his crash?" Marcus asked. "Did he do anything unusual that night?"

"Are you a cop?" the bartender asked cautiously.

Marcus shook his head and the bartender continued.

"I told them everything I knew, which wasn't much. I told them he was on his cell phone before he left the bar, but I must have been mistaken because when they checked his phone records, there was nothing. Pretty much cut and dry accident, I guess. I think the district attorney was more interested in busting us than Simon. I heard the only reason Simon had to do as much time as he did was because the dead people's lawyer was ruthless on the D.A. and judge."

Marcus cringed at his family being referred to as "the dead people" but he listened intently. Allison was a fantastic attorney and, like the bartender said, he bet she could be ruthless. This bartender was a talker. Marcus could always get information from a talker. That was part of his job. Talkers always wanted to babble even when they thought they didn't.

Marcus tapped his glass.

"What did Simon do to you?" The bartender asked as he poured some whiskey into Marcus's glass. This time he left out the water. Marcus shrugged. "He owes me, that's all. Room 134 - Deters," he said as he stood up from his stool, gulped his drink down, and exited the bar.

"Goodnight, Mr. Deters."

14

Allison woke up on Sunday morning feeling a little bit groggy. She looked around and realized they had both fallen asleep on the couch. She smiled as she thought about the last thirty-six hours. Unbelievable, she mused. She was not this person. She was not like the boy-crazy girls she'd known in college whose only goal in life was to get married by age twenty-five, have kids, and be a stay-at-home mom. She had a good head on her shoulders. She had a great career. She didn't fall for guys she just met. She was stronger than that. Allison looked to her right and watched Darrin still sleeping.

Who are you kidding, Al, she thought to herself. You're in love.

Allison kissed Darrin on the cheek and stood up. She smiled as she looked at him. What a night. They had gotten back to the cottage reasonably early, had enjoyed some wine and great conversation together, but then they must have both nodded off. She had slept so soundly. She went into the bathroom and looked in the mirror. Her hair was a mess. She needed to get back to Marcus's cottage and shower.

"I'm making coffee," Darrin called out.

She could hear the sleep still in his voice. Allison left the bathroom and went to the kitchen. There he was, in jeans and a t shirt, making coffee. She smiled and wrapped her arms around him from behind. "What time did we fall asleep?" she asked him.

Darrin shrugged, "I was going to ask you that," he laughed. "We must have been tired."

Allison squeezed her arms tighter around him. "I was thinking of going back and taking a shower. May I come back for that coffee in half an hour or so?"

Darrin turned in her arms and faced her. He bent down, gave her a kiss and a smile, and said, "Hurry."

"Count on it," she said, excitedly dropping her arms. Allison left the rental and headed back to Marcus's place. As she walked up the sidewalk, she started to worry again. What is Marcus up to? Did he have any luck? She should give him a call.

"After my shower," she said aloud.

15

Marcus woke up around 9:00 a.m. with a pounding headache. He hadn't drunk like that in years, and he was paying a price now. He quickly showered and dressed before heading down to the restaurant and taking a seat. He picked a booth in the back, as far away from the other customers as he could. The rage Marcus felt the night before had turned into sadness, and the knowledge that the crash was in fact murder had been turning his mind inside out. Marcus had to piece some more things together.

"May I help you, sir?" This time the accent went unnoticed as the waitress asked to take his order.

"Coffee, black, and a plain bagel with butter," Marcus replied.

She hustled off and Marcus looked around the restaurant. He saw a family of five sitting a few tables away. They seemed to be enjoying themselves. They were eating as a family, maybe on vacation, maybe locals who liked this place's breakfast, who knew, but they were happy. Marcus suddenly yearned to be at Chick-fil-A.

The waitress was back now and set his bagel and coffee down in front of him. "Here you go, sir," she said softly.

Marcus was sure she had seen his tears. He said thank you and grabbed his coffee as if nothing was wrong.

"You're welcome. If there's anything else you need, ya'll just let me know." She smiled and walked away.

Marcus went over everything in his head, what he had remembered about the crash and what both Simon and the bartender had told him. Suddenly something in him snapped and he had some focus. He called the waitress over. "Sorry to bother you, but could I get a paper and pen?"

"Sure," she said. "I'll be right back."

"We had this at the counter—will this work?" She handed Marcus a pen and a children's paper menu. "You can write on the back." She pointed for him to flip it over.

"This will be great. Thank you."

Marcus was about to do something he hadn't done in three years. Make a list. He was big into making lists when he had been working. Back then he would make lists every day. It always helped him focus and bring his thoughts together. Only thing was, this list wasn't for him; it was for Allison. On the top of the menu he scribbled "New Things" and he started writing.

1. *My family was asleep.*
2. *I changed lanes to avoid Simon.*
3. *Simon came at me and wrecked us on purpose.*
4. *I saw the Wainwright's Yukon.*
5. *Simon said he "had to" hit us and "he didn't want anyone to die".*
6. *Bartender told me Simon may have made a call.*
7. *Simon acted more nervous than drunk.*
8. *The cops never really investigated it as anything more than an accident, there was no foul play suspected.*

After writing bullet number eight, Marcus paused and thought. No one had ever said anything about foul play—not the police, not Allison, not the Wainwrights. No one. That is, until now. Marcus's head was spinning. Why not? Marcus had always refused to call it an accident, but in his mind, that was because Simon was a driving drunk. Marcus thought about what Simon had said the night before and added to his list.

9. *Someone made Simon crash into our car.*
10. *I believe Simon.*

He folded his list and put it in his shirt pocket. He placed a ten-dollar bill on the table and left to go back to Simon's apartment. He was now investigating a case. Not just any case, but the most important case he'd ever had. A case that would pay no money but would give unlimited satisfaction, assuming he could keep himself together. He stopped at the front desk, checked out of the hotel, and located his car. He very methodically headed to Simon's apartment complex.

He arrived to find pandemonium in the parking lot. There were four patrol cars with their lights on, right in front of building 3217. He could hear a siren coming closer from behind him, a sound he knew all too well from his ride in 2013. Instead of stopping, he drove right past 3217 and exited the apartment complex. He knew he needed to leave; he couldn't risk hanging around. He glanced at the clock in his car and calculated he should be able to get home before midnight.

His phone rang and when he saw Allison's picture, he answered it quickly. "Hi, Allie. How are you?" Marcus said, trying to sound casual.

"Never mind me. How are you?"

"I'm good. On my way home. I should be back late tonight."

"Ok. How was your trip? Did it do any good? What did you do?" Allison bombarded him with questions. She wanted to know everything.

"Hold on, Allie. Let me get home. Then I'll tell you all about it. Honestly, I need to tell you all about it."

"I can't wait until tomorrow!" Allison shrieked. "Besides, I'm not coming home tonight."

"Where are you?" he asked. He was surprised she wasn't home.

"I'm up in Pentwater. I thought I would take a long weekend. Didn't I tell you that last time we talked?" She knew she hadn't but played a little dumb, knowing she just revealed that she had been checking up on him.

"No, you didn't," he answered sternly. "Do Mom and Dad know I'm not there?"

"Well, not exactly, they have their suspicions but they don't know for sure." Suddenly, she felt guilty. She hadn't called her parents and told them if Marcus was there or not. They must be so worried.

"Well, that's good at least." Marcus breathed a sigh of relief and said, "I hated to lie but I knew they would worry themselves sick. Anyway, I really need to see you tomorrow. Can I meet you at the office?"

Allison's heart sank and rose simultaneously. She didn't want to say goodbye to Darrin and yet she was thrilled Marcus wanted to go to the office. He hadn't been to the office since the accident. "Ok," Allison said. "I'll meet you there, but I won't be in before ten."

"Great, see you then."

Allison hung up the phone and walked out the door. She headed over to see Darrin. She would have to tell him she had to work tomorrow. She could stay the night and get up early and leave around seven in order to drive home, change, and still be to the office by ten. Maybe she could come back afterwards. "It's not that far." She told herself. Allison knocked on the door as she walked into the rental.

"Hello," she called out. "Darrin?" She called out again. She walked over to the bathroom and heard the shower running. She knocked on the bathroom door. "Darrin? I'm back!"

"Be out in a minute." She heard Darrin's voice and it put her at ease.

"Ok! I'll be on the porch." The water stopped in the shower as she walked away. She went and took a seat on the porch and waited.

Darrin came out, his hair still a little wet, with some comfy looking jeans, a tee shirt, and flip flops. "Ready for a great day?" he asked with a big smile on his face as he leaned down and gave her a peck on the forehead.

"Sure," she said slowly, "but I'm afraid I have to go in to work tomorrow."

Darrin's smile disappeared. "I thought you could take a few days off?" Allison looked at him and noticed he seemed concerned.

"Yeah, I know. Marcus called and said he needs to meet me at the office. I would put it off, but he hasn't been to the firm since the accident, so I'm excited to see what's gotten into him. Don't worry—I can come back at night if you want! It's not that long of a drive."

Darrin looked at her for a long moment. "Ok," he finally said and smiled at her again. "Come back after work. So, what do you think your brother wants you for?" he asked.

"I'm not sure but I think it's about the accident. He may have thought of something in the last few days he wants to discuss. Maybe it's about the Daniels case." Darrin knew what she meant by "the Daniels case." She had told him all about the accident and the court hearing with Simon Daniels yesterday.

"Really, you think he found something out?"

"Oh, I doubt it, but I'll meet him if that's what he wants to do. Obviously, he hasn't been himself. I think going back to the office is a huge step. I also think it could be just what he needs to help him move on."

"I suppose you're right," he replied with a sigh.

"It's ok. I'll only be gone for the day." She smiled and moved in for a hug. "Let's enjoy the rest of today."

16

On Monday morning, Allison woke at 6:30 a.m. to the sound of the alarm on her phone. She rolled out of bed and went into the kitchen. First things first: make coffee, she thought. She was excited about Marcus coming to the office today. The others were going to be so thrilled to see him there.

She had slept by herself at Marcus's cottage last night. She had told Darrin that she didn't want to wake him when she left, which was half true. She really just wanted a break to gather her thoughts about everything that had happened the last few days.

He had seemed fine with that, which was good. He didn't seem overly aggressive and he totally respected her wishes. Allison grabbed her coffee and headed out to her car. She started down Beach Street and turned down the main road toward the highway. There was not another car in sight. This place is so quiet in the off-season, she thought with a smile. What a coincidence meeting Darrin now. Fate, she thought.

Marcus arrived in the parking ramp under the firm's building at 7:00 a.m. He knew he would be the only one in the office at that early hour, and that's the way he wanted it. It would be easier to see everybody one by one as they came in instead of walking in once they were all already there. Plus, he was anxious to get started on his case.

He pulled in and found a spot, one of many that said, "Reserved: Davis, Hayes, and Deters." He parked and walked to the elevator. Their firm had half of the fifth floor. They shared it with GRT Development, a real estate company that bought old commercial buildings and turned them into condos and apartments. Downtown living had become very popular with young professionals in the area. Allison had bought her place through them; she got a great deal and in turn, she agreed to do legal work for them once in a while.

Marcus pushed the button for the elevator, and out of the corner of his eye, he noticed a car parked a hundred feet or so away with two people sitting in it. Weird, he thought as he got in the elevator.

Exiting the elevator on the fifth floor and entering the offices of Davis, Hayes and Deters, Marcus felt strong. He felt capable. He felt a sense of purpose. He had no idea what his day would bring, but he was looking forward to it immensely. He was going to try and get some answers.

The office was the same. The old entry code still worked. The reception area where Jessica and Laura sat was virtually unchanged. There were the familiar eight chairs in the lobby and a couple of tables with magazines. There was a large conference room with a richly gleaming mahogany table. Allison's office was next to that, and past hers was Marcus's. Both their offices had windows facing east with ample views of the sprawling city.

The original partners, Michael Davis and Robert Hayes, had offices on the other side and had beautiful views of the Grand River and downtown Grand Rapids. There were also six large cubicles for paralegals in the middle of the four sumptuous outer offices. They were just a small firm with three partners. Allison was being groomed to be the fourth, and that would happen soon, Marcus was sure of that.

They had done really well considering the size of the firm. Not many three partner firms had such prime downtown office space, especially not right on the river. But they were good attorneys and had highly qualified people working for them. They had been on a rocket ship journey up, before his family had been murdered. He felt he was letting the company down by not being there, but he was grateful to know no one else in the firm felt that way about him. Marcus unlocked his office door and looked around. "Still the same," he was relieved to note.

"They kept up on the cleaning; that's good," he said aloud to himself with a little bit of a smile. As he sat down and took out his list, his mind went back to Simon Daniels and the police scene he had left behind just yesterday morning. Marcus was smart enough to know that if something had happened to Simon, it wouldn't be long until they contacted him. If they found out he was down there, his coming week would not be good.

Marcus put that out of his mind and instead focused on his list. He went over every bullet point in his head. He stopped at number four: He saw the Wainwright's Yukon. He thought back again and could picture the crash clearly: he saw the Yukon and noticed the interior lights were on. Marcus took out a pen and after # 4, "I saw the Wainwright's Yukon," he added, "The interior lights were on."

"I wonder if John remembers this," he said out loud to himself. Marcus then logged on to his computer, determined to find out everything he could on Simon Daniels—everything. He would look as deep as he could, maybe even pulling together another list before Allison arrived.

17

Allison entered the office at 9:45 a.m. and was greeted by a number of excited and curious coworkers.

"Did you know Marcus is here? He's in his office on his computer. He was in there before anyone else arrived. I think he's working!" Jessica was so excited to see Marcus she could hardly control her enthusiasm.

The entire firm had been crushed by the tragedy. Marcus was loved by all, and, everyone would agree, was critical to the success of the company. He was the backbone of the firm. His numbers were huge both in billable hours and percentage fees. His work ethic set the bar high for others. Without him there, the firm had been left sputtering.

The biggest blow was losing the lawsuit Marcus had been working on for the eight months prior to the crash. Afterwards, the firm didn't have the knowledge or manpower to take the case to court, so the client decided to accept a settlement offer of four million dollars. A win in court would have meant a considerably larger payout. Marcus found out about the settlement two years later, after all his surgeries and rehabilitation. He was furious, not about the settlement so much, but because he felt he let the client down.

Allison knocked on Marcus's office door and he motioned for her to come in.

"Shut the door, please." he stood up and gave her a hug. "Thanks for coming. I know you deserve the time off."

Marcus waved in acknowledgement at the faces looking through the office windows. Allison started in on him, "Great to see you here, Marcus. I have so many questions for you. I want to hear about your trip. Was it useful to you? It must have been; this is the first time you've been in since the accident." Marcus glanced up in disdain at the word "accident" and Allison knew she had made a mistake.

She amended, "I mean event."

"Sit down." Marcus pulled a chair up next to his and motioned her to take it. "I need to tell you something, and it's going to be hard for you to hear, but you have to believe me."

Allison sat down without saying a word. She looked at him totally tuned in to what he was about to say, curious beyond belief and just as nervous.

"My family was murdered."

Allison's heart sank. All her hopes for Marcus coming to work and starting to overcome the trauma were trampled. He's lost it, she thought. God, what am I going to do?

Marcus could tell Allison was skeptical about his proclamation. "Just listen to me a minute Allie. I remembered the crash, and I talked to Simon Daniels. I know he did it on purpose. He told me he did. I found out more than that—there was someone else involved as well."

"Hold on, Marcus." Allison had both hands up and extended toward him. "You talked to Simon Daniels?"

Nodding, and behaving way too calmly for Allison's liking, Marcus answered her, "Yes, I went to his apartment."

"I'm sorry, Marcus. This sounds crazy. You went to Simon Daniels' apartment and he told you he murdered your family? Why would he do that?" Allison felt faint. Had her big brother finally given up and checked out? He had been through so much, more than anyone could fathom, and this is how it was to end? With him cracking?

Marcus sensed her growing panic and tried to calm her. "Allie, I know this is a lot to take in, but you must trust me. I'm not nuts. I'm more together now than I have been in three years. I need your help. Can I please tell you everything I know before you pass judgment on me? If you don't believe me after that, I'll be disappointed but I'll understand. Just give me a chance."

Allison studied Marcus. She knew him well and recognized his seeming to have his old focus back. She wanted so badly to believe he wasn't going crazy. She made up her mind. "Ok, tell me everything."

Marcus told her about driving to the crash site and how he remembered seeing his family sleeping, the Yukon in front of him, and Simon crashing into the right side of their van to cause them to spin out of control. He told her how Simon had purposely looked at him before he swerved into them.

Allison turned white when he told her about having gone to Simon's apartment and holding a gun to his head, and hearing Simon's claim of, "I had to do it," and, "I didn't want anyone to die." By the time Marcus finished telling her what the bartender had said she was starting to see some plausibility in Marcus's theory. She didn't fully buy in, but enough coincidences were falling into place to chip away at her doubt. Marcus told her everything he had seen, remembered, and heard, except the last morning when he saw the police at Simon's apartment complex; he knew if she knew that he might lose her right now. He had to get her on board with his investigation first.

Allison sat back in her chair. They had been facing each other and she had been leaning farther and farther forward the more he talked. They sat silent for a couple minutes. Marcus was dying for her to say something, but she had to be the first to talk.

Finally, Allison spoke. "Why would he want your family dead?"

"C'mon, Allie. Think! He didn't want anyone to die. He said that and I believe him. He also said he had to do it, which means either someone was forcing him to do it, or he was crazy and couldn't help but do it. I'm inclined to believe someone forced him."

"But who? And why?" Allison was really starting to believe. This was the old Marcus. He was totally engrossed and completely focused on the task at hand.

"Well, why do people harm or kill? 1—They do it for love. That doesn't fit. 2—They do it because they need to, as in serial killers. Having met Simon, that doesn't seem to fit either. 3—They do it in anger. I can't think of anyone who was angry at me or my family. I don't believe that fits. But, 4, let's talk about reason number 4—THEY DO IT FOR MONEY." Marcus said this slow and loud to let it sink in.

"Who benefited from my injury or death? That's what we need to figure out. Who would benefit, how would they benefit, and why would they benefit?" Allison looked at Marcus with respect. He'd always been a gifted attorney because he was so sharp. In ten minutes he had convinced her that not only was he not crazy, but that together they had to find his family's killer or killers.

"I'm in." she said. "Where do you want to start?"

18

The first thing Detective Bruce Harper did that Monday morning was to tackle the Daniels file. He had been with the Marietta police force for eight months, and as far as police work goes, it had been a relatively quiet transition. He was forty-one years old, stood about six-foot-four, and weighed two hundred and sixty pounds. He was an imposing figure; he knew that, so he would call upon his broad smile every time he met someone new. Any intimidation his size provided would usually fade away at the sight of his infectious grin.

He had moved from Dawson, a small rural town, population five thousand or so, where he had served for ten years on the force. When a detective position opened up in the Marietta police department, he was fortunate enough to get hired. He didn't know if the city was pressured to hire him because he was black, but he didn't really care. He knew he would prove his worth. Yet he couldn't help but feel a little added pressure to succeed. He had been happy in Dawson—great people, excellent community to live in—but he wanted a little more action. He wanted to test his skills.

Now, the Marietta crime log wasn't exactly on par with Atlanta, but compared to Dawson, it might as well have been. So, when an execution-style murder that has a victim with three shots in the face and four in the back, you go to work. It was 5:37 a.m. Sunday morning when he got the call to go to 3217 Whiting Drive, Apartment 2B. When he arrived, three cruisers had already beaten him there. There were a few neighbors gawking in their doorways and he told them to go inside. The door to Mr. Daniels' apartment was wide open and he was just inside, on his stomach. Forensics was there taking pictures and dusting for prints. Bruce had spoken briefly to the first officers on the scene before returning to pump the neighbors for information. Apparently, both had been sleeping when they heard the gun fire. When they ventured outside, they saw Mr. Daniels' door was open and he was lying in a pool of blood.

Now it was Monday morning and Bruce was going over the file. He noticed immediately that Mr. Daniels had a criminal record. "No surprise there," he said quietly to himself. But what he saw next made him sit up straight in his chair.

Guilty of DUI, manslaughter with ordinary negligence, sentenced to three years. Manslaughter, that's a good place to start. Bruce looked over as there was a knock on his door. He motioned the young officer in.

"Brian Cambridge, sir. I have the forensics report for Daniels." He held out his hand and gave the folder to Bruce.

"Thank you," Bruce said with a smile. He had been in that boy's shoes before. A young cop trying to get his feet wet. The kid was twenty-four-years-old, fresh from the academy. He was skinny with dusty blonde hair and blue eyes that showed excitement every time he was given something to do.

"Wow, they got a match." Bruce was shocked. A 9mm pistol was used and there were prints on the shell casings that matched a print that'd been lifted from the buzzer to get in. This didn't make sense. He had been trained to know what a professional hit looked like and although this initially seemed to fit the bill, it now appeared to be too sloppy. There was a finger print on the buzzer? No one, professional or not, would use the buzzer without gloves if they were planning a murder. Also, there would be no prints on the casings from when they loaded the gun.

When a gunman loads a gun with his bare hands, sweat is left on the bullets. When the gun is fired, heat is transferred to the metal which sets the salt from that sweat. A chemical reaction with the metal etches the prints permanently into the casing. A smart killer would know this.

Bruce had a feeling this case was not going to be cut and dry. Like most murders, he needed two things to solve it: the murder weapon and a motive. He would start by finding out all he could about Simon Daniels. Bruce looked up and saw officer Cambridge still there waiting for him to respond.

"Hey Brian, help me find out everything we can about Mr. Simon Daniels."

"Yes, sir!" Brian said with a smile. "I'll get right on it." Bruce smiled as Brian practically ran out of his office.

Bruce began pouring over the manslaughter case. He wrote on a note pad: "Marcus Deters - survivor. Sheila, Dustin, Dillon - deceased." "Contact," he wrote with an arrow to the top name. He readily found contact information for Marcus Deters. It was a 616 area code. No cell number listed, just a land line, officially listed under the name Brian Deters. He knew he should start by giving them a call. The sooner the better, he thought. The media would be releasing Mr. Daniels' name soon and he wanted a jump on that.

19

Marcus and Allison were busy researching Simon Daniels when Allison's cell phone rang. It was Darrin.

"Hi Darrin! Miss me already?" Allison looked at Marcus with a sheepish smile as he gave her an I'm-totally-confused look, the same look he would give the paralegals when they tried to explain something poorly.

Darrin responded bluntly, "Like crazy. I don't know what to do with myself today. Would you mind if I drove in and we saw each other in Grand Rapids tonight?"

"That would be great. You should come to the office, but I don't know what time I'll be done. I'm working on a case with Marcus." Darrin paused for what seemed to Allison an odd amount of time.

"Ok, send me a text later with when and where to meet."

"Will do," she said, still looking at Marcus as she disconnected the call.

"Ok, I give. Who was that?" Marcus asked with a mix of curiosity and worry.

"His name is Darrin Warner. I met him in Pentwater. He's staying in the rental at the end of Beach Street."

Allison expected the third degree from Marcus. She was extremely surprised when all he said was, "Oh, good for you. Shall we proceed?" Allison stared at Marcus for a second and nodded.

"I'm on it, Boss," she said with a playful military salute. Marcus smiled back at her before they both turned to concentrate on their computers. After another hour of research, they paused to compare notes.

"Let's make a list," Marcus said, which came as no surprise to Allison. "What do we know about Simon Daniels?"

Allison started: "He's twenty-eight years old, married in 2011, divorced in 2012, and has a four-year-old daughter. He works at National

Wholesale in Marietta as a forklift operator where he makes $23.00 per hour. He lived in Atlanta prior to the crash. He was convicted of minor manslaughter, served a partial sentence starting in March of 2015, and was released in February of 2016. His ex-wife's name is Elizabeth Daniels. She sued for sole custody of their baby daughter in 2013, citing alcohol abuse, lack of finances, and stability as grounds. She was granted full custody after his arrest. He lives at 3712 Whiting Drive, Apartment 2B, in Marietta, Georgia. He has six months remaining on his lease. He owns a 2008 Ford F150 pickup, color is red. His parents live in Macon, Georgia in the house that Simon grew up in. Simon has a business degree from Vanderbilt University."

Marcus raised his hand and stopped her. "He has a business degree from Vanderbilt? Why is he working as a forklift operator?"

Allison held up a finger as if to tell him, "Hold on," and continued. "He graduated in 2009 at the age of twenty-one." Allison looked up and said, "He's no dummy. He worked for Lambert Securities in Atlanta as an investment advisor for a year, but appears to have been terminated right before the crash."

After stopping to finally take a breath, Allison looked at Marcus and said, "That's about all I got."

"Well," said Marcus, "Where do you think we go from here?"

Allison looked at Marcus fondly; she knew he already knew where the next steps were leading, but he was letting her call the shots. That is, as long as she stayed on the same page as him.

"We need to talk to his ex, Elizabeth Daniels, and to find out more about Lambert Securities and why he was fired."

Marcus nodded and said, "I'll have Jessica get two tickets to Atlanta for tomorrow morning. Don't stay out too late with this Darrin guy," Marcus said, trying but failing to not sound overly protective.

"Ha ha," Allison said, smiling back at Marcus. It was so good to see him working again, even if only temporarily.

"Have fun, Allie. I have to go meet with the partners and let them know I plan on being around more."

"Good luck," she winked at him as she left his office. "Let me know what time I need to be at the airport."

"Will do, Allie," he called out as he headed to Jessica's desk. "Hey Jessica, I need two round trip tickets to Atlanta tomorrow. Can you see what you can find? I'm going to see Michael in his office. Let me know when I come back."

Jessica nodded and started to look. Jessica had been with the firm as long as Marcus had and had become very close with him and his family. She had been devastated along with everyone else at the firm after the crash. She was always eager to help him with anything and was delighted to see him in the office again.

Marcus knocked on the door of Michael Davis, senior partner at the firm. He was a handsome man in his late fifties with silver hair that made him look distinguished instead of old.

"Come in, Marcus," Michael said as he motioned him to enter. "Great to see you here. How are you doing? Are you coming back to work?"

Marcus always hated that question, "How are you doing?" He was sure that most people that lost loved ones probably hated it as well. He's doing shitty, and as far as he knew, that would never change.

"Well," Marcus replied, "I'm doing ok and I do have some things to do in the office, but I don't think I will be coming back officially for a bit yet. But I do plan on coming back."

Michael paused as if he was carefully choosing his words. "Ok, Marcus, do what is best for you, but we really could use you here. I know you've been through a lot and you are still suffering terribly, but maybe it would be good for you to get back to work."

There it was. The old it-would-be-good-for-you speech. He had heard that so many times in the last couple years, and he knew everyone meant well, but still... What the hell do they know? Nobody could possibly have any idea what would be good for him unless they'd suffered a tragedy of their own.

"I'm sure you're right, and I plan on getting back to work soon," Marcus said assuredly. "I just have some things to take care of first."

Michael looked at Marcus sadly. He felt so bad for Marcus and yet he needed him working. The firm was struggling, profits were down, and expenses were up. Marcus had been drawing a salary the whole time he'd been off. Michael knew Marcus hadn't needed the money with the life insurance policies and compensation on the accident. But the firm couldn't stop paying him. They wouldn't stop paying him. He was a part of their family and a huge part of the success they had enjoyed. But they had taken a hit financially the last three years. There was no doubt about that.

"Ok, Marcus. You take care of those things. After that, we would love for you to come back. We miss you around here."

"Thanks, Michael. That means a lot to me," Marcus replied softly. Marcus started to leave but paused and turned back. "I am so sorry about the Peters case. I know what that meant to our firm. I heard about the settlement, and I know it's not what we wanted, but I'm glad we at least profited." Michael looked at Marcus in a way that made Marcus question, "We did profit, didn't we?"

Michael shook his head slowly.

"But our percentage would have been almost one and a half million dollars! That would have covered the salaries, expenses, and then some!" Marcus half shouted.

Michael looked at Marcus and could see the lights going on as it dawned on him what must have happened. Michael nodded and explained, "After your accident, Mr. Peters had thought that without you, we wouldn't be able to emotionally or mentally handle the suit properly—and he was probably right—so he decided to settle. The defense attorneys knew this as well and only offered four million and wouldn't budge. Mr. Peters would only accept it if we would change our percentage. We were not in a good position to argue the case well without you, so we agreed and lowered the percentage."

"Lowered it to what?" Marcus was getting agitated over what he was hearing. He and a team of three paralegals had worked on this case for over eight months.

"Ten percent," Michael blurted out, almost embarrassed.

Marcus looked at Michael in bewilderment. "Ten percent? That's only $400,000!"

Michael nodded at him in agreement. "We decided it was in our best interest to cut our losses and walk away. The client recouped some damages, and we all moved on. I'm sorry, Marcus."

Marcus was fuming. "They dropped their percentage from thirty-five to ten? I'm sorry, Michael. I didn't know."

Michael nodded. "Don't worry about it. What's done is done and we must move on."

Marcus stood up, wished Michael a good day, and left the office. He had a busy night ahead of him and he had to get ready for Atlanta.

20

Allison was busy touching up her hair and makeup when the intercom sounded. She was instantly excited. It was Darrin. He had driven down to see her and they were going to go get a bite to eat. She was going to take him to her favorite spot to eat downtown. It was a little Mexican place only a short walk from her condo called Luna where both the food and the margaritas were excellent. She went to the intercom and looked at Darrin through the camera system the condo had set up in every unit.

"Come on up," she said as she pushed the five-digit code that unlocked the front door.

Her condo was on the seventh floor. It was an industrial-style loft with polished cement floors and high, open ceilings with exposed heating and cooling ducts. It had two big bedrooms, two bathrooms, a big open kitchen with nice stainless appliances, and a large family room with a fireplace. It was city living at its best as far as she was concerned. You could keep your suburbs—she loved being around everything.

She knew Grand Rapids was no Chicago but boy was it changing. What a transformation downtown had undergone in just the last fifteen years. An eclectic variety of restaurants and bars, great entertainment, art, museums—you named it, Grand Rapids had it, and it was only getting bigger and better all the time. She was excited to show Darrin a little bit of its appeal.

She walked to the door and let him in. He reached out and gave her a big hug. She looked up and kissed him.

"Welcome to my home," she said happily.

Darrin looked around quickly. "Wow, it's really nice. How long have you lived here?"

"Four or five years," she answered. "You hungry? Cuz I'm starving." She smiled and grabbed his hand. "Let's go get some dinner."

21

Marcus pulled into the driveway of his parents' home and could see his mom looking out the window. She had a look on her face that Marcus knew all too well; she was worried. She was very worried. He knew it right away. Her eyes were squinty and her lips pursed, but even worse, she was pacing, back and forth, in front of the window, nervously glancing out of it as if waiting. Waiting, he assumed, for him.

"Oh boy," Marcus thought as went to the door. He stepped into the house and his mom was right there.

She didn't waste any time. "Marcus, a detective from Marietta, Georgia named Bruce Harper called and wanted to speak to you. I told him you weren't here but you would call when you got back. He said you could call at any time. What's going on?"

"I don't know," Marcus replied. "He didn't say anything else?"

"Nope, just that it was important." She had tears in her eyes and Marcus felt terrible.

"Where's his number? I will take care of it," he said as he walked to the kitchen. He already knew where the number would be, right on the note pad next to the phone. The same place the note pad had been as long as he could remember. He picked it up, went outside, and dialed the number. The phone rang a few times before he heard a friendly sounding voice with a heavy southern accent answer.

"This is Detective Harper. How may I assist you?"

"Detective Harper, this is Marcus Deters. I was told you had called."

"Yes, Mr. Deters. Thank you for returning my call so promptly. If it's ok I would like to take a few minutes of your time and ask you a couple questions. I will try and be brief."

Part of detective training had been studying voice inflection, the tones and tendencies reflected in a person's voice when they are startled, lying, or nervous. He had wondered if he would pick something up in Marcus's voice but there was nothing—no pause, no waiver, nothing.

Marcus simply said, "Sure, I hope I can help. What are they pertaining to?"

The detective started off, "Well, Mr. Deters, I would like to ask you about Simon Daniels."

Marcus knew where this was going. "What about him?" he asked, sounding curious.

"Well, Mr. Deters, Simon Daniels was found dead in his apartment Sunday morning."

Marcus paused and then spoke, "Good."

Now it was the detective's turn to pause. He was a little surprised by the candor but perhaps shouldn't have been. "I understand you probably have no sympathy for him considering the situation, but I wondered if you knew about it. From your reaction, I don't believe you did."

"Were you thinking I may have had something to do with it?" Marcus asked.

Bruce needed to be careful here. "Well, it's my job to explore all avenues and your name was on the top of the list of people that were affected by Mr. Daniels."

"I'm sorry, Detective, but I'm not sorry he's dead. I only wish it had happened more than three years ago."

"Of course, Mr. Deters," the detective said slowly. "We're all sorry for your loss."

Marcus paused and said, "Thank you, I'm sure you are, and I'm sorry I couldn't be of more help to you."

"That's quite alright, Mr. Deters. Oh, and by the way, do you own any guns? It's just a routine question."

Marcus quickly thought of the gun under his seat. "Yes, I own several: a few rifles and shot guns for hunting and a small pistol collection which I use for target shooting."

"Do you own any nine millimeter pistols for target shooting?"

Marcus thought this question was a little sarcastic and was not impressed. "Of course I do."

The detective concluded the conversation politely with, "Thank you for your time, and I may be in touch if we find anything that seems relevant to talk to you about."

After Marcus hung up he wondered how he would explain this to his parents. He finally resigned himself to the fact he would lie, but just a little. He simply told them that Simon Daniels had died and the police thought he should know, and that's it. They were taken back by the news, but Marcus felt they believed everything he said.

.

22

Darrin and Allison were enjoying their dinner at Luna when Allison got a text from Jessica saying their plane would be leaving at 8:15 the following morning.

"Not terribly early," she said out loud, knowing Darrin would want to know what she was talking about.

"What's that?" he asked.

"Marcus and I are flying to Atlanta tomorrow morning at 8:15. We'll have to turn in early," she said with a smile as she looked at him.

Darrin seemed not to notice her smile at all. Rather, he simply asked, "What's in Atlanta?"

Disappointed, Allison replied, "We need to interview some people for a case we are working on."

Darrin continued to stare at her and asked, "What case?"

Allison started to feel a little uneasy at his prying and she shook her head as if to say I don't want to talk about it, but he continued. "Al, you said Marcus hadn't been working. Now you're going to Atlanta on a case?"

Allison looked at him intently. Was he worried about her or did he think she was lying? Which was it? "Look," Allison said, "he hadn't been working but now he is. There is some new information on the accident he was in, and we are just going to do a few interviews tomorrow to follow up. It isn't a big deal and you shouldn't worry about me. I'll be fine."

Darrin stared back at her with a very concerned look on his face. Allison was confused; why would Darrin be so uptight about them going to Atlanta? She decided to let it go and focus on the night that they were going to share together. "So, what do you think of the food?" she asked, wanting to change the subject.

"It's great, this place and the food are great." He was smiling again. "We should get the check. I'm ready to go back to your place." They were both smiling now.

23

Allison woke up early on Tuesday to get ready for her flight. She packed a small bag in case they decided to stay the night. Darrin had volunteered to bring her to the airport, so she woke him and they headed out. He was acting odd. They rode in virtual silence the whole way to the airport. Allison had a strange feeling come over her. It's like he knows something that he's not telling me, she thought. She knew that had to be impossible; they had just met. She scolded herself, thinking, stop it, Allison, you always do this. Darrin is perfect for you. It's all in your imagination. He's just worried about you.

They arrived at the United Airlines terminal at Gerald R. Ford International Airport by 7:30. Darrin pulled up to the curb in the passenger drop off zone and parked the car. He looked at Allison with concern.

"Promise me you'll be careful. If you think something seems dangerous, just come home."

Allison was agitated now. "I'm a professional attorney; I've been on hundreds of interviews. Nothing dangerous is going to happen. But if something does happen, I assure you I can handle it." She paused, hating the idea of leaving on a negative note. "But to ease your mind, I'm always careful." She winked, gave him a kiss, and said, "I'll call you later." Allison looked back as she entered the airport and saw Darrin driving away. She suddenly felt oddly alone.

"Allie!" Allison heard her brother calling from the ticket counter. He waved her over. "I guess we don't rate first class anymore," he said with a smile. "But I got an exit row, so that's something!"

Allison shrugged. She didn't care about being in first class. Honestly, she always thought that was a frivolous expense, more of a status thing for the partners. They rarely flew outside of the Midwest anyway. It didn't bother her in the least to fly coach. She was just happy her brother had a pulse again, that he was breathing in life instead of just air. But she knew that if things started unfolding like he had suggested, it may be hard for him to continue. Proving the accident was in fact no accident would be a difficult task, but learning the truth may be even harder to accept. All she knew was that she was going to do her best to follow this through for Marcus and see where it ended up.

They grabbed their boarding passes, breezed through security, and entered the plane. Allison was looking forward to this time with Marcus. As the plane left the runway and headed up into the clouds, Marcus began to speak to her quietly, like he didn't want anyone else to hear.

"I talked to Michael about the Peters case yesterday."

Allison knew where this was going.

He continued. "I heard about the lowered commission. We took a bath on it; our expenses were more than that! I feel terrible about the loss, but I understand the client's position on the percentage. I know something was better than nothing, but it stings to have had to settle after putting so much time and effort into it."

Allison nodded. She knew Marcus was bound to learn the details of the Peters settlement eventually. It was the case that Marcus had invested months of effort into but had to be basically abandoned after the accident. Marcus was an incredible attorney but he was also a loner. He never shared with the partners or other attorneys any of the details of his cases. The paralegals knew pieces of the case, but only Marcus knew his plan on how to argue it. Without Marcus, the Peters case was doomed, and the client, needing the money, had no choice but to settle.

The defendant, GR Financial, had been a small wealth management and financial advising company. Though they were small, they seemed to have been extremely well funded and had hired the impressive legal team from US Law, a national firm with five locations and over a thousand attorneys. It held licenses in almost every state and billed in the two to three billion dollar range annually. Allison had always thought it strange that such a large and expensive firm had taken on such a relatively small case.

Before the crash, Marcus had branded this case as a "home run" and was obsessed with it. After the crash, he wouldn't speak of it. Allison had tried once but he had just waved her off and turned away.

Marcus continued, "The four million was enough that the client could put back what had been lost in the company's pension fund, so I'm happy for them, but I'm really disappointed with the outcome. It could have been huge." Marcus looked at Allison, moved close to her, and in a low, stern voice said, "It seems to me somebody there benefited from my not being able to finish the case after of the accident."

Allison looked at him and couldn't help thinking again that he was losing it. He actually looked crazy. Maybe this was a mistake coming down here. Was Darrin right?

"Come on, Marcus," Allison pleaded. "Why would they do that? I don't think any company would kill three people just to win a lawsuit. Remember they still paid four million dollars. That's a lot of money to a small firm like GR Financial."

Marcus calmed down a bit. "Ok, Allie. Just promise me you'll keep an open mind and do your due diligence in the investigating. I need you at your best."

Allison felt better immediately. He had calmed down and was Marcus again. "I will be your Sherlock Holmes," she said smiling. Allison sat back in her chair and closed her eyes. In what seemed like only minutes, she heard the flight attendant announce, "We are beginning our final descent into Atlanta. Please put your seatbelts on and tray tables up."

24

Bruce Harper was examining the Simon Daniels file when Officer Cambridge joined him at his desk. "How's it going with the Daniels homicide investigation?"

Detective Harper looked back at the young officer and shrugged. "What do you think happened, Brian? Do you have any thoughts on the matter? Do you have any ideas to share?"

"Well, the toxicology report came back negative, so I don't think it was drug related. I don't know, maybe a jealous boyfriend?"

Detective Harper shrugged again. "Maybe a possibility, I guess, but I don't think so. It seems to be more like a professional hit than an emotional reaction. That's not to say a jealous boyfriend couldn't have been trained to kill. He could be active duty or ex-military. But something just feels out of sorts. The victim's name was released last night, so I'm betting we'll get some leads today. That being the case, I'm going to need your help from here on out until we get this solved."

Brian was thrilled to be able to help on a real homicide case. Now he just needed to make a difference. "I'll do my best, sir." He tried to sound serious but it was hard for him not to smile. Bruce smiled at the young man's exuberance and recognized in that moment that he was going to be the officer's mentor. It was a task he planned on doing well.

Selma from the front desk walked in. "Sir, there is someone here to see you. He wants to talk about the Daniels murder."

Bruce knew not to get excited about a visitor prematurely. There would be plenty of people coming in. Most wouldn't help at all, but you must listen to all of them, he'd learned. You never knew when you'd get some breakthrough information.

"Please send him in, Selma," he said calmly.

Bruce leaned back to look through the glass next to his office door to see if he could get a glimpse of who was coming. It was a younger man, maybe thirty, with a thin build, dark brown hair, very pale skin, and tattoos on his arms. He had a serious demeanor about him that right away made Bruce hopeful this would be worthwhile. The young man came into the office and took the seat Bruce offered, right next to Brian.

Bruce shook his hand and introduced himself. "My name is Detective Harper and this here is Officer Cambridge. What can we do for you?"

The young man grabbed Bruce's hand and gave it a shake. "Well, sir, I heard about Simon, and I may have some information for you."

Bruce nodded. "Did you know him?"

"Yes, sir. My name is Dale Coffman. I am the bartender at The Marietta Oasis Hotel. I talked to a man the night of Simon's death who was very upset with him.

Bruce leaned forward in his chair a little; he was interested now, very interested. Bruce had all kinds of questions flowing through his mind but he knew he must let this man tell him everything he could before asking anything. Bruce nodded for him to continue.

"Well, he said that Simon owed him and that Simon was a fuck, and he asked me questions about the night of Simon's accident. He wanted to know everything I could tell him about that night."

Bruce looked at him and asked, "Did he leave a name?"

The bartender nodded. "I don't recall what it was, but I remember he asked me to bill his room. He was staying at the Oasis."

Bruce glanced at Brian and Brian left the room to chase down the lead. He was going to call the Oasis. Good boy, Brian, Bruce thought to himself. Way to take charge.

Bruce turned back to Dale. "Anything else?"

Dale shrugged and answered flatly, "He seemed to be drunk. Not falling-down drunk, just drunk. He was drinking whiskey. He left around 1:30 am."

Bruce stood up and held out his hand. "Thank you, Mr. Coffman, for coming in. Please leave your information with Selma when you leave so I can get in touch with you if I need to."

Dale left, leaving Bruce thinking that this could be something substantial. But it seemed too easy. Maybe it was easy. Maybe the drunk guy at the hotel had a beef with Simon and went and shot him. It was interesting and they'd certainly pursue it. But already it didn't sit right with Bruce.

25

"Two cars?" Allison asked Marcus as he signed an agreement at the rental car desk.

"Yep. You have two places to go, and I have two places to go. We need two cars to get there."

Allison looked at him, confused. "I thought we were doing this together?"

"C'mon, Allie. We'll cover more ground separately, and, besides, I want you to talk to Simon's wife alone. I think she will respond better to you."

Allison was astonished by what Marcus was suggesting. Marcus had given her no indication she'd be doing the interview alone. "Am I going to Lambert Securities alone as well?"

Marcus smiled and nodded at her. "That's the plan. Do your best—I know you will." Marcus handed her the keys to a 2016 Impala. "Good luck, Sherlock," he said with a grin.

"Where are you going to go?" Allison was a little ticked off now.

Marcus was amused by her reaction. "I have an appointment with a detective in Marietta, only he doesn't know I'm coming. Just go do your interviews. I have complete trust in you. That's why you're here. I can't think of anyone I'd rather have on this than you."

Allison's head was spinning now. "What's going on Marcus? Why do you need to go to Marietta? What did you do?"

"Nothing, Allie. I just want to talk to someone about Simon. Stay focused, sis. I need you to stay on your game. Go find something out about Simon."

Allison sighed and nodded. She took the key from Marcus and headed to her car. Marcus watched as she drove off. He knew what lay ahead. She was going to discover that Simon was dead at her first stop and it was going to floor her. He wanted her to have an honest reaction when she found out. It would develop some trust right away with Simon's ex, and that could help her out. However, Marcus was not looking forward to dealing with Allison when they met up later. She would be livid that he'd kept her in the dark.

Allison headed first to meet Elizabeth Daniels, Simon's ex-wife and mother of his four-year-old daughter. Allison was interested to see how Elizabeth would react to her being there. She assumed she would have to talk her way in. As Allison followed her GPS to the address they had tracked down, she couldn't help but notice the size of the houses she was driving by.

"Wow," she said to herself. "Where did you get all your money?"

Her phone indicated her destination was on the right. She pulled up to a large gate with a security camera and a small but unmanned guard house. Allison pushed the call button on the intercom and after a few short seconds, a voice responded. "May I help you?" It was an older woman's voice with a heavy southern accent.

"Yes, hello! My name is Allison Deters. I would really like to talk to Ms. Daniels. Is she available?"

After about thirty seconds, Allison was relieved when the woman finally answered. "Come on in. The gate will open shortly." As promised, the massive gate moved inward and Allison proceeded up the long entry toward the residence. Although less than twenty years old, the home was styled to replicate a stately southern plantation and it was beautiful. The driveway split near the house to a wide circle drive surrounding the fountain in the front, and an expansive four-car garage in the back. There was a huge front porch with massive columns that reached the second story roof.

Allison's mind was racing. How did Simon's ex-wife afford to live here? Did she remarry? Had she come from money? If so, it must have been big money. Allison pulled up the circle drive to the impressive front entrance. As she got out of her car and walked up the porch steps she took in all the intricate details and especially admired the phenomenal flowers and lush green bushes that highlighted the property's landscaping.

She was definitely interested in meeting Elizabeth now. She rang the bell and waited in anticipation. The door opened and there stood an older woman wearing a sixties-style maid uniform: a gray shift, mid-shin in length, with a wide, white collar and matching bright white apron tied tightly around her waist.

"Come with me, please," the woman beckoned in a rich southern drawl.

Allison followed her into the enormous foyer. The housekeeper stopped and warily looked Allison up and down.

"Can you tell me what this is about? This is a really bad day," she said.

"Well, ma'am, I came a real long way just to speak with her, and if she could just give me a few minutes, I sure would appreciate it."

The housekeeper looked down her nose at Allison; she wasn't convinced.

"Well, Elizabeth agreed to see you, but don't you upset her any more than she already is."

The housekeeper led her to a comfortable sitting area and motioned her to take a seat. Allison obliged and as she did, the door at the other end of the room opened. Allison could only assume the younger woman standing in the doorway was Elizabeth. She appeared to have been crying heavily as the light streaks of mascara on her cheeks betrayed her. "Ms. Daniels?" Allison asked, rising to greet her. The young woman nodded and asked, "What can I do for you?"

"Ms. Daniels, my name is Allison Deters. I'm an attorney, and I've come a long way to ask you some questions about Simon. Would you mind?"

Elizabeth held open the door and signaled for her to follow. Allison complied. "Thank you. You have a beautiful home."

Elizabeth politely acknowledged her compliment and led her to another room off the back of the house, this one with windows on three sides. It had nice wicker furniture with extremely thick cushions and an old, rugged coffee table in between. Allison couldn't help but feel at home.

"Would you like some coffee? Or tea perhaps?" Elizabeth asked her. She was talking so quietly, Allison could tell that she was still terribly upset.

"That won't be necessary, but thank you. I'm sorry to ask, but are you alright?"

Elizabeth looked up at her with her red, tear-stained eyes. Instead of answering the question, she asked her own. "Why did you come here? I know who you are. You're the sister."

Allison was taken aback at first, but her mind quickly processed what was now obvious; Elizabeth must have recognized her name from the court appearances after the crash.

"Yes, I'm the sister. I'm the sister of Marcus Deters who was severely injured in a crash three years ago. I am also the sister-in-law of Sheila Deters who was killed in that same crash and aunt to the two boys who died with her. I am here to ask you some questions about Simon because, to be perfectly blunt, we feel evidence has shown that it might not have been an accident after all."

Elizabeth's reaction terrified Allison. Not because she grew angry or defensive, but because she barely responded at all. Allison instinctively concluded her lack of emotion gave credence to Marcus's theory; Simon really may have done it on purpose. Elizabeth hung her head low, and without looking up she asked, "Why now? Why right after he's been killed?"

Allison looked at Elizabeth, shocked. "Who's been killed Elizabeth? Who's been killed?"

"Like you didn't know." Elizabeth was again in tears. "Simon was killed on Saturday; it's all over the news. He was shot at his apartment."

Allison was horrified. Her mind was reeling. Marcus was there Saturday night. He came down to see Simon. What did he do? He couldn't have, could he? Even as Allison stared at Elizabeth, her fear was replaced with sympathy. Elizabeth was obviously devastated by Simon's death. For a second, Allison thought of Darrin and missed him.

"What do you know about what happened, Elizabeth?"

"Nothing really," she sobbed. "A detective from Marietta called and told me. He said Simon had been killed and that they were still investigating. He also asked if I knew anything that might help. I couldn't think of anything just then, but I can tell you that Simon was devastated by the deaths of your family members. He was such a good person, and our lives had been changed so much. He really didn't care what happened to him anymore, but I did. I cared a lot." Elizabeth had stopped sobbing and her bloodshot eyes caught Allison's. "It's all my fault; nothing ever would have happened if it wasn't for me." Allison placed her hand on Elizabeth's knee and gently squeezed it.

"Why would you say that? It's not your fault. How could it be?" Allison could tell there was something behind Elizabeth's words. She believed all this was somehow her fault - whether it was or not, she believed it.

"I fell in love with Simon, that's why. I thought we could stay out of it, but I was wrong."

Allison's heart was pounding. What was going on? She didn't expect this. What was this woman talking about? Stay out of what? Allison wanted to get some information, but she could tell Elizabeth was becoming more upset again, so she decided to direct her another way.

"Elizabeth," Allison said softly, "what happened between you and Simon?"

Allison had doubted Elizabeth would answer, but she looked up at her and began to tell her story.

"I loved him." She sobbed. "We met at college and I fell for him right away. I was a sophomore and he was a junior. He was sweet and so smart. He had such a fire and drive in him but always such a kind heart. I was smitten. We knew right away we would eventually get married."

She stopped to see if Allison was listening. Allison silently bobbed her head in encouragement, hoping to hear more.

"I should have stayed away from him. It was unfair of me to bring him into my world. I told myself it would work, but I was blinded by my feelings for him. I think I always knew it would end badly. I knew it, but I ignored my head and followed my heart, and now three innocent people are dead and so is Simon. Believe me when I tell you—I'm so sorry about your family and so was Simon. But also believe this: if Simon and I hadn't met, your family would still be alive."

Elizabeth buried her face in her hands and wept inconsolably. Allison was torn. She didn't know if and how she should continue. She obviously wanted more information, but at the same time, felt so sorry for Elizabeth and didn't want to cause her more pain. She decided to keep gently pressing while remaining sympathetic to Elizabeth's grief.

"How could that possibly be true, Elizabeth? How could Simon's meeting you be responsible for the crash or his death? Maybe you can help me understand what happened? Maybe together we can find out what happened to Simon?"

Elizabeth lifted her head and this time Allison could almost feel the pain she saw in her eyes. She reached out and placed her hand on Elizabeth's.

"I know who killed Simon," Elizabeth said curtly. "Just because I told the detective I didn't know anything doesn't mean I really don't know. I also know your brother was with Simon the night he died."

Allison was sick to her stomach. Marcus had seen Simon and Elizabeth was well aware of it. That had to be bad news. She suddenly wondered if Marcus knew Simon was dead. Of course he knew. The police would have called him right away. And it also occurred to her why he hadn't told her. It made sense. He wanted Elizabeth to see Allison's initial reaction of shock and disbelief, ultimately leading her to confide more of her story in Allison.

It appears Marcus's plan worked. As much as she hated being blindsided, she could at least agree that it was a smart approach to take. At the same time, she also knew that when the police found out Marcus was at his apartment, he would be brought in for questioning and probably held for Simon's murder. She needed to find out all she could from Elizabeth now, anything that would help Marcus either legally or emotionally.

"Marcus saw him?" repeated Allison.

"Not only did they see each other, but Marcus pulled a gun on him. He pulled it on him and put it to his head, and Simon told him to shoot." Those words terrified Allison.

"Elizabeth," Allison said softly, "how do you know Marcus was there?"

"Because I was there, too."

Elizabeth spoke in a tone that left no doubt she was telling the truth. "I was waiting for Simon. I showed up about ten minutes before Simon got home and was hiding in the bedroom when your brother came up. I thought we were both going to die, but then he left without hurting Simon and he never even knew I was there. I left shortly after Marcus did. Simon was killed later that night, but I know your brother didn't do it."

"How would you know for sure?" Allison asked. "How do you know he didn't go back?"

Elizabeth shrugged. "He didn't have it in him. I could tell by his tone. His demeanor. When he let Simon go, I knew he was devastated. But he is not a killer."

"I'm sorry, Elizabeth, but I have to know one more thing. Why did you and Simon get divorced when it's clear how much you cared about him?"

"We have a four-year-old daughter together. Did you know that?" Allison nodded. "We couldn't let anything happen to her. She was Simon's whole world. We love her and would do anything to keep her safe. We had to divorce to protect her." Elizabeth looked at her intensely. "There are evil people in this world. People that all they care about is money and power. People that don't care who they hurt, or who they steal from, or even who they kill. As hard as it is for you or me to comprehend, there are people that care more about money than their own families. There are people who will never, and I mean never, have enough money no matter how rich they are. I happen to be part of a family with members that think and act this way. I am a member of the Dean family. My maiden name is Elizabeth Dean."

Elizabeth stopped and waited for Allison's reaction. Surely she would know who she was talking about. Allison hesitated for just a few moments before the name clicked. "Jeremiah Dean?" she ventured.

Elizabeth nodded. "That's right. Jeremiah Dean, one of the most ruthless men you will ever come across. He has politicians on his payroll. Senators and members of the House of Representatives call him all the time. He's even met presidents."

"Right from the start, he felt that Simon wasn't good enough for me because Simon's parents were poor and didn't come from money like we did. My father despised Simon, so naturally he was vehemently opposed to our marriage. When we married against his will, he set out to ruin Simon. I had no idea the lengths my father would go to. He is a dangerous man. He can have anything done or anybody killed. He will stop at nothing to keep what he has and to gain even more."

"When our daughter, Anna, was born right away, he softened for a bit. I thought we might be able to work things out between us. For a little while, at least, he was tolerable. He still hated Simon, but he was civil to us. He gave us this house even though Simon didn't want it. I made Simon try and appease my father."

"But then something happened at work and Simon got fired from his job. My father and Simon had a huge argument, and Simon told me he even threatened to take Anna away from us. Can you imagine taking your daughter's child? He could have done it, too. Power and money can get anything done, and that's who he is. Simon and I separated and then got divorced after he'd been sentenced for the crash. Simon would never tell me the details of the crash. But I can promise you, if it wasn't an accident, my father was involved and Simon had no choice. He would never have hurt anyone on purpose."

Allison had heard of Jeremiah Dean. He was one of the richest men in the Midwest, if not in the entire United States. So that explains this mansion and the housekeepers. But she admitted she had no idea what he'd done to earn all his money, only that he had it.

Something about the story still didn't make sense. "Why would a man like your father have his son-in-law smash into an innocent family's vehicle? They were just four people on vacation," Allison asked her. Elizabeth trembled and began to cry again, more softly this time.

"I'm sorry. I don't know why. I can just promise you that Simon wouldn't do that on purpose unless, like he told your brother, he had to."

Elizabeth stood up and Allison knew it was time for her to leave. Elizabeth looked exhausted. Allison stood up as well and leaned over to give her a hug, which she returned with a full embrace.

"Thank you for sharing with me," Allison whispered into Elizabeth's ear. "I'm so sorry for your loss."

Elizabeth pulled back and looked Allison in the eyes. "And I'm sorry for yours. If there's anything else I can do for you let me know, but please be careful. You have no idea the kind of people you're dealing with."

Allison thanked her and they exchanged cell phone numbers in case Elizabeth thought of something else that may be helpful for her to know. As they made their way to the front door Elizabeth asked her where she was going next. Allison mentioned her plan to visit Lambert Securities.

"I figured you might. Ask for Diane Parker. She would be your best source, I would guess."

"Thank you," Allison smiled. "Thank you for everything."

As Allison drove away, she thought about everything she had just been told. It was a lot to take in, especially the fact that Simon had been killed. She felt a little guilty for thinking, even for a second, that Marcus could have done it, but who knew what he would be capable of now? And she now began to feel a little nervous for her and Marcus's safety. If the people Elizabeth thinks are involved in this, as Elizabeth seems certain they are, they could be in danger. She desperately needed to go over all of this with Marcus. But since she knew he would still be tied up with his own agenda for the day, Allison decided to grab a bite to eat and take some notes to help organize her thoughts better for when they would finally sit down together. But before that, she wanted to call Darrin.

26

Bruce was pondering what the bartender had revealed when Brian came back in. Bruce looked up at him and noticed he looked a tad excited. He was obviously anxious to tell him something.

"Ok Brian, what did you find out? Tell me before you pass out," Bruce laughed. He enjoyed seeing the animation in the young man's face. He surmised that after a while, the thrill of detective work would likely fade and be replaced with disgust and discouragement. After a few years in law enforcement, you tend to start losing faith in humankind a bit.

"Guess who was at the hotel bar Saturday night? Guess who I think it was that talked to Dale the bartender?" Bruce motioned Brian to continue. He was afraid Brian would explode if he wasn't allowed to continue. "Marcus Deters was there. Marcus Deters, 'THE' Marcus Deters from Michigan. The man you called yesterday was here last weekend. I confirmed it with the hotel desk; they have him on file. He was there for two nights and had a tab Saturday night at the bar."

To Officer Cambridge's bafflement, Bruce showed no surprise at this revelation. Instead, he became deep in thought. When he talked to Marcus just the day before, he never mentioned having been to Marietta. He must have known they would find out. Why wouldn't he have said anything?

"OK," Bruce said, "let's try to reach him again on the phone. You know where this case is going to go, don't you?"

Brian looked at him and shook his head.

"To the FBI," Bruce frowned. He quickly explained their dilemma. "The FBI will have to get involved unless Mr. Deters comes back down to Georgia on his own, and the chances of that happening are almost nil. Why would Mr. Deters, the prime suspect, and an attorney, voluntarily come down? He wouldn't. He knows the whole procedure: he knows we won't have enough evidence to arrest him, and if we can't arrest him, we can't get his prints. Without his prints, we can't cross reference the ones found at the scene. So even if the prints on the bullet casings and door buzzer are his, we can't prove it. And if we somehow obtain his prints illegally, they'd never make it to the inside of a courtroom."

"Brian, at least let's run a search on the data base to see if he has any prints on file. It's a long shot, but you never know."

Brian nodded and left the office. Just as he was leaving, Selma poked her head inside Bruce's office.

"Hey Bruce, there's someone here to see you. He says his name is Marcus Deters. Should I show him in?"

Bruce stared at her in amazement and simply said, "Please do."

27

Marcus sat calmly in the drab lobby of the police station. When the woman behind the window had told him to take a seat, he knew he wouldn't be sitting there long. As soon as they discovered Marcus had been in Marietta the night Simon was murdered, he would undoubtedly become their number one suspect. He was quite positive they knew by now. They'd want to bring him in for questioning anyway, so why not beat them to the punch? Marcus knew, too, that because he was from out of state, the FBI would have to be the ones to bring him down here. He wasn't too worried about that, but it seemed like a good idea to delay their involvement as long as possible. Once they were called in, he'd likely be under surveillance non-stop, and he needed to have some freedom to move about on his own without being seen for a while yet.

"Mr. Deters, will you follow me please?" The woman had returned.

Marcus got up and followed her down a hallway and into an office with a "Detective Harper" nameplate stuck on the door.

"You must be Detective Harper." Marcus reached his hand out to greet the detective.

"You can call me Bruce," the detective answered somewhat cautiously. "Please sit down. Officer Cambridge was just leaving."

The young officer stood up and looked at the detective, hoping he would change his mind and let him stay. But Bruce was clearly waiting for Brian to leave and close the door behind him.

"Well, Mr. Deters, I must admit I'm very surprised to see you here. Is there something I can do for you?"

Marcus took stock of the gentleman behind the metal desk. The detective was a pretty imposing person, about six-foot-four or so, maybe 250 pounds. He kept a very neat appearance with a nice suit and starched shirt. He had an honest look and a very calm demeanor about him. Marcus hoped that this man would be just the vehicle he needed to help him with his plans.

"Well," Marcus started, "I guess I thought I would save you the trouble of trying to get me down here. I'm sure by now you know I was here on Saturday night, and that must have put a target on my back. I thought I could help myself by coming to you first and telling you everything that happened that night. I know it doesn't look good for me. But I'm going to have to trust a complete stranger to get to the truth."

Marcus looked at the detective to try and get a read on him. Nothing, he just stared back at him with a solemn look on his face.

Finally, Bruce broke his stare and said, "I assume I am the complete stranger you're referring to?"

Marcus nodded.

"Well, Mr. Deters, I wouldn't get too confident in that just yet. But I will admit I am intrigued that you're here, and I can't wait to hear your story, so why don't you begin by telling me what brought you to Marietta last weekend."

Marcus liked the detective right away; he was going to be perfect.

"I came to see Simon. He killed my family and I wanted to see him, to see what he was like, how he acted in his everyday life. I wanted to find out why he did it."

Bruce held up his hand, an indication for Marcus to stop talking.

"Mr. Deters, are you suggesting that Mr. Daniels hit you on purpose? I've gone over that file, and as I recall it, every determination was that it was an accident. A very, very unfortunate accident and I am truly sorry for your loss. But Mr. Daniels pled guilty and served his time, and now he is dead too. My priority is to find out how and why he was murdered. Right now, you are suspect Number One."

"Well, if you think I'm suspect Number One right now, wait until I tell you the rest my story. I'm sure you'll be even more convinced that I did it."

Bruce raised an eyebrow at that. "Ok, Mr. Deters. Continue."

Bruce had no plans on interrupting Marcus again. He couldn't wait to hear what it was that would be coming out of this smooth-talking lawyer's mouth.

Marcus could tell he was going to have a hard time getting the detective to believe him, but he knew it could be done. Trial law had taught him that people's minds can be changed. You just need to give them an explanation that makes sense. If it's possible, it can become probable. If it's probable, it can become truth. It's just one step at a time. Marcus took a deep breath.

"As I said, I came down to see Simon, but I also wanted to see the crash site. I'd lost all memory of that trip, including the crash itself, and I hoped being there would jog something for me. When I got to the location, I was suddenly able to completely recall the events leading up to the catastrophe. I saw Simon in his truck as he came at us, on purpose. I am absolutely sure of that. I saw it just as clearly as if it was happening right at that moment.

So, my original plan had been to observe Simon, maybe follow him for just a little bit to see what he was like. But I was enraged when my memory came back, so I went right up to Simon's apartment that night. I rang the buzzer a bunch of times and he let me in. He had no idea who I was. I pulled out my gun and he knelt down in front of me. I told him who I was and he broke down in tears, saying he was sorry, he hadn't wanted anyone to die. When he ultimately blurted out the truth by screaming that he 'had to do it!', I put my gun to his head. And that's when he begged me to kill him."

Marcus was crying now. He looked at the detective and sobbed, "Believe me - I wanted to kill him so badly! But I couldn't. I just…couldn't. So I left. I ended up back at the hotel bar and got drunk. In the morning, I headed home. So when you called, I was surprised to hear Simon was dead but I was definitely not unhappy about it."

Bruce handed Marcus a tissue to dry his eyes and patiently waited until he'd regained his composure.

"So, you're saying that you brought your gun down with you to 'study' Mr. Daniels, but when you were able to remember the night of the accident and realized Mr. Daniels purposely caused the crash that killed your family, you went to his apartment in a rage and put said gun to his head. But then you just left without hurting him and got drunk in a bar. Then, coincidentally, four hours later, someone that is not you found Mr. Daniels still in his apartment and shot him? Wow, Marcus. That's an interesting story. Either you did it and you're turning yourself in to look innocent, or you didn't do it and you're turning yourself in to look innocent. Well played, Marcus. Tell me, though, if you will. If you are telling me the truth, then who do think killed him? What's your theory on that?"

Marcus looked at the detective and sighed, "Someone who wanted him dead more than I did."

Bruce just stared at Marcus, "Brilliant, Marcus. Someone that wanted him dead more than you did. Ha! Do you actually expect me to believe all this?"

Marcus lowered his head a little and spoke softly. "It gets worse. It gets even harder to believe."

"How, Mr. Deters? How could it possibly get harder to believe?"

Marcus paused for a minute as if the next words he would say were to be his last. "I'm pretty sure whoever killed Simon used my gun."

Bruce shook his head in exasperation. "What? Why on earth would you think that?"

Marcus took a deep breath to try and settle down. He looked at the detective, afraid he was blowing it. Maybe he shouldn't have come? Too late now, he thought. I need to convince him I'm innocent.

"Well, because after you called and asked about my owning a 9mm pistol, I checked my vehicle, and it wasn't there. I know I put it back after going to Simon's apartment and now it's gone. I think someone broke into my car, stole my gun, went to Simon's apartment and shot him."

Now Marcus and the detective were caught in a stare down. Bruce was trying to absorb the magnitude of what Marcus had said while trying to get a read on Marcus and to figure out if he believed him or not. His first reaction was not to believe him, but his resolve was quickly deteriorating. His story, though farfetched, made some sense too. It had been his experience that 'farfetched' that makes sense can sometimes out-trump the more typical excuses and alibis.

"Ok, Marcus. Are you going to be in town long?"

Bruce was hoping Marcus was staying a couple more days so he would have time to go over his statement and to meet with the district attorney.

"I'm planning on leaving tonight." Marcus could see the detective frowning at this. "We have a flight back to Grand Rapids this evening."

"We? Who's we?" Bruce asked quickly.

Marcus smiled a little; this guy was sharp. He was going to be perfect. "My sister came with me to keep me company."

"Really? And where is she now?"

"She's just taking care of a few loose ends down in Atlanta."

Bruce was curious again. "Loose ends. What kind of loose ends?"

Marcus answered vaguely, "We're just trying to wrap up a case we're working on, that's all."

Bruce looked at him and shrugged his shoulders as if to say whatever. "So, Mr. Deters, would you let us take your fingerprints and schedule a polygraph?" Bruce asked, realizing the answer would be no.

Marcus shook his head right away. "No polygraph. I've seen too many of my clients get mixed results. I won't take one. But I will give my permission for fingerprinting."

Bruce was pleasantly surprised at his response. "Fine, I will have Selma take you down for prints and then I will be in touch. I trust you will come back here if we need you. I would hate to have to get the FBI involved."

"I'm at your beck and call," Marcus said with a smile. "But I have to ask. Why are you letting me go? It seems a little unusual, considering."

"It does, doesn't it? Well, I guess you should know. When I spoke with Elizabeth Daniels, Simon's ex-wife, yesterday, it just so happens that she was also at the apartment when you were last Saturday. She was in the bedroom and heard absolutely everything."

Marcus stared blankly at him while trying to process this startling information. Meanwhile, Bruce wasted no time calling Selma in to get Marcus down to fingerprinting.

"I'll be in touch," he said sternly.

Marcus waved goodbye as he walked down the hall. That went well, Marcus thought to himself. At least he didn't arrest me.

28

"It's going good, thanks. I'm learning quite a bit, especially things I didn't know about my brother."

Allison was happy to talk to Darrin. She needed a little boost after the morning's conversation with Elizabeth.

"Like what? Do you want to talk about it?" Darrin asked, but he knew the answer before she spoke.

"Not right now, but I will tell you all about it when I get home. You're still in Grand Rapids, aren't you?"

Darrin laughed, "Of course. You're not getting rid of me that easily. I have some exploring I want to do today, and then I'm still planning on picking you up at the airport tonight. I have to admit, I miss you already."

Allison could feel herself starting to blush. She wanted to be home right now. She missed him too.

"Aw, you're sweet. I'm looking forward to seeing you, too. After today, I'm sure I'll be needing a nice glass of wine. Can I count on you for that?"

"That's right here on my list of things to do. Number 5: Get Allison a perfect cabernet for tonight."

"Number 5, huh? What's number 6?" Allison laughed.

"Well…" Darrin paused and then demurred, "You'll just have to wait and see."

Allison laughed again. "Fine, I guess I can do that. Hey, I'm pulling into my next stop and need to let you go. Can't wait to see you tonight!"

Allison had arrived at Lambert Securities.

"Gotcha. Same here, Beautiful. See you tonight."

Allison said goodbye and sat in her car for a few minutes pondering over her life. Darrin is amazing, she thought. So that's good.

Marcus is still a mess, though, and that's not. She couldn't get over how he'd brought his gun down here with him and had actually pointed it at Simon's head. While it was loaded, no less! They needed to get all this figured out before Marcus finally did go crazy or ended up in jail.

She walked through the visitors' entrance of the Lambert offices. It was a typical financial building; it had a well-appointed lobby, a rounded reception desk with a pretty, young lady perched behind it and an impressive bank of shiny elevators beyond that. There was a directory on the wall with names and corresponding floor numbers. Allison scanned it and looked under P for Parker. She spotted it quickly. Diane Parker was on the second floor. Allison glanced at the reception desk and saw the girl engrossed in something on her computer screen. Funny, Allison thought; she has no idea I'm even here. Allison pushed the button on the elevator and got in.

In a moment, when she arrived on the second floor, there was another pretty, young receptionist. This time, the girl greeted her as she walked up and asked if she could help her.

"Diane Parker, please," Allison said expectantly.

The girl regarded her sweetly and asked, "Do you have an appointment?"

Allison shook her head. "No, I don't, but I would like to talk her if she's available. It will just take a few minutes."

The young girl smiled. "Of course. Please take a seat and I'll ask if she can see you. What's your name?"

"Allison Deters," Allison smiled back and sat down. She watched as the girl talked on the phone. The young girl looked at her and shook her head.

Covering the mouthpiece, she raised her head toward Allison and asked, "Ma'am, what is this regarding?"

Allison walked back to the desk. "Tell her I want to talk about Simon Daniels."

It was obvious to Allison that Simon's name meant nothing to this girl. Which, as young as she obviously was, she had to assume the two of them had not worked here together.

"Unfortunately, Ms. Parker is busy and can't see you right now. If you leave your business card, she will call you to set up a meeting."

Allison grabbed a business card out of her purse and wrote her cell number on the back. She handed it to the receptionist, said thank you, and went back to the elevator, disappointed at the outcome.

Once back in her car she sat back and wondered what to do next. What's her next move? Marcus wanted her to interview someone at Lambert to find out more information. She'd reached a dead end with the one lead she'd been given so far. Was there someone else she could contact?

"I'll call Marcus," she said aloud.

Just then her phone rang, indicating a call from an Atlanta number.

"This is Allison Deters," she answered.

A woman's voice on the other end told her, "There is a coffee shop at 645 Riley Street. I'll meet you there in fifteen minutes. That's 645 Riley Street." Click.

Before Allison could ask who was speaking, the woman hung up. She called the number back and was sent to a messaging system for Lambert Securities. She was a little freaked out. She hoped it was Diane Parker deciding to talk to her.

She arrived at 645 Riley Street in less than ten minutes. She wouldn't call the place a hole-in-the-wall, but it wasn't much better than that. There was an old, porcelain sign out front, faded and dirty, that read "Mama's Cup O' Mud".

There was no parking lot, only street parking, so Allison drove past the Cup O' Mud about a block before finding an open spot. As she walked to the restaurant, she held her purse a little tighter than usual. It didn't seem like a terrible area, but the circumstances of the day made her a little uneasy. She walked by a small group of kids hanging out in front a tiny grocery store, but they seemed not to notice her at all as she hurried past. Allison entered the Cup O' Mud and looked around. She was nervous about meeting with a stranger all alone, but her fear evaporated when she walked in.

There were about twelve tables in the place, a coffee bar in the front, and a big chalkboard with the day's food and drink specialties written on it. The place was old but very clean and bright, and it had a hometown feel to it. There were people sitting at four different tables, all in groups, no one alone. They were all smiling and talking away. Allison felt very comfortable there.

An older lady from behind the counter yelled out to Allison, "Find a seat, darlin'! I'll be right there."

Allison picked a table that seemed to be somewhat private and sat down. The lady from the counter came to Allison's table.

"Hi, darlin' and welcome to Mama's. What can I getcha?"

Allison smiled back at her. "Sweet tea with lemon. Actually, can you make that two?"

"Sure thing, darlin'. Would you like to try a piece of Mama's pie? We got eight kinds, and they're all spectacular."

Allison shrugged and smiled. "I'll start with the tea and see where it goes. Thanks so much."

"You're welcome, darlin'. I'll check back when your date arrives." She winked and headed off to get the tea.

Just as the waitress returned, setting down two glasses of sweet tea, a tall, thin woman walked up to the table with her hand held out.

"Allison Deters? I'm Diane Parker. Thanks for meeting me here."

Allison took her shook her outstretched hand. "No, I should thank you for meeting with me."

Diane smiled. "Mama, could you grab two pieces of sweet potato pie with whipped cream, too, please? Thank you." Diane took a seat across from Allison. "Best pie around. You simply must try it."

Diane was smiling at Allison, and Allison felt immediately at ease. Diane seemed to be a few years older than Allison. She looked very professional with her pant suit and medium heels.

"So, Allison, I know who you are, and I know what happened to your brother and his family. I remember seeing you at the courthouse. Elizabeth called me and said you were coming by. I know you're aware of Simon's death."

Diane was not smiling anymore.

"I want to tell you a few things that Simon had shared with me, but you can't tell anyone that you talked to me. It could be very dangerous for me."

Allison could tell that she was serious. It was clear that whatever she had to say would have to remain confidential, or, at the very least, she couldn't let anyone know where she'd heard it. Diane absolutely believed she could be in danger. Mama came back and set the pie in front of them.

"Thanks, Mama," Diane smiled at her.

Mama nodded as she left. Allison took a bite of her pie. Wow, she thought. It was delicious.

"So how well did you know Simon?" Allison prompted Diane.

Diane looked at her and frowned. "Look, like I said, I know who you are, I know all about the accident, and I feel terrible for you and your brother, but let me start by saying this: no one felt worse about it than Simon."

I doubt that, Allison thought to herself. Sure, Simon may have felt bad about it, but nothing compared to what Marcus was enduring.

Diane continued, "Now, I know that you're probably thinking, whatever, my brother lost his family, and that's true; there is no way anyone can even imagine what he's going through. I'm just saying, after the crash, Simon's life was over too, and he never recovered."

"Simon was a brilliant kid. He joined us at Lambert right after college. He married Elizabeth, the daughter of Jeremiah Dean. She is a great woman and a wonderful mom. They were extremely happy together. Simon worked directly under me. I was assigned to train and mentor him. It was an easy assignment - he caught on quickly and was a natural with the clients. We became very close friends, and I got to know Elizabeth well, also."

Allison was listening intently but was anxious to get to the accident. She wanted to find out what Diane knew about that. "So, what do you know about the accident?" Allison broke in.

Diane gave her a look that made Allison regret interrupting her.

"I'll get to it," she said, annoyed.

"After only six months, I had Simon in charge of a few smaller business accounts, and he was doing well with them. One of his accounts was a medical clinic for which Lambert handled their pension plans, 401k's, and Roth IRA's. These smaller-sized businesses, typically with 500 or fewer employees, constitute the bulk of our customer base. Of course, a successful rep at Lambert needs to be a good salesperson even more than he needs to be a good investor. Once the accounts are acquired, we manage their investments, mainly pension funds. What funds or stocks they invest in is decided by our parent company, Pine Harbor Corporation. They own Lambert Securities as well as another thirty brokerage firms which are all about our size. Once we sign a client to an investment agreement, the account is actually managed by Pine Harbor. They decide what to buy and when to sell. The employees of the companies we represent get a quarterly statement about their funds. They really have no idea what their money is specifically invested in nor do they generally care. They are interested in what it will be worth in the long run. Sometimes a company we represent will want to invest extra capital over and above their employee pensions, and we handle that, too."

"This medical clinic was one of these companies with extra capital to invest. They had been meeting with Simon and had agreed on a specific plan for the investment. It was an unusually large amount of money for a single client of ours to want to invest - close to forty million dollars."

Diane paused for Allison's reaction.

And when Allison whispered back at her, "Forty million?", Diane nodded and continued. "That's a big number for one of our clients, especially when it's not invested on behalf of the employee benefits program. But Pine Harbor rejected Simon's request, commiserate with the client's desire, to invest in a particular stock. They told him to push the client in a different direction, and they made it clear what that direction was."

"Simon came to me and complained about it and asked me if that was typical. He was understandably worried about losing his client. I must admit, I agreed with him and thought it was crazy for us not to comply with the client's wishes. I decided to call my Pine Harbor contact and discuss it with him on Simon's behalf. He sided with Pine Harbor and was adamant about not letting clients pick their specific stocks. He said it would set a precedent that Corporate would not want to have, no matter how big the investment. I was ok with the philosophy behind his statement to an extent; you wouldn't want a bunch of different investors trying to dictate your company's investments. Our main objective is to provide benefit for the full collective of our investors. What did bother me was his reference to 'Corporate,' as if someone else, beyond Pine Harbor even, was dictating what we had to do."

"I relayed that conversation with Simon and he was very upset. Not only did he risk losing a large commission, but he wanted to do right by the client. Something just didn't make sense. Why would Pine Harbor risk losing such a big investment, precedent-setting or not? And who is 'Corporate'? My associate at Pine Harbor had never used that term with me before. He'd always referred to Pine Harbor simply as 'we,' or 'us'. Simon and I decided to pursue it further."

Diane smiled at Allison as she finished her pie. "I told you it was good."

"Incredible," Allison said as she pushed her empty plate away.

Diane looked around the restaurant to see if anyone else was listening to her. Satisfied everyone was minding their own business, she continued. "And so, for the first time, Simon and I investigated Pine Harbor. What we discovered was very surprising at the time, but the more we thought about it, the more it made sense."

Allison was intrigued, but since nothing had connected Simon with the crash yet, and she was starting to get antsy. "What? What did you find out?"

Diane was not smiling anymore, "Guess who owns Pine Harbor Corporation?" She didn't wait for Allison to respond. "Dean & Warner Worldwide owns Pine Harbor."

Allison shrugged, "Dean & Warner?" She looked at Diane for more.

"Dean & Warner. Jeremiah Dean, you know? Elizabeth's dad, Simon's father-in-law? Jeremiah Dean and Phil Warner, who are two of the richest men in the U.S., own over forty corporations like Pine Harbor. Are you following?"

Diane was impatiently waiting for Allison to piece things together.

"I'm sorry, Diane. Why is that important?" Allison thought she was catching on but decided to let Diane tell her everything to be sure.

Diane looked around again before saying softly, "Just think, Simon's father-in-law is half owner of forty-two corporations that each own at least thirty investment firms. That's a minimum of twelve hundred firms which are all being told by one corporation what stocks to buy for every one of their clients. That's billions of dollars being invested at their discretion."

Diane looked for a glimmer of acknowledgement from Allison. Nothing. She shook her head and continued. "There is nothing legally wrong with that; a firm can buy whatever stocks for their clients that they see fit. However, let's say one corporation buys stock at a low price, and then has all its independent clients buy the same stock, driving the value of that stock upward. When the corporation sells its stock, they enjoy a huge profit. But since that causes the stock to drop sharply again, those smaller investors are left suffering a significant loss. That's illegal, albeit very profitable."

"We're talking hundreds of millions, if not billions, of dollars of profit each year. When Simon compared the stock history of Pine Harbor clients with that of Dean & Warner, and he found a correlation, possible evidence that Dean & Warner was profiting at the expense of their clients. He couldn't prove it with the limited access he had to company stock reports, but he knew that the government probably could."

"Simon had shared the information he had gathered with me, and it seemed very likely to be true. Dean & Warner could have made hundreds of millions of dollars every year off their clients' losses in addition to the percentage they earned in normal commissions. Simon was conflicted at what to do."

"At the time I suggested that we both let it alone. After all, I was making very good money, and he would be, too, soon enough. Why risk that? But Simon couldn't do it; he felt he needed to talk to someone about it, and unfortunately for him, he chose the wrong person. He chose to go to his father-in-law."

Allison was listening intently; she couldn't help but think of Marcus's list of reasons people commit murder, and his reason number four in particular when Diane was talking about money. Financial law wasn't her strong suit but she did know enough to understand that if what Diane was saying is true, if Dean & Warner was in fact manipulating the stock market at the expense of others, they could face serious jail time. White collar crime wasn't tolerated like it used to be; it carried stiff penalties now. Very stiff penalties. Allison also realized that Diane could have helped Simon expose them is she'd chosen to.

"So, what did Mr. Dean say when Simon confronted him?"

Diane sighed, "Simon didn't tell me what happened. He just said that he was going to drop it. But I've got to tell you, that's when Simon changed."

"How do you mean?" Allison asked.

"Well, he got quiet and standoffish. He started to drink a lot, and his work began to suffer. A couple months later, he got fired."

"Did you fire him?" Allison asked, but she already suspected the answer. "No, it came from much higher up than me. Afterwards, I tried to keep in touch but he shut me out. He and Elizabeth got separated, and then after the crash, they divorced. I had seen him once after he was released from jail, and he was just a shell of his old self. It was really quite sad."

"Do you have any information about the crash itself?"

Diane shook her head. "No more than you, I suppose. Just a tragic accident, I guess."

Allison could read people well. That was one of her gifts that made her a good attorney, and until Diane's last statement, Allison had believed everything Diane had told her. Now Allison was sure Diane knew more about the crash than she was saying, but Allison let it rest for the time being. Instead, she got up and set a twenty on the table.

"That should cover it. Thank you for your time. You have given me some good information. It's definitely worth checking into."

Diane frowned. "Ok, but remember - I never told you anything."

"Right." Allison nodded in agreement. "Just answer one more thing for me. Do you regret not confronting someone with Simon? I mean, do you think it would have made a difference if you had collaborated with him and backed him up in his theory?"

Diane angrily snapped at Allison. "It probably would have made a huge difference—I would be dead as well."

Allison overlooked the outburst and handed Diane another card. "If you think of anything else, please give me a call."

On the slow walk back to her car, Allison poured over their conversation. "This is big," she said aloud.

Diane walked quickly to her car. It was after four o'clock already, and she figured she should at least make an appearance at the office again. She had talked with the lawyer for over an hour and was starting to regret it a little. What was to be gained by that? she thought. It wouldn't bring Simon back and it wouldn't bring the lawyer's family back. In fact, it just might open another can of worms all together.

She needed to ensure the conversation remained confidential, she was sure of that. She wondered if anyone else already knew. As she approached her car, she convinced herself that no one else could possibly know. It'd just been her and Simon. Now that she'd shared her piece, she would just forget about the lawyer and her brother and go about her business as usual.

Still lost in thought, she never noticed the person step out of the nearby doorway. She never saw them walk up behind her as she slid into her seat to head back to work. She never even saw them raise the 9mm pistol and shoot her in the side of the head, and she certainly never saw them calmly walk back to their car and drive away. By then, she was already dead.

29

Detective Harper was concerned. Going over the facts of the Daniels murder, he was starting to think he'd made a mistake in letting Marcus Deters go free. It'd been confirmed that the fingerprints from the casings and the buzzer at Simon's apartment were Marcus's. He had a motive—revenge for the death of his family—and there were witnesses who saw him in town and drunk around the time of the shooting. He had an alibi that couldn't be proven, that he left the bar and went to sleep in his hotel room. All that, combined with the fact that Marcus was from out of state had Bruce worried that he'd eventually have to call the FBI.

Still, there was something about Marcus that made Bruce want to believe in him. He seemed honest and caring, and he had been through so much, more than Bruce knew he could possibly understand. How does someone handle something like that, losing their entire family?

So, despite having been taught explicitly not to trust anything a suspect said without solid proof, Bruce was banking on Marcus. Yet, Marcus was a lawyer—a lawyer who knew the system. A lawyer who knew what Bruce would be looking for, who knew his rights and how to use them—leaving Bruce to find himself, for the first time in his career, doubting his decision-making skills.

To distract him from this line of thinking, Bruce called Elizabeth Daniels. He needed to ask her a few more questions. For some reason, he thought Elizabeth may have been one of the "loose ends" Marcus had mentioned.

Bruce dialed the number and an older woman, presumably someone who worked for the Deans answered, "Dean Residence."

"Elizabeth Daniels, please. This is Detective Harper from the Marietta Police Department. Is she available to speak?"

There was a pause from the other end, and then, "Just a minute, please."

Bruce could hear echoing footsteps over the phone. Knowing what he knew of the Deans and their wealth, he envisioned a black woman carrying the phone across the cool marble floor of a large open room to her employer. Her short heels clicked beneath her weight as she moved through the house, and he imagined her feet must ache by the end of day. The picture of it in his mind pained him, too reminiscent of old southern plantations with their ancestors forced to do the bidding of the rich, white people without any power to leave.

"Hello, this is Elizabeth Daniels."

Her voice snapped him back to the task at hand. "Hello, Ms. Daniels. This is Detective Harper from the Marietta Police Department. I was hoping to ask you a few more questions, if I may?"

Elizabeth paused. She'd known this was coming but didn't really want to deal with it right then; she had her hands full with other matters and, frankly, didn't feel like spending any more time on the phone with some detective she didn't think could help her anyway.

"I'm sorry, Detective. I'm pretty busy right now, and, besides, maybe we should talk in person? I have some questions for you as well. I will be in Marietta tomorrow to arrange Simon's funeral; would it be ok if I stopped there in the afternoon?"

"That would be great. I'll look forward to it. One quick thing though—did you meet with an Allison Deters today?"

"Yes, as a matter of fact I did. Is that a problem?" Elizabeth asked this only because she thought he expected the question, not because she particularly cared about the answer.

"No, not a problem. I was just curious, that's all. Until tomorrow," Bruce said politely.

"Until tomorrow, then. Good day, Detective," Elizabeth replied.

30

Allison had arrived at the airport, returned her rental car, and now found herself sitting at a bar drinking a $12.00 gin and tonic. She was disgusted by the price, but the drink was going down just fine. She had sent Marcus a text that she was waiting for him there, but he hadn't yet replied.

She was tired and ready to head home. That was a lot of travelling for one day, and she was done, ready to rest and decompress in the comfort of her home. It'd been an interesting day, for sure, and she had certainly learned more than she had expected since their arrival just this morning. Her mind was trying to put the pieces together, but she resisted. She wanted to hold off on that right now, and wait until she'd had a good night's sleep and a clearer head. She thought about Darrin and how she going to see him soon. Allison smiled. She'd never felt this way before, and it was exhilarating. Being away from him today had seemed like forever.

"Can I get you another?" the bartender asked as he took away her empty glass.

"Why not?" she ventured.

As Allison was finishing her second drink, Marcus walked up with a grin on his face. He pointed to the bartender with two fingers in the air. "Two more, please."

Allison waved one finger at the bartender and he nodded. Marcus sat down beside her easily.

"I know. You want to wait and talk tomorrow."

Allison gave Marcus a smirk of appreciation and nodded. Although it went without saying, he continued anyway, "I know you too well. You want to sleep and rest your mind so you will be more focused. Can I just ask you one question?" he pleaded with just enough insistence in his voice that Allison relented.

"Go ahead, Marcus. We can talk about it now."

Marcus downed his drink in one big gulp set his glass down. He looked at Allison intensely and asked, "Did you hear anything that makes you believe me? That makes you think Simon killed my family on purpose? That the crash was not an accident and that there were other people behind it, not just Simon?"

Marcus gave her the same look he gives the jury when he's giving closing arguments at a trial. It was a look that Allison and everyone else at the firm knew well. It was a look that confidently conveyed to its recipients the message, "It's obvious that I am right, so let's get down to it." Allison deftly avoided his gaze by staring at the bottles behind the bar instead.

She chose her words carefully. "I now believe you were hit on purpose. I suspect someone else may have been behind it. I can see it's definitely going to take more questions and research to find out the reason or reasons why they did it. I, for one, am not prepared to figure that all out right now, without the aforementioned sleep and a clear head. Most surprisingly, I learned something about my brother's recent activities that I didn't know before we landed today."

Marcus forced himself to not look away, even though he was a little ashamed for having purposely set her up for the shock. So, he already knew what she was alluding to, but he waited for her to explain how she'd found out.

"You were in Simon's apartment the night he was murdered. You proceeded to put a loaded gun to his head and threatened to kill him. I'm guessing you decided to withhold that crucial bit of information from me so my reaction would be real or sincere or whatever, but never mind that! Marcus, what were you doing?!? Why did you even have a gun? Were you really thinking about killing him?"

Marcus looked around quickly to make sure no one was paying attention to them. "I don't know what I was thinking, to be honest. I don't believe I ever had it in me to kill him. I just wanted some answers."

"Well, unfortunately, you'll never be able to ask him now," she quipped. "C'mon, the plane is boarding. We'll go over everything tomorrow at the office. I want to take a nap on the plane."

It was a pretty smooth flight home. Allison caught a quick cat nap, and she felt at least a little refreshed. What a day, she thought as she watched the lights of Grand Rapids getting closer and closer. The moment the plane was on the ground, she sent Darrin a text.

"We're here!"

Darrin answered right away. "Sorry, babe, I can't pick you up. Something came up. I'll call you in the morning." Allison's heart sank, but she figured at least this way, she would be able to go right to bed when she got home.

She turned to Marcus. "Do you mind bringing me home tonight?"

Marcus rolled his eyes in jest. "Of course I don't mind," he said with a smile.

As they left the gate area and headed to the exit doors, Marcus made a move toward the luggage claim area. "Where are you going?" Allison asked.

Marcus nonchalantly shrugged. "I just need to grab my bag."

Allison was confused. Why did he have a checked bag? We didn't stay the night, and if he'd wanted a change of clothes, why not just put them in a carry on? She followed Marcus to wait by the carousel.

"I didn't know you checked a bag." She casually observed. Marcus turned toward her and smiled. "Yeah, I did. I must have done it before you got here this morning. I had extra clothes and my bathroom stuff in case we had to stay longer. You know my hard-sided carryon is a pain to bring in the plane. What's the big deal?"

Allison nodded, "No big deal, I'm just looking forward to getting home, that's all."

Marcus grabbed his bag and they headed across the road to the short-term parking ramp to get his car. For some reason, Allison couldn't get her mind off his suitcase. She was certain he didn't have it when they picked up their rental cars in Atlanta. Either he went back and got it after she'd left the Enterprise counter, or he bought a new bag in Georgia. Why would he do either one? She watched as he put it in the trunk. Stop it, Allison, she thought. You're making something out of nothing. He must have had it. He has no reason to lie.

The ride to Allison's condo was quiet. They had a lot to talk about, but both wanted to wait until morning.

"See you tomorrow?" Marcus asked as he pulled in front of her building.

"Of course. I'll be at the office by eight. If you can start that early, I really should get some real work done tomorrow as well." Allison smiled at Marcus as she said that. "Love you," she said as the door shut behind her.

31

John Wainwright had had a good night; he had just won a couple grand. He played cards at the country club with the same group of guys every Tuesday, and he was in a good mood. It wasn't the money; he had plenty of that. It was the winning itself. He was so competitive, it didn't matter what it was, he just needed to come out on top. He was the same when it came to his job.

He was an attorney, and he had moved up the ladder at his firm quickly. He left a few good people in the dust as he went, but as he liked to say, "You end up where your feet take you. If you stop moving your feet, someone is bound to pass you." He had an opportunity a few years ago that would ensure his rise to the top and make him financially set for life, and he grabbed it. He had some regrets about it, but the new house and cars made it easy for him to justify. After all, he hadn't known all that would happen. He was only protecting the owners of his law firm.

Card games where he could take money from some other self-proclaimed "big shots" and "high rollers" were just another boost for his never-ending ego. He played golf with them during the warmer months, but as soon as the weather turned cold, the game of choice was poker. Tonight, he had done well and was pleased with himself.

It was well after dark when he left the clubhouse. He didn't notice the person behind him. When he reached his car and someone called out, "John.", he turned, expecting to see one of his card buddies. What he found instead was someone wearing a hooded sweatshirt and a baseball cap on backwards. "Yes?" he said, surprised. "Who is it?" He came closer, moving quickly, and John caught a glimpse of the gun wielder's face only for a moment. He knew immediately who it was. It didn't matter, though; it was the last thing he would ever see. The silencer on the gun served its purpose, and the shot went unnoticed. The shooter searched John's pockets and took all his cash before leaving his lifeless body lying on the pavement and disappearing as quickly as he had come.

32

Allison got up early when her alarm woke her at 6:00 a.m. that Wednesday morning. She jumped in the shower. The hot water felt so good and melted the aches of plane travel away. She took her time as she tried to organize her upcoming day in her head.

She knew she had to sort out everything with Marcus first, and who knew how long that would take? She really needed to get some billable hours in as well. With the time off she took going to Pentwater and Atlanta, she had some hours to make up. Keeping up her billable hours was crucial to making partner, and that was one of her goals. She sensed this investigation with Marcus was going to take up considerable time and she knew it was very important to him. If she was honest with herself, she would admit she was consumed with it as well.

She knew that something dirty was going on and she wanted to know more. She believed that Simon had indeed caused the crash but only because he was made to do it. Maybe he and his family were threatened with bodily harm or he was being blackmailed in some other fashion. Either way, the facts were starting to unfold and with a little work, they could hopefully piece them together.

The first major issue bothering her was, why a car crash? The possibilities of something going wrong seemed high. To swerve into another car going seventy miles per hour on the highway seemed likely to cause a fatality, so someone apparently wanted them dead. Yet Simon was adamant that that was not his intent.

Furthermore, how could anyone know that Simon would not also get hurt? What made the most sense to her was that someone actually assumed Simon would die as well, and when he didn't, that may have caused additional problems.

Her next serious question was, had Marcus been targeted? And if so, why? Or was it a coincidence? Was he in the wrong place at the wrong time? She didn't think so.

She reviewed again what Marcus's theory was for the motivations behind murder. People kill for love, necessity, anger, or money, and as he said, the first three didn't fit their circumstance. It had to be reason number four. The only thing that made sense was the money, and the only thing that Allison could think of in that regard was the lawsuit Marcus had been working on. She had to connect the dots, and so far, she wasn't having any success.

Allison turned the water off and got out of the hot shower. With a little sigh, she predicted the best part of her day was over. She wiped the mirror of its steam and looked at her reflection. "You can get through this, Allie," she said aloud.

33

Skip Lamont was in his thirteenth year with the Federal Bureau of Investigation, the last seven of which had been served in Atlanta. His real name was Nicholas Carl Lamont. He had been known as Nicky throughout his childhood and high school years, but his college teammates gave him his new nickname. Of course, his name wasn't legally changed, but it might as well have been.

He'd gone to Georgia Tech and played on the baseball team. He was a catcher, a very good catcher. In fact, he considered himself one of the best defensive catchers in all of college. Unfortunately, he was as bad of a hitter as he was good on defense, so Coach would frequently have someone pinch hit for him. Most times, he would have a designated hitter in his place for the entire game. His teammates came up with Skip since they always skipped his at bat. He hated it at first, but eventually he got used to it, and before long he embraced it. He felt that his nickname set him apart and it was easy for people to remember. Plus, if someone ever asked him about the name, he would just say, "My teammates at Georgia Tech gave it to me." It was an easy way to let people know that he was a college athlete without having to sound like he was boasting. Now practically everyone he knew called him Skip.

He liked his post in Atlanta; work there was never dull. It was, in his opinion, the greatest city in the United States. On some occasions, the FBI would be contacted by the Atlanta police to help with a case, like when a crime had been committed on federal property, if it involved drugs, or if it crossed state lines. Rarely, however, did he get called in on a homicide case. Typically, the local police would handle those investigations.

Today, though, afforded one of those rare opportunities. The Bureau had gotten a call from the Atlanta Police Department asking for an agent to come down to their station to discuss a case, a case that may involve crossing state lines, and it was Skip who had been assigned to help.

He liked helping the police on investigations because most of the time their cases seemed to be a little more interesting and almost always had less red tape to go through to get things accomplished. He knew the reaction to FBI help wasn't always a positive one, but he didn't care. He had worked hard to get where he was and felt he was destined to go farther. If he had to work with police officers, well, so be it.

He always tried to include the police officers as co-investigators instead of replacing them on a case, but that was often easier said than done and quite a hot topic for argument between agents at the bureau. Some agents believed that the police should be seen and not heard, and Skip, in some cases, tended to agree with them. You would think that working together would be the quickest way to resolve a case, but sometimes egos intervened and officers could intentionally be uncooperative. Never the less, Skip was excited to go to the 3rd Avenue station to meet with Detective Gaines about the homicide.

Detective Gaines didn't fall into the category of incompetent or difficult. Rather, Joanne was smart and talented, and Skip knew her well. He had worked a case with her before and had enjoyed it.

Today they were going to discuss a new case—some investment banker had gotten gunned down while sitting in her car, in broad daylight, with no witnesses and not much for leads. Reportedly, all they had so far was a business card from a Michigan attorney. When they'd run the lawyer's name, they found she'd flown to and from Atlanta that same day. They wanted Skip to go over the case with them and, if warranted, head to Michigan to interview her. As an FBI agent, if Skip were to go to Michigan, he would also have the authority to bring her back. Before this, his week had been shaping up to be quite boring. Now he was happy to help and excited by the prospect of traveling.

He arrived at the police station at 9:30 sharp and parked his Buick in the visitors' parking section. His wasn't the stereotypical government-issued vehicle peddled by Hollywood. Rather, it was nice-looking and comfortable model personally preferred by most of the agents down here.

He chuckled when he thought about how movies portrayed agents driving big, shiny, black SUV's with darkly tinted, presumably bullet-proof windows, but at eighty thousand bucks apiece, and with budget constraints a priority out in the field, agents like him were happy to have any decent vehicle to drive.

Another thing in the movies that bugged Skip was the fact that agents almost always had a partner. In real life, that was not the case. He had been on the force thirteen years and had yet to have one. Sometimes the Bureau would assign him some help, but that was rare, and again, it came down to the budget. Why pay for two agents when one could do the job?

Skip locked his Buick and walked into the police station. He took a left at the main desk and followed the long row of fallen officers' portraits that were hanging on the wall, making his way to the crowded bullpen area the officers shared. At the common desk, he introduced himself and asked for Detective Gaines. The young lady sitting there nodded and called the detective for him. After she hung up she smiled and said, "She's expecting you. Do you know the way?"

"Thank you, yes, I do," he said smiling back at her, and he walked himself to the back.

"Come in, Skip," the detective said quickly when she saw him. She waved him into her office and got up to shake his hand. "Thanks for coming in. I think we have an interesting case here."

Skip raised an eyebrow and looked at her as if to say, tell me more.

"Well," she continued, "this lawyer came down to Atlanta and went to the Lambert Securities office and asked specifically to see the victim. The receptionist turned her away and the lawyer left without contact. But then the owner of a coffee shop around the corner from the crime scene said that the victim had been there with another woman. We showed her a picture of the lawyer and, low and behold, she was the one with her. After their meeting, the victim was shot in her car. No witnesses.

Obviously, that's why we need you. Can you go to Michigan and interview this lawyer? I've already contacted the Grand Rapids police, and they have agreed to cooperate fully with our investigation."

Skip watched the detective closely as she spoke. He heard every word, and they registered, but he also was a little sidetracked by her. She wasn't a model-type beauty, but there was something about her that Skip was attracted to. She was strong, intelligent, to the point, pretty, and, luckily for him, single. He would never dream of acting on his interest for fear of appearing to disrespect her position or abilities on the force. As such, Joanne and Skip would continue to be colleagues, and only colleagues, for the foreseeable future.

Skip sighed in quiet resignation to himself before replying. "Ok, Joanne. I'll drive up tomorrow. Is there anything else I should know?"

Joanne looked at him in astonishment. "You're going to *drive* all the way to Michigan?"

Skip smiled back at her. "I enjoy the time on the road, and it's not that terribly far. Besides, then I'll have my own car. I can leave early and get there by afternoon."

"Suit yourself," Joanne said, shrugging her shoulders. "Do you want me to call and try to set up an appointment?"

Skip shook his head quickly. "No, I like to see their faces when I show up. A person's initial reaction can tell you a lot."

"Ok, keep in touch, and call me anytime." Joanne smiled at him and handed him a folder. "This has all the information we have on her. I'll have the digital files sent to you via email. We're waiting for phone records and should have them soon. I'll send that to you as well. I would be shocked if there wasn't a phone call or two exchanged by the two women."

Skip nodded and couldn't help but to smile back. "I have a better idea. I'll go pick up lunch, and when I come back we can go review everything over a burger." He opened the door and headed out to his car. He was keyed up about this case; something told him it was going to be very interesting.

34

"Ok, Darrin, what was sooo important that you couldn't pick me up last night?" Allison teased, trying to sound casual even though she seriously wanted to know.

Darrin was silent on the other end of the phone for what seemed to her as far too long. Finally, he answered, "Well, Al, I had some family stuff to take care of."

He didn't offer any more information which sort of perturbed her. Allison didn't want to pry, but she wanted to know more. "Is everything ok?" she asked, hoping for a little more disclosure.

"Yep, everything's cool now. When can I see you again?" He was very flippant with his answer, and Allison was getting a little mad.

"Can we do dinner tonight?" Allison asked.

Darrin answered quickly this time, "Sounds great. Can I cook at your place? I'd love a nice evening alone with you."

Allison couldn't have been happier to hear that; she would love a night at home just the two of them. "Absolutely, that sounds wonderful. I will text you the code to the condo and you can go there whenever you want and start. I hope to be home by seven."

Darrin laughed a little. "Sounds great, Al. I'll see you then."

Allison hung up the phone and concentrated on the task at hand. She knew she should do some billable work, of course she planned on it, but right now she chose to dig a little more into Dean & Warner. She had a bunch of dots she wanted to connect. She figured she would start from the bottom up and see how far she could get. When she hit a dead end, she would begin this time from the top and work her way down through the connections, and hope the two lines would meet somewhere in the middle. If there was a gap between the lines, she would just have to find more dots. Allison decided to take a page from Marcus's book and make a list.

She opened the file on her computer named "Reason Number 4." In the file, she had written everything Marcus had told her. Yesterday she had added everything else she'd discovered about the case from her own inquiries. Now she wanted to make a clearer picture out of it. She started her list.

35

Marcus was on his way in to work. He was running late because he had decided to go to breakfast with his parents at the spur of the moment. His dad enjoyed "Rick's," a favorite among the locals. A lot of the customers would eat there every day, his dad being one of them. This morning he and his mother both went along with dad. He'd been wanting to spend a little time with them, and it had proven to be a good diversion.

Just as he pulled into the parking ramp at the office, his phone rang. It was Nick Thomas. Nick and Heather Thomas were one of the other couples they had traveled with to Florida every Spring Break, before, but Marcus hadn't heard from them in a while.

"Hey, Nick, how are you?" Marcus answered warily.

There was a short pause and then Nick spoke quietly. "Hey, Marcus. I don't know if you heard this yet, but I figured I should check with you. I know we haven't talked in a while. I've had a hard time knowing what to say to you. Sorry. I needed to call and tell you the news before you see it online or on TV."

"Ok, Nick. What is it?" Marcus asked.

"Well, there's no easy way to tell you so I'll just say it. John Wainwright was shot and killed last night." Marcus was silent for a bit and Nick seemed to be waiting for him to respond.

"What happened, Nick? What have you heard?"

"Well," Nick replied, "they think he was robbed on the way to his car last night. Someone shot him in the head and took all his money. It's just awful, Marcus. His poor kids."

Marcus was having a hard time wrapping his head around this news. Finally, he said, "Thanks for calling me; I will be praying for his family. I should go."

Nick quickly spoke. "Marcus, I'm sorry we weren't there for you more. I have no excuse other than I was scared. Scared to not know what to say and even more scared to say something wrong."

Marcus sighed. "It's ok, I understand. I do. Just try to be there for Sandy and the kids because I don't think I can. Thanks again for calling."

Marcus hung up, left his car, and went up to his office. He needed to talk to Allison. When he got to Allison's office and he saw she was working on a list, it made him smile despite his shock and grief.

"Hi, Allie. We should talk about everything we know so far."

Allison looked up at him. "Absolutely, let's do that."

They talked for an hour. She told him everything she had learned from her interviews with Elizabeth Daniels and Diane Parker. How Simon's father-in-law was Jeremiah Dean, one of the most powerful men in the Midwest, maybe even the country. How Simon had confronted Jeremiah about the presumably illegal activities of Dean & Warner. She told him that Diane Parker, Simon's mentor and a friend to both him and Elizabeth, had also known about the corruption but had advised Simon to ignore it. She relayed how Elizabeth suspected her father had influenced Simon to cause the crash. She confirmed that Elizabeth had been at Simon's apartment at the same time Marcus was.

In turn, Marcus discussed his meeting with the detective in Marietta, his agreeing to have his fingers printed but refusing the lie detector test. How he told the detective his gun was missing and that he was afraid it was used as the murder weapon. And how he told the detective everything he now remembered about the crash and how he was sure it was not an accident.

After laying out everything they knew of the case, Marcus told Allison about John Wainwright.

"I don't think it was random, Allie," Marcus said with a stone-cold look on his face and tone in his voice.

Allison felt disconcerted at the news. She managed to look at him intensely to attempt to read his expression before talking. "Do you think it's related to your crash and investigation? Why? Why would someone kill him? What could he have had to do with it?"

Marcus sighed, "That's what we need to find out."

Allison shuttered as the reality of John's death hit home. This is getting absurd, she thought to herself. How many different directions can this go? "Any ideas?" Allison asked, hoping in vain he had more insight than she.

"Maybe," he replied. "you should look into his law firm and see how they were originated. You may be surprised."

"What do you know?"

No answer.

"Marcus? What do you know? You need to tell me everything you know!" At this point, Allison was angry and overwhelmed. *Does he know something important that he won't tell me? That would be crazy, after everything they'd done and with everything they had yet to do.*

"Trust me, Allie. I need *you* to research it. You're smart; I know you'll figure it out."

Allison was frustrated. "Can you at least tell me why?"

"Are you seeing that guy tonight?" Marcus asked coldly.

"As a matter of fact, I am. Why so snotty? And don't change the subject."

Allison was a little hurt at Marcus's tone of voice but forgot that disappointment quickly when Marcus rose to leave.

"Marcus! Come on, Marcus!"

Marcus looked at her sadly and handed her a cell phone.

"This is Sheila's phone. Check out the pictures from the last trip down. She took quite a few before the crash. See if anything pops out at you."

Allison took the phone from Marcus without saying another word. He left her office and she sat staring at it in her hand. It felt strange it was Sheila's and that she had had it with her when she died. She noticed it was fully charged; Marcus must have charged it in anticipation of giving it to her today. She took a USB cord out of her desk drawer and plugged the phone into her laptop. After accessing Sheila's photos, she went to Friday, April 5, 2013. Marcus was right; she had taken quite a few pictures that day.

Sheila had been a big picture taker; she always had a camera with her, well before you could take pictures with your phone. Allison felt tears well up in her eyes as she looked at photos of her nephews in the Meijer parking lot, obviously excited about the trip. There were pictures of all three families ready to have a good time. It was eerie to look at the photos and know they had had no idea no one would be enjoying that Spring Break. As she scrolled through the photos, she saw many pictures of the kids in the back seat, Marcus behind the wheel, and the "Welcome to

Indiana" sign, captured twice by the ambitious photographer. Allison smiled at the pictures in the Chick-fil-A restaurant. Sheila always raved about that place.

Allison's thoughts went to Darrin. She wanted to have her own family and, although she hadn't known Darrin long, she felt sure that he would be a part of it. For a minute, she forgot about the pictures and smiled as she thought about him. She was anxious to see him tonight. Allison shook her head and told herself to focus. Sheila wasn't shy about taking pictures; there were even some of the kids running to the bathrooms at a rest stop.

Allison looked over the pictures for quite a while and, at first, she didn't notice anything out of the ordinary. But then it hit her: there was a picture taken at 12:54 a.m., an hour or so before the crash. Marcus and the boys were in front of the map at the rest area. Sheila had them pose with Marcus pointing to the "You are here!" star.

That was all normal and cute enough; it was what she saw beyond them that gave her pause. The map was inside the rest area lounge, and while Marcus and the boys were in front of that, you could see John Wainwright on a cell phone. Not only was it odd that he would be making a call at 1:00 a.m., but he was obviously talking on a flip phone. It seemed particularly unusual for someone like John, an attorney, not to have a smart phone of some kind to check emails and such. Even Allison had been using a smart phone by that time.

Allison felt a sudden chill. She scrolled back through all the pictures again. There! She pointed at the screen as if she was showing it to someone else. There was another picture, and it showed John in the background on his phone. His iPhone! John must have called Simon from the flip phone! The call the bartender had talked about. John would have called Simon to let him know where they were. John was a part of it.

Allison was thinking frantically now. What did Marcus say? The Wainwright's Yukon had its interior lights on. He was signaling Simon. Simon must have waited at the onramp until he saw the lights on inside the Yukon! He then went down the ramp and caused the crash. The phones they used were disposable so they couldn't be tracked! What in the world? Allison's mind was spinning. Why would he do that? Why in the heck would he help someone kill his friend's family? The rush of questions without answers was infuriating to Allison.

"Reason number 4," she said aloud.

The anger she felt quickly morphed into concern for her brother. Marcus obviously knew this already; he'd probably known for some time. Maybe even since he'd come home from the hospital. Of course, he had. She felt dumb for not picking up on it earlier. He absolutely knew the connection to John Wainwright but he wanted her to find it on her own. Why? Did he know he was in danger? Why wouldn't he be? Someone already tried to kill him via the crash, and now both Simon and John had seemingly been eliminated; it only made sense that he might be in danger, too. Was he afraid that if they came after him, she would have to finish the task alone? Allison had to connect the dots quickly.

"Sooner or later, we will need to talk to the police," she said aloud without even realizing it.

36

Detective Bruce Harper saw something come across his computer screen that made him sit up abruptly in his chair. It was a bulletin to all Georgia departments about a murder in Atlanta. Not an unusual occurrence, of course, as Atlanta had more than its share of murders, but this one struck him right between the eyes.

"Diane Parker, forty-four, was shot in her car on the corner of Riley and Dulles Avenues Tuesday afternoon. She was an investment broker at Lambert Securities..."

"Lambert Securities," Bruce repeated aloud. "That's where the Daniels kid had worked."

Bruce picked up the phone; he had a weird feeling that this murder of another Lambert Securities employee wasn't a coincidence. He didn't know why, but he had to call and ask a couple questions. There was a phone number on the bulletin for a Detective Gaines. He dialed the number and, after a couple of rings, a man's voice came across from the other end.

"Atlanta P.D., 3rd Street Station" he bellowed.

"Detective Gaines, please. This is Detective Harper from the Marietta Police Department. I need to talk to her about the Parker murder."

"Detective Gaines is in a meeting right now. Do you want to leave a message for her?"

Bruce couldn't wait to talk to her; he wanted to talk to her right away.

"I really need to talk to her now. Could you please let her know I'm on the phone?"

The man on the phone was quiet for a moment, weighing his response. "Ok, sir, I will let her know. Hold on a minute, please."

Bruce waited for a couple minutes and expected to hear the man's voice again but instead he heard, "Detective Harper? This is Joanne Gaines. I am with Agent Lamont of the FBI. We are discussing the Parker murder now. You're on speaker—what can we help you with?"

Bruce's mind quickly processed what she had said. She was with an FBI agent. That meant the case most likely crossed state lines. Now he was even more interested.

"Ok, no problem, thank you for taking my call. We're in the process of investigating a murder in Marietta that took place Sunday morning. The victim's name was Simon Daniels, and he was an ex-employee of Lambert Securities. Now, I'm not saying that the two murders are related, but I am trying to find any lead I can for my case. Do you have any information that could be relevant? I know it sounds like a long shot, but it's oddly coincidental to me that the only suspect in my case has a sister that I know for a fact went to Atlanta that same day. It's probably nothing, but it has me curious."

Detective Gaines looked at Skip and tilted her head as if to ask, Should we tell him anything? Skip nodded, giving her the go ahead without having to say a word.

"Well, Detective Harper," she started, "our victim had a meeting with an attorney at a coffee shop right before she was killed. It was a little odd because according to the receptionist at Lambert, the attorney had asked to meet with the victim and then left a business card for her after being denied the meeting. At the murder scene, the victim was found with another one of the attorney's business cards. We find it strange that after turning down her meeting request, Ms. Parker went right out and saw her."

"Her?" Bruce asked quickly.

"Yes, the attorney was a woman," Detective Gaines answered.

Bruce asked a question he already knew the answer to. He knew the answer as much as he knew his own name, as much as he knew anything.

"Was she from Michigan?"

There was silence on the other end. Detective Gaines and Agent Lamont looked at each other in surprise. Finally, the FBI agent spoke. "Why would you ask that, Detective?"

Now it was Bruce's turn to pause. He was certain his suspicions would now be confirmed. "Well, let's just say our two cases may be connected. If the attorney's name is Allison Deters, I think we should meet."

Skip and Joanne looked at each other, and then Skip took the lead.

"I think you're right, Detective; we should meet. I can be to your office in a couple hours. One more thing, though—what was your victim's name again?"

"His name was Simon Daniels. Why?" Bruce asked.

"The receptionist at Lambert had said the lawyer asked to talk to our victim about someone but couldn't recall the name she'd used. I think we'll call her again. Thank you, Detective. I'll be there shortly," Skip answered then hung up the phone.

Bruce set down his phone and pondered the situation. FBI involvement—this may be big. Who would have thought? Marcus may be right, maybe there was a lot more to the crash that killed his family.

Although Bruce's first priority was the homicide in Marietta, he realized this was going to be a lot bigger than the murder of an ex con in an apartment building. He was looking forward to meeting with the FBI.

37

Darrin was walking the aisles of the grocery store, picking up ingredients for tonight's dinner with Allison. He planned on making a chicken parmesan recipe they had had at his house growing up. It had always been his favorite, and he decided to make it for Allison and pair it with a nice Caesar salad. He'd already called Paula, his family's personal chef, for the recipe. He was disappointed that Allison had to work so late, but he supposed it gave him a little more time to prepare. As he walked toward the checkout, his phone rang. He saw that it was his brother Blaine. He didn't want to answer, but knew he had to, so he ducked down an empty aisle and took the call.

"Hey Blaine, what's up?" Darrin asked casually while bracing himself for the response.

"What do you mean, what's up? Why are you not here yet? What the hell are you still doing in Michigan? Dad wants you here now! We have a lot of things for you to do, and we don't want you up there complicating things. You need to get back here and get to work. Did you hear me? You shouldn't still be up there; you have to come back to Indianapolis now!"

Darrin waited for Blaine to take a break from his tirade and stop yelling. He responded calmly, "Look Blaine, tell Dad I will be there by the end of the week. I need this break. I know that what I'm doing worries you, but I have everything under control; just give me my space."

"Brother or not, I won't let you put some girl before our family."

Blaine was practically screaming at him and Darrin was getting annoyed.

"What? Do you have your thugs following me, Blaine?" Darrin did his best to yell back at Blaine without anyone in the store hearing. "I know what I'm doing. I'll come home when I want to and there's nothing you can do about it!"

This time Blaine calmed down a bit and replied in a softer, yet scarier tone, "There's always a way, Darrin."

Blaine hung up, leaving Darrin fuming. He had a plan and they should just accept it. He would go back to Indy when he was ready. Darrin gathered himself and went back to the checkout, trying to put Blaine out of his mind so he could enjoy tonight.

38

Skip Lamont pulled into the parking lot of the Marietta Police Department. He had spent the entire drive thinking about the case. He was a little disappointed because it looked like he wouldn't be working directly with Joanne much, but he had a feeling this case could be big, so he was excited about what was to come.

If he was to be totally honest, which is something an agent really couldn't afford to be, he wanted to solve a big case. Doing so meant more notoriety in the Bureau, which in turn brought about promotions and more authority. Law enforcement is supposed to be a service job, a calling if you will, but he would bet his last dollar that ninety-five percent of the agents felt the same way he did. It's human nature to crave more, and the law enforcement profession wasn't any different.

Skip walked right into the station and showed Selma his badge. "Detective Harper," he stated in a way that struck Selma as rude.

Before she responded, he continued on his way past her so she spoke to his back, saying, "Second office on the right."

He raised his hand in acknowledgement. He opened the door with an engraved metal plate that read Detective Harper.

There was a large black man sitting at a desk.

"I'm looking for Detective Harper?" The confusion in Skip's voice gave Bruce pause. It was one he had heard many times before.

"Yes, can I help you?"

Skip recovered quickly and said, "I'm Agent Skip Lamont from Atlanta. I came to talk about the case."

Although Bruce was anxious to hear about the case, he felt the need to pursue the agent's tone a bit further first, both to amuse himself and maybe even embarrass the agent a little.

"Ok, great, I'm looking forward to it, but I need to ask you something. You sounded surprised when you came into my office. How come?"

Skip laughed, "Oh, it was nothing. I was just a little surprised that you were black."

Bruce raised an eyebrow at him.

"I mean to say, you didn't sound black on the phone."

There it was—Bruce had heard that comment before, from others who also lacked the depth to realize how offensive that might be.

"Well, if I didn't sound black, what did I sound like?"

"Err, it's not that you couldn't have been black," Skip stammered. "I, uh, just mean you don't have a black accent."

Oh, Bruce was going to have fun with him now. He scowled at Skip who was starting to turn red. Skip knew he was in a spot that was going to be impossible to get out of.

"Did I sound white? Please don't tell me that I sounded white," Bruce said seriously.

Skip was starting to panic now, and Bruce sensed it was time to let him off the hook. He smiled and said, "Don't sweat it. Just jerking your chain a bit. I had to have a little fun. You set yourself up for it."

Skip was taken aback at the attempted humor. "I'm really sorry; I didn't mean to offend you."

Bruce motioned him to take a seat, "Really, forget it. Let's talk about the case. Why don't you start?"

Skip was relieved to change the subject. He told him about Diane Parker's murder, how she had been shot in her car in broad daylight but no one saw a thing, or at least no one claimed to. He told him about Allison Deters, the lawyer from Grand Rapids, Michigan who had met with Diane for over an hour just prior to the murder. They had pie and tea in a little shop right down the road from the scene. Witnesses say the lawyer was walking in the opposite direction after leaving the coffee shop, and the shooting had happened so quickly afterwards, that there was seemingly no way she could have been the killer.

He told Bruce how they had contacted the receptionist at Lambert and asked if she had recognized the name Simon Daniels as the name Allison had mentioned, but she couldn't say either way. He had researched Simon Daniels as an employee of Lambert Securities and was able to verify that both victims indeed had known each other and had, in fact, worked very closely with one another. Other than that, they didn't have much. No motive, no suspects, and no leads except for the Michigan lawyer.

"So here I am to see how you can help me with my case. And hopefully I can help you with yours."

"Well," Bruce asked, "when are you going to Michigan? I assume that's where you're headed next."

"Right after I leave here," Skip said eagerly.

Bruce could tell he enjoyed to travel.

Skip continued, "I'm going to drive a few hours and grab a hotel tonight. I should get there before noon tomorrow. I was hoping you would have some more information for me first."

Skip's initial awkwardness with Bruce was all but gone now. Bruce looked at Skip and gave him a wry smile. Bruce had an inordinate gift of reading people. It was a skill that had helped him excel at his job. He figured Skip out within five seconds of his entering his office. Bruce would never show it, but he disliked him immediately. He could tell right away Skip was all about Skip. But if Bruce could use him to help with the Daniels homicide, he would.

"I think I should start from the beginning. Three years ago, there was an accident in your city of Atlanta…"

Bruce told Skip everything he knew about the crash. How Marcus was critically injured and his family had died. How Marcus had been in Marietta and went to Simon's apartment with a gun on the night Simon had been killed. He told him about the bartender and Marcus being drunk. He told him about the phone call to Marcus's home and how Marcus was glad to find out Simon was dead. Then he told him about how Marcus's gun was missing and how Marcus thinks it could have been used in the Deters murder. His theory that someone was possibly setting him up to take a murder rap to get rid of two problems at once.

Finally, he told him about Marcus coming back to town the day Diane Parker had been killed, how Marcus drove up to Marietta to meet with him, and how he let him take his fingerprints but refused the lie detector test. Then Bruce told Skip that while he was meeting with Marcus, his sister Allison visited both Elizabeth Daniels and Diane Parker in Atlanta.

Skip had listened intently to what Detective Harper said. No matter what anyone thought of him personally, there was no denying he was good at his job.

"So, what were the results of the fingerprints?" Skip asked. He assumed they weren't a match or they wouldn't have let Marcus go.

"They were an exact match," Bruce said, and, fully anticipating what Skip was thinking told him, "I let him go because, for one, I didn't have the results yet, and two, I had a witness collaborating his story. Elizabeth Daniels was in the apartment when Marcus visited Simon. She was hiding in the bedroom and heard Marcus threaten him. The prints were a match on the buzzer—which makes sense as he admitted to touching it—and on the bullet casings, validating his story about his gun being stolen."

Skip was having a hard time with this. "His prints matched the buzzer and the bullet casings? And you let him go? Don't you think you should have detained him while you waited on the results?"

Bruce knew that was a legitimate question, but it irritated him none the less.

"I know it's not textbook police procedure, but what would it have helped to detain him? There are multiple witnesses to back up his story. He left the apartment, went to the bar, and got drunk. He was extremely drunk according to the bartender. I don't think holding him was an option that would have helped me in the long run. At the very least, it may have pissed him off, and he is a very accomplished lawyer. I prefer an agreeable suspect or witness. Besides, I know where he is if I need him."

"You mean if you need me to get him?" Skip clarified. But he said it with a smile.

Bruce ignored him. "It may seem farfetched, but his story could have merit. He may be right; there may be something bigger behind the crash and someone's busy trying to keep it all quiet. Maybe Diane Parker knew something about it as well. Maybe they didn't want her talking to anyone about it, especially that lawyer. Maybe someone followed Marcus to Simon's apartment, or maybe they had been watching Simon already and it was a lucky break that Marcus showed up. They followed Marcus back to his hotel, grabbed his gun out of his car, and went back and killed Simon. They would get rid of two problems if Marcus got convicted. They would not have known that Elizabeth Daniels had been there to corroborate Marcus's story. Elizabeth swears she doesn't believe Marcus killed Simon; he just didn't seem capable, even when he had the chance. I believe whoever killed Simon also killed Diane Parker. It just makes more sense, and besides, I like Marcus Deters and I believe him."

Skip waited to make sure Bruce was done.

"That's a lot of maybe. I tend to look at the facts and not what may have been possible. To me, that's a pretty thin line you're walking. I'm willing to buy it for now, but I must say, I'm skeptical. It's been my experience that if someone says they didn't do it but evidence says otherwise, even circumstantial evidence, they usually did it. Either way, it looks like we may be hunting the same animal. Is there something I could do for you when I'm in Grand Rapids?"

Bruce looked at him and raised an eyebrow. "How are you at surveillance?"

39

Allison arrived at her condo at a quarter to seven. She had used the last four hours of her day to work on a couple briefs for clients. She was able to get some billable hours in, but she knew pretty soon she was going to pay; she would have to pull some long hours to catch up to her quota. She was ok with it, though, because she was absolutely enthralled in her brother's quest. She wanted to get to the bottom of it.

It was getting to be bigger than she thought they could handle, and she wanted to go to the police, but Marcus would have none of it. He wanted the two of them to do it. He said he couldn't trust anyone else to carry it through to the end. He said he had to find out the truth and didn't care how far up the power ladder he had to go.

Right now she just wanted to see Darrin, or "that guy" as Marcus called him. Allison was amused when she thought of Marcus calling him that. She was sure he didn't mean anything bad by it; it was just that in his mind, no one was ever good enough for his little sister.

Allison opened the door to her condo and instantly smiled. Darrin was busy in the kitchen mixing a salad together. Something cooking in the oven smelled wonderful, and she saw a bottle of wine on the counter. Darrin had already poured a glass for himself and appeared to be enjoying it as he prepped dinner. Allison dropped her purse on the sofa and walked over to Darrin. He looked at her and smiled but didn't say a word. She put her arms around his neck and gave him a long kiss hello.

"Missed you," she said after reluctantly pulling away.

"Same," Darrin agreed. "I hope you are hungry."

Allison nodded and gave him another kiss. "Smells amazing."

She was thrilled to have him make a nice meal for them at home. It was such a nice change from going out.

"Sit down. I'll bring out the salads and some wine. The chicken still needs a few minutes yet because I wasn't expecting you quite yet, but I'm happy you're here now."

Darrin poured her a glass of wine and dished out two Caesar salads, and they sat down to eat. Allison enjoyed the meal immensely. The food and wine were great and the company was even better. Allison reached over to Darrin and grabbed his hand.

"So, tell me more about Darrin Warner. You really haven't told me much. I mean, I know you have a brother and sister and that you're from Indiana. You also said you were in the military for ten years—what did you do? Where did you live? Were you able to travel? I want to know more."

Darrin shrugged his shoulders a bit. "Hmm. Like I told you before, I am the youngest of three kids. My brother is a vice president at my father's company; he's worked there since college. He's married with no kids, which is for the best because his wife is a total B..." Darrin mouthed the word conspiratorially.

Allison laughed and Darrin continued.

"My sister is married and has two great kids, Austin and Haley; they're both in high school in Carmel, Indiana. Her husband Gary sells real estate and does very well for himself. My parents still live in Carmel. My father works every day even though he doesn't need to. I think he just likes to get away from my mom."

This time Darrin added a wink.

"Ha ha," Allison laughed again. "What about your time in the military? What did you do?"

Darrin's smile faded.

"Nothing too exciting really. I was stationed in Virginia for the first two years, did a couple years in Iraq and one in Afghanistan, from 2008-2011, and after that, I was stationed in Fort Buchanan, Puerto Rico until I got out last year."

"Are you kidding? You were in the war! What's not exciting about that?" Allison couldn't believe he hadn't mentioned that before. "How was it? What happened? Were you in combat?"

Darrin rolled his eyes to tease her. "So many questions. Don't you know that's all classified?"

Darrin was smiling from ear to ear. Allison got up, walked over to him and gave him a playful punch in the arm. Darrin grabbed her and pulled her into his lap.

"You," Darrin paused for effect, "are in trouble."

40

The lights were still on at the law firm of Davis, Hayes, and Deters. Everyone was long gone except for Marcus. He wanted to be somewhere quiet to think about the letter he was going to write to Allison. He turned on his laptop and started typing.

Dear Allison,

There is no question that the last three years have been hard on all of us. I know the loss of Sheila and the boys was devastating for you, just as it was for me. There are mornings when I get up and I wonder if I'm going to be able to make it through the day. Many times, I have thought about just ending it all. I catch myself thinking about it quite often, actually. I'm sure that's not a complete surprise to you, but I'm also sure that it's not what you want to hear. I know Dr. Bryant said I wasn't a suicide risk, but sometimes doctors are the easiest people to fool. The fact remains that I am not, nor will I ever be, the person I was. I am so very appreciative of the love and support that you, Mom, and Dad have showered on me, but I feel that's not enough. The hole in my life is being filled by my quest to uncover the mystery that surrounds the crash and bringing those involved to justice. Please do not be alarmed; this is not a suicide note. Rather it is a letter to express the feelings of love and appreciation for you that I struggle to say in person, and I would also like to use this letter as a means of explaining the next actions I will be taking and the action that I need you to be taking as well.

Before that, I need to bring you up to speed on all I know about the crash. You have done amazingly well in your investigating, of course. I knew you would, and I know you will continue to do so. You may not understand why I didn't just tell you everything in the first place, but trust me—you will figure it out eventually.

As I'm sure you've figured out already, I already knew about John Wainwright's involvement. When I saw Sheila's pictures, coupled with evidence from Simon's court hearing, I figured it out right away. I just didn't know why. I started to dig. I had been researching all I could for the last couple of years. With your help, I finally think I have enough information to move forward. I had remembered more right away than I let on. Then I remembered even more things on my trip to the crash site, but none of it really surprised me.

You asked me how John was connected, and I told you to check out his law firm's origination. Well, here it is: John Wainwright's law firm is one of many firms owned by U.S. Law Conglomerate. U.S Law is another company that is owned by, guess who? That's right, Dean & Warner. Turns out that John plays golf with an executive from U.S Law every week, wouldn't you know it, not even a month after the crash, John was promoted from partner to managing senior partner, a title that paid him three times his former salary. What's more, his big new house has no mortgage—turns out John received a million dollar bonus when he took his new position.

Remember when we talked about motives for murder? Reason number 4 seems to be stronger than friendship in this case. But still, why me? What did Dean & Warner have to gain from the crash? Of course, it all came down to the case I was working on.

I know you didn't know all the details, but I was going to blow the cover off Dean & Warner and their illegal activities. Our lawsuit would have opened a Pandora's Box for them; we would have won big, and class action lawsuits would have almost certainly been filed by hundreds of companies, sure to have brought Dean & Warner crashing down. As dirty as they are, not even their political connections could have saved them from bankruptcy and, most likely, incarceration. Obviously, that would have been huge for our firm, but more importantly, it would have brought money back to the small companies they had been stolen from.

Dean & Warner recognized the imminent threat, and that's where Ken Stark came in. Ken Stark is a high-ranking executive at U.S. Law, and he also happens to be the personal attorney for Jeremiah Dean. You see, Ken Stark is another one of the men that played golf with John Wainwright. One can only guess how that conversation started, but evidentially, John was asked to help. I want to think John didn't realize the crash was going to be so devastating. He was probably told that they were just going to try and scare me, to send a warning to me and my family to get me to settle the case. Maybe their plan was to threaten me the next day, maybe tell me that next time they would finish the job, but as it turned out, it worked out even better for them, didn't it?

Not only was my client forced to settle, but I was out of commission for almost two years, plenty of time for them to recover and strengthen their legal position. As far as I'm concerned, those lawsuits are dead. I'm certain they've covered all their tracks by now and are continuing business as usual.

So, Ken Stark convinced John to help them, and according to his ex-wife,

Simon was threatened by his father-in-law to carry out the plan. I'm not so sure that Simon was threatened; maybe Jeremiah had told him he could get back into his good graces if he helped carry it out. Either way, it doesn't matter now because Simon is dead. Which brings me to his murder—there is still an investigation going on into that, and I'm probably the only lead they have. I'm certain the detective in Marietta, Bruce Harper, will eventually be calling me to go back down there.

I'm not ready to go back; I must get solid proof linking Jeremiah Dean and Ken Stark, and I need my freedom to do so. I know how I'm going to do it, but I can't have the police getting in my way right now. I want to connect things to the top. I want to connect them to Jeremiah Dean; I know he's involved, but I don't have enough proof yet. I want him to pay. I know they are nervous right now because people are dying - people that were connected to the crash. Someone is killing everyone who knows about their fraud. That makes me a big target. That's why I need to disappear for a while. I'll check in on you every so often, and if I think there's a chance you're in danger, I'll come back immediately; right now, I don't believe you are.

I need to finish this, Allie. I need to settle the score.

It's Wednesday evening as I write this. If you don't hear from me by next Wednesday, bring this letter to the Grand Rapids police department and ask for Captain Lewis. Also send a copy to Detective Harper in Marietta. Please continue to research the case, but do it discreetly. When you get a chance, check out the Dean & Warner assets list that's on the desktop in my office. I think you will find it interesting. I called in a favor with someone I know at the IRS and had him get me a copy from their tax returns. It is under the file named Spring Break.

Be safe, Allie. I love you.

Marcus

When he finished the letter, Marcus printed a copy and slid it into an envelope. He brought it into Allison's office and put it in her top desk drawer. Marcus took off for home. He wanted to let his parents know that he would be leaving town for a week or so. He also wanted to tell them that when he returned, he was going to look for a house. He was ready to be on his own again.

41

Skip Lamont was enjoying his drive north. He didn't go as far as Michigan very often, and he found the drive wasn't too bad. He was about to leave Kentucky and enter Indiana. He considered driving straight through the night and skipping the hotel room, but he thought better of it. He figured he had a couple hours yet to his hotel room, putting him there around midnight. He could unwind with a drink or two and then go to bed.

He worried the next couple days might prove boring. Normally he didn't take any instructions from a local cop, but for some reason he had this time. Detective Harper asked him to follow Allison for a day or two before he made himself known to her. The request seemed a little odd to Skip until Bruce explained his reasoning. Initially Skip had expected to contact Allison Deters and question her about Diane's murder per his conversation with Detective Gaines of the Atlanta PD. If all went well, he could probably turn around and come home the next day. But there was something to Detective Harper's methodology that grabbed his full attention.

He'd pointed out, "If you question Allison, you already know what she will say. She will say that she's shocked and that she has no idea who killed Diane—maybe that's true and maybe it's not—but other than seeing her reaction to the news of the murder, it seems a fruitless endeavor. But if you follow her for a while, see where she goes, who she interacts with, it may lead you to something. If our cases are connected, which I believe they are, I think there is a lot more going on than we know so far."

He'd gone on. "I believe that the two attorneys are conducting their own investigation; I think they're investigating something big, really big even, based on what Marcus told me. For some reason, they haven't asked for police help directly, but he did reach out to me unofficially. Right now, we have basically nothing. If you take a little time and follow her, you may find something you wouldn't have otherwise. Either way, all it would cost you is a couple extra days in Michigan."

Detective Harper's argument made sense, but what had ultimately convinced Skip to humor the guy was the part about the whole thing being "big". This could be the break he'd been waiting for, the case that would put him on the FBI map. So, for now he'd listen to the black guy from Marietta. Skip laughed out loud when he thought of that. At some point, he'd have to show that small-timer how to investigate a case.

42

On Thursday, Allison woke up to sunshine coming through the living room window. They had fallen asleep on the sofa watching a movie on Netflix. She peeked over her shoulder at Darrin, still asleep. She'd snuggled into his arms during the movie and they both slept so soundly, they stayed that way all night. She wiggled out from under Darrin's arm and stood up. Darrin stirred but didn't wake. She went to the kitchen and made some coffee. She had a twinge of a headache from the wine last night, but all in all, she felt great. She was giddy about her relationship with Darrin. She had never felt so comfortable with someone before. It was as if they were meant to be together, and she was so thankful they had met. How lucky, she thought as she looked at him.

Strange how things work out; if Marcus hadn't lied about where he was going last week, she and Darrin never would have met on the beach that night in Pentwater.

Allison let Darrin sleep as she got ready for work. She wondered how long he was going to stay around. He had said he needed to go home and start working, but he had delayed that already. Maybe he would stay longer. Allison was conflicted; she had so much she could do at work, and with the investigation for Marcus on top of that, she really needed to be focused all weekend. If Darrin was around, she knew he would take precedence with her. She walked over to the sofa and gently shook him awake. He opened his eyes and smiled at her. Allison handed him a cup of coffee as he sat up.

"Rough night?" she asked, smiling back at him.

Darrin took a sip of the coffee and moved his head from side to side. "Neck's a little stiff, but other than that, I'm good," he said, still smiling.

"So, I need to go in to the office. What's your plan for today?"

Allison asked him with a little disappointment in her tone.

Darrin took a gulp of his coffee. "First, I have to go to the bathroom."

Darrin got up and ran off down the hall. Allison laughed and gathered her coat and gloves. The forecast for the day was chilly with a chance of rain that could turn to snow—typical Michigan spring, trying to squeeze in a last few days of winter.

Darrin came back and looked at her coat. "Leaving right away?"

Allison nodded. "I really have to go. What about you?" she asked again.

Darrin looked at her and his smile was gone. "I need to get to the airport soon. I have to go home." He paused for a moment and then continued, "I have to be home this afternoon for a few reasons, but we'll see each other again soon."

Allison gave him a big hug. "You better come back up here quick. After all, it's only a four-hour drive."

Darrin kissed her on the cheek. "Of course I will, but I'm leaving my truck at the airport," he said with a laugh. "And you need to come to Indiana soon, too. I have to show you off!"

Allison hugged him hard. "I love you."

She was almost shocked to hear those words come out, but she knew she wanted to say them. She did love him, crazy as it was. Knowing him a week and falling so hard was not her personality, but she didn't care. She wanted him to know.

"You know I love you, too," he whispered in her ear.

Allison squeezed him harder before pulling away. She could feel tears welling up in her eyes as she looked at him. "Will you call me tonight?"

Darrin's smile had faded and been replaced by a frown. "Of course I will."

Allison forced a weak smile and left the condo, wiping the tears away as she rode the elevator down to the parking level. She told herself to relax; she would see him again.

43

Ken Stark was on a plane heading to Chicago. It was only a three-hour drive from Grand Rapids, but why would he drive when he could take the company jet? He was the Vice President of Business Development for U.S. Law Conglomerate. U.S. Law owned thirty-five law firms across the country, and it was his job to help startup firms get their businesses running. It was more or less a figurehead position as the business plan he'd developed was provided to each new firm and had been proven to be effective. U.S. Law was, to put it simply, franchising law firms, and he was the person that oversaw the transition teams. It was a high-ranking position that paid him an annual salary of two million dollars plus bonuses.

He would never say it out loud, but he knew his real job was babysitting the owners. He was a Harvard Law graduate and one of the top attorneys in the country. He handled all the legal issues that Jeremiah Dean and Phil Warner had, and in the last few years, that had been more than enough work to keep him busy. He had kept them out of jail for the last twenty years. But now it was getting crazy.

He had his hands full with all that was happening. Everyone associated with the Deters case was suddenly being wiped out. He hadn't been told of any plan to that end, and he was thankful for that; he had already done more than enough unethical and illegal things to protect them, but the fact that he was out of the loop also made him nervous. He feared that he may be next, and why wouldn't he be? He knew about everything. He wasn't that scared of the old men, but the kid…he was a wild card. He was ruthless.

So here he was, on a flight to the corporate office in Chicago to attend a supposed "regional meeting" for U.S. Law and discuss future expansion. He knew better. He was heading to Chicago to talk to the owners about their own issues. They always picked Chicago to meet. It was close, but it wasn't home. They hated doing dirty business in their own city. Ken always assumed that their meeting away from home made their actions seem more tolerable to them.

As the plane approached Chicago, Ken predicted their meeting would revolve around preparation for if and when they got caught. Who would they have to get rid of? Was there a politician they needed to pay off? The same old questions they always asked.

He was sick of it. He had just lost a friend when John was murdered after his poker game the other night. Police said it was a robbery, but he knew better. John was killed because of the Deters incident. John had been greedy; it'd been easy to convince him to participate in the ruse. Of course, John had had no idea how bad the crash was going to be.

John was brash and selfish, and also, it turned out, stupid. To think that no one was going to die was naïve at best. All it had taken was a tiny puncture in the gas tank and a jar of accelerant for the van to catch fire upon impact. It was a tactic the boss's kid had used at least two times prior to the Deters crash and it was always successful. Especially since the accelerant burns off, and with it goes the evidence of foul play.

It was a convenient coincidence that Ken played golf with John and that John went on Spring Break with the Deters every year. It was that information that Ken had mentioned in a meeting with the bosses that set the whole disastrous plan in motion. It was information he desperately wished he had never shared.

The bosses had told Ken to approach John with his new compensation package. John had jumped on it right away, and he'd ended up dead. Ken's real fear now is whether or not the bosses think he is a risk. If so, he could be next.

The plane was on the ground now. Ken grabbed his laptop and exited the plane. The airport was busy, so much so that he didn't notice he was being followed.

There was a limousine waiting curbside for Ken, and the driver held the door open for him. His tail climbed into a waiting taxi. Both vehicles merged effortlessly onto the highway in the direction of downtown Chicago. After a twenty-minute ride, the limo pulled in front of a tall building. It had large gold letters above the entry door that read "U.S. LAW Co." Ken Stark got out and went inside. About fifty feet further back, the patron paid their fare, exited the cab, and headed in as well.

Ken, completely unaware of the danger he was in, boarded the first available elevator. Unbeknownst to him, his tail was there right beside him. Many people were in the elevator, but Ken was lost in thought about the upcoming encounter. He was oblivious to everyone around him. As the elevator went higher and higher, people exited to their various floors. Soon there were only two of them inside.

Ken felt a sharp pain in the back of his neck. His hand automatically shot up and he turned in terror to look at the person behind him. Ken recognized him instantly. "What are you doing here? What was that?" His assailant didn't answer. It wouldn't have mattered anyway—Ken Stark was already dead. The needle, strategically inserted right beneath his skull, contained liquid cyanide. The killer pushed the button for the fifty-fifth floor. He got off there, went to the elevator across the hall and pushed the down button. When the elevator containing Stark's dead body arrived at the top floor, it would look like he'd died from a heart attack. If anyone suspected otherwise, the murderer would be long gone.

Ken Stark's elevator reached the sixtieth floor and when the door opened, no one exited. The receptionist glanced up but couldn't see Ken's crumpled body from behind her desk. She never thought anything of it. The killer was back in a cab heading back to the airport before the body was even discovered.

44

Allison was busy at work. She was surprised to be so focused on the task at hand, considering all that was going on in her life. She was doing very well until she opened her top desk drawer. She saw the envelope right away and noticed her name written in Marcus's handwriting. Her mind was spinning as she slowly removed the letter. She started to panic.

She cried right away as she read the opening paragraph. She knew that Marcus was devastated, that went without saying, but she had no idea he'd been suicidal. As she read on, she was comforted when he promised he wasn't going to do anything brash. Her crying subsided and she even grinned a little at what he had figured out when about their case.

She nodded with understanding as she read about Ken Stark and John Wainwright's connection. It was all making sense. Those greedy, disgusting people, she thought. It was infuriating. She was ready to get the police involved, thinking they might have an advantage in solving the remaining loose ends, but she now knew why Marcus wanted to wait. She would respect those wishes, but it would be hard. She prayed it was the right thing to do and that nothing bad would happen to them before they did.

When she finished the letter, she put it back in the envelope and went straight to Marcus's office to check out the list Marcus had on file. Getting something from the IRS was next to impossible. She didn't know who gave it to him or why, but she was very interested in looking at it. Marcus had a good reason for her to, or he never would have mentioned it. It was just like Marcus not to tell her what she was looking for but rather to make her put in the effort to find something herself.

She fired up the computer and dutifully opened the file named "Spring Break". The name gave her chills; after all it was the Spring Break trip where all this had started. The list was long. The amount of assets that the Dean & Warner Company owned was astronomical. And presumably these were only a portion of the ones that were listed in what must have been a comprehensive and expensive IRS audit.

Allison poured over every line, but nothing jumped out at her. There were pages listing companies with the different assets allocated to each one. Dean & Warner Securities held the majority of the assets, followed by U.S. Law Conglomerate. The assets were broken down separately even though the primary owners were the same.

Allison found looking at the list mundane until suddenly she saw what she was supposed to all along, and it terrified her. She had to look twice to see if it was real. Under the Dean & Warner Securities assets, there was an "Employee Vacation Property" purchased in June 2012. The address of the property was what startled Allison: 233 Beach Street, Pentwater, Michigan. That was the rental Darrin was in!

Allison felt sick and she started to panic again. How did she not see it? How could she have been so dumb? She'd never put it together, but now she moved the cursor to the Google search and typed *"Phil Warner family"* and hit the images tab. Up popped a picture of the Warner family at what seemed to be a black tie event. Phil and his wife were sitting down, and there were five people standing behind them, all posing for the picture. The guy on the far left grabbed Allison's attention. The young, handsome man in his Army dress uniform. Darrin.

She'd known all along that Darrin's last name was Warner, but never once had the thought that he was a part of *THE* Warner family crossed her mind. It couldn't be! There was no way he is a part of all of that. She knew him!

Or did she? She tried to remember what all they'd done together this past week. Everything she had told him about Marcus and the crash, he'd already known! Allison was fuming, but she still wanted to believe he couldn't possibly be involved. No matter what, though, she couldn't deny that he'd lied to her. So where did that leave her?

"Think, Allison. Think," she said aloud, trying to force herself to concentrate on what she must do and not on her impending heartache. She mulled over this upsetting revelation.

The Dean & Warner Company purchased the cottage just after Marcus began work on the lawsuit; they most likely used it as a cover to keep tabs on Marcus. But why? What would having a cottage close to Marcus gain them? Allison was going over different scenarios in her head. Were they watching him to find an opportunity to kill him? That didn't make sense; they wouldn't have to buy a place to do that.

Allison was racking her brain trying to come up with a reason that fit. Suddenly a horrible thought came to her that positively made her shudder, in part because she knew right away it was true. They were watching him, and they were listening. They would have bugged his cottage and possibly even installed cameras. She was certain that's what happened; it was the only possibility that made sense. They were listening to his conversations with his wife and they were also assuredly listening to his cell phone conversations. That would be easy from that close proximity.

Allison went back to the Spring Break file. She had a feeling that the Pentwater property wasn't the only real estate that Dean & Warner owned in West Michigan. She opened it up and searched; it was only a matter of minutes until she found what she'd expected.

There was a house listed at 3600 Maplewood, East Grand Rapids. Maplewood was right behind Marcus and Sheila's old house, and, as their address was 3612, 3600 had to be behind them and one house to the east. Allison knew the house instantly. She remembered Marcus and Sheila talking about it when it sold; they had been surprised that it had sold the first day it'd been listed, and for more than the asking price.

Allison wondered if any cameras and microphones would still be in the East Grand Rapids home. She had to assume that they wouldn't leave something like that behind that could be found later. Surely they must be able to install and remove devices unnoticed.

But back to the question at hand. Why was Darrin here now? There was no way it was a coincidence. He must have a mission. Was he there to keep an eye on her?

Allison became agitated as another thought struck her: was her parents' house under surveillance? If so, whoever was listening would have known she was going to Marcus's cottage in Pentwater. They would also have heard her and her parents talking about Simon Daniels and Marcus going to Georgia. Allison's wheels were turning. Why would they care if she went to Pentwater? Why would Darrin intercept her? Were they afraid she would find something? Could the cameras still be there? Allison jumped up when she looked at her clock. 2:30 already?

"Where did the day go?" She left Marcus's office and went up to Jessica's desk.

"I'm taking off for a while Jess; send all calls for me to voicemail please."

Jessica nodded. "Yes, of course."

Allison headed out of the building down to the parking ramp. As she pulled out, Skip Lamont, who had been sitting in the ramp watching Allison's car for over an hour, started his car and waited for her to get a little distance apart. As he followed, a Ford pickup pulled out in front of him. He wasn't worried; he could still see her and, besides, he had put a tracking device under her car. It was standard FBI issue, simple technology, just a magnetic box that stuck to the car that he could track with his own onboard computer. As Allison jumped onto Highway 131 North, Skip was still behind the pickup. Skip stayed a safe distance behind. He couldn't help but think he should be watching the pickup as well.

As Allison was driving, she called a friend. He was more of an associate she knew through the firm. He had been a State Representative from their district, and Marcus and he had become well acquainted. Since then he had been elected to the House of Representatives and had served there for four years now. It was nice to have the cell number of a member of the House, even if she rarely called it.

"Michael Heyboer speaking," the voice on the phone came blaring through.

"Hi, Michael. It's Allison Deters. How are you?"

"I'm doing well, Allison. How about you and Marcus, how are you guys doing?"

Allison could hear the real concern in his voice, and it made her feel good for a moment.

"He's doing well, only…"

When she hesitated, he prompted, "Only what Allison?"

"Well, Michael, we need a favor."

"Ok," Michael said. "I'll try to help. What do you need?"

Allison paused for a minute. "I need some information about a soldier. His name is Darrin Warner. He was in the Army until last year, and he's the son of,"

"Phil Warner," they both said simultaneously.

Allison was surprised. "How did you know that, Michael?" she asked curiously.

"C'mon, Allison. Everyone in Washington knows the Warner family, including Darrin. I can tell you some information about Darrin that is widely known in the congressional circles but is really meant for military ears only. What I'm telling you is mildly classified so you need to promise to keep it to yourself."

"I swear, I won't say a word."

The congressman took a deep breath and began. "Ok. Here we go. Darrin made quite a name for himself helping in the war effort. Everyone noticed his accomplishments because of who he is; after all, most of Congress knows his father. Anyway, he was a highly decorated soldier. He was used on many special missions and his team, nicknamed "Death Unleashed" by their commanding officer, never failed. And I can tell you this, Allison: Darrin was extremely skilled in hand to hand combat and marksmanship. He is very highly thought of in the Army and by other government agencies. That's as much as I can tell you. Why? What's up?"

Allison was afraid of this question, for what could she say?

"Oh, it's nothing important. I had met him and he asked me out, he said he was in the military, and that was it. I was just curious to know more about him, that's all."

Allison waited for either laughter or a big "bullshit" from the congressman, but neither came. He simply said, "Oh, ok. I hope I helped."

Allison knew he hadn't bought it, but she didn't care. She was just glad he didn't press the issue. "Thanks so much, Michael. I really appreciate it."

"No problem at all. Please give Marcus my best, would you?"

"Of course I will," Allison replied sweetly.

"Wow", Allison said aloud, hanging up the phone. She took a minute to absorb what she had heard. Although she'd known Darrin has served overseas, it hadn't dawned on her the extent of his involvement. Darrin had killed people. It sounded like he had killed a lot of people. It was hard for Allison to picture the man that she thought she was in love with killing anybody. She didn't know what to think.

She looked to the right and saw a sign for her exit. "Monroe Road Next Right."

45

Skip Lamont was curious about the pickup truck that had accompanied him and the attorney from her office all the way to Pentwater. It was clear that it was following her. The field agent in Skip was dying to confront the driver, but he knew that would be stupid. If something was going to happen, he would just as well like to catch them in the act. He had been hanging back a good quarter mile so as not to be seen. When he got a chance, he would run the plate.

Both vehicles exited up ahead. Skip put on his blinker and headed down the exit ramp. He came to the stop sign at the end of the ramp and turned left, heading west toward the lake. He couldn't see the cars now but he had her marked on his computer. She was just over a half mile away. The map on his phone showed a lot of turns; there was a lake on his left and he saw a sign that said Pentwater Lake. What a beautiful area, he thought as he drove past. He could see a channel that connected the smaller lake with Lake Michigan. He drove through the little town of Pentwater as he followed his tracking map.

He turned onto 1st Street and started to slow down. He could see the pickup parked up ahead. Allison's car was around the corner to the right on a street called Beach. It was obvious that the pickup still wished to remain undetected; why else would it be parked around the corner? Skip drove by slowly. The license plate was from Indiana, number GS9397. Although the driver was faced the other way towards Allison's car, Skip could tell it was a man. The man had on a baseball cap and a sweatshirt with the hood bunched down around his neck.

Skip continued down the road to the state park and drove in. As long as he was here, he was going to take a look at Lake Michigan, and boy, was it amazing. He'd seen it a few times before but never got tired of it. He left the park and headed back on the road facing the pickup. He parked in front of a cottage on 1st Street. From here he could observe the truck, but he had no visual on Allison's car.

He typed the pickup's plate number in his computer and waited for the results. The truck was registered to a Darrin Warner of Carmel, Indiana. No warrants, no arrests, nothing on his record. Skip got on the phone and called Detective Harper in Marietta. When the Marietta homicide detective answered, Skip told him what he was doing, where they were, and finally, what he wanted Bruce to do.

"Can you find out all you can about a Darrin Warner of Carmel, Indiana? Someone else followed the lawyer up here, and I think it's him. He seems to be watching her at a cottage. If you use your resources to get me some information, maybe I can figure out what this guy wants."

Bruce was writing down all the information Skip had given him. "Ok, I got it, Skip. I'll get back to you soon."

Skip said thanks and hung up the phone.

Allison was frantically running around the cottage looking for proof of surveillance equipment. She'd become certain the cottage had been bugged. She found it very unlikely that anyone who'd infiltrated the cottage would not have also taken the time to remove everything, but you never know. They may have missed something. She looked in every room, under lamps, beneath furniture. She removed the clocks from the walls; she even searched all the picture frames. She found nothing.

"That doesn't mean anything," she said aloud. "You have no idea what you're even looking for."

Suddenly, she was sorry she had said anything. What if they're still listening? she thought. Then she saw it. Her eyes fixed on the mug on the desk. It was a large mug shaped like a monkey with its arms crossed. It contained pens, pencils, paper clips, and various other junk.

What caught her eye was the flash drive that was also sticking out of it. Normally, she wouldn't have thought anything of it, except for the fact that there wasn't a computer at the cottage. There never had been. Marcus wouldn't even bring his laptop up there. He had always been adamant about it - the cottage was for family time; television and computers were strictly prohibited.

Allison grabbed the flash drive and studied it closely. She knew that such a device could be used for surveillance. This one seemed legit enough, though. Maybe she was wrong and it wasn't a bug. Maybe Marcus or Sheila had brought up a computer and she didn't know it. Maybe Marcus had forgotten he had a flash drive in his pocket and had taken it out and tossed it there on the desk. She didn't know, but she was going to get it checked out.

Skip was shifting around in his seat; he had been in the car for a long time and was starting to get antsy. Suddenly, the pickup was backing up, obviously to keep from being seen. Skip watched intently and then saw Allison's car leaving Beach Street and heading toward town. Why was she leaving already? Was she going home? Why would she drive up here and only stay for half an hour? Skip waited while the pickup pulled out and started following her again. He slid onto the street behind them. They made their way through town and back to the highway.

"She is definitely heading back to Grand Rapids," Skip said aloud.

He couldn't see Allison's car and he could barely see the truck. He wanted to leave room so he wouldn't be seen, but he was afraid to let them out of his sight, especially since he had no idea what the driver of the pickup was up to. He checked the tracker. Allison was heading south on Highway 31 about a mile ahead of him. Skip's phone rang; it was Detective Harper calling back.

Skip answered, "Hey Bruce, did you find anything?"

Bruce's bellowing voice sounded intimidating through the speakers of Skip's car. "Yeah, I did. Darrin Warner, thirty-one years old, is the son of Phillip Warner, co-owner of Dean & Warner Securities, one of the richest families in the country."

Skip interrupted, "Seems strange for him to be driving a 2014 Ford pickup."

Bruce ignored him and continued. "He graduated early from Butler University and then enlisted in the Army where he served ten highly decorated years. He served on special task forces in Afghanistan and Iraq, the details of which I couldn't get any info on because they are classified. It sounds like he's a talented soldier, a real mercenary type."

Skip's mind was racing. What the hell was he doing following a lawyer from Michigan?

Bruce continued, "He left the Army less than three months ago. No arrests or warrants; I couldn't even find a speeding ticket."

"A real boy scout, huh?" Skip asked.

"Well, that appears to be the case, but who really knows? There is some more news that you need to know."

Bruce waited for Skip to speak.

After an awkward silence, Skip asked, "Well, what is it?"

"Well," Bruce began, "the forensics on your victim Diane Parker came back."

"And?" Skip said impatiently.

"She was shot using the same gun as Simon Daniels. No prints on the casing, but the bullet markings indicate that it was definitely the same weapon."

Skip thought about that for a bit. "Didn't you say your suspect thought Simon was killed with his gun?"

"Yes," Bruce answered, knowing what was coming next.

"Do you still think it was smart to let him go back to Michigan? Could he have killed Diane Parker?"

"It's possible I suppose, but extremely doubtful. He would have had to have immediately left my office, driven all the way over to Atlanta and then located and shot her within ninety minutes. Plus, you need to remember I have two witnesses - one in Simon's apartment and the other the bartender – who both doubted my suspect's involvement. For Mr. Deters to pull off both murders within the timelines we have would be remarkable."

Skip wasn't convinced yet, "So you're saying that although Mr. Deters went to Marietta to kill Mr. Daniels, he only threatened him and left. Then someone else stole his gun, went back to the apartment and shot Daniels. Days later, that same person went to Atlanta and killed Diane Parker with that same stolen gun on the very day that Mr. Deters happened to be back in Georgia with his sister who just happened to have coffee with the victim?" Skip whistled, "Seems a little farfetched to me."

"I stand by my decision; to believe Mr. Deters could plan and execute those murders on those tight timelines is much more unlikely." Who does this guy think he is? Bruce thought. Bruce was not ok with someone questioning his decisions as a detective. If someone disagreed with him, that was one thing, but to talk down to him about his decision was an altogether different animal. Bruce kept his calm and with his best southern charm, he said, "Well, sir, I do value your opinion, and I will definitely keep an open mind as we both move forward with our investigations."

Skip could tell when he was being talked down to and he didn't like it, but for once he held his tongue and simply said, "You're right. If you find out anything let me know. In the meantime, I'll keep following Allison, at least for another day, and then I'm going to interview her."

"Understood," Bruce said and hung up.

46

"That small town son-of-a-bitch, what does he know?" Skip screamed in his car. He hated being talked down to. "I'll be the bigger man, that's for sure."

Even though no one could hear him, Skip felt better after yelling out. Deep down, he sort of believed Bruce; he thought it was plausible that the murder weapon had been stolen from Marcus and could have been used to try to frame him. Skip looked at the tracker; he had been distracted talking to Detective Harper and needed to regroup. Allison's vehicle was just ahead about a quarter mile.

The traffic was heavier now than it had been on the way up, so Skip thought he would take advantage of it and try to drive by the pickup. The driver shouldn't think anything of it with the traffic being so thick, so maybe Skip could get a look at him. Skip sped up, closing the distance between them. The truck was in the far right lane, as was Allison, and Skip was in the left lane. As he pulled alongside the pickup, he knew to be subtle when he looked over. Skip slowly glanced over at the pickup but couldn't see anything. The driver had slowed down and had his head turned to the right. Skip saw the same thing he had seen in Pentwater, the back of his baseball cap.

"What the heck?" Skip said aloud. "He must know I'm following her, too."

Suddenly the pickup was behind *him*. Skip maintained his speed and was quickly gaining on Allison; the pickup was keeping up with him. Skip put on his blinker and moved back into the right lane; he was only two cars behind Allison. The truck got over as well and was right behind him again.

Skip thought back to what Bruce had said about Darrin Warner; he was basically the Army's version of a Navy SEAL. Maybe an Army Ranger or a Green Beret, Skip didn't know, but he knew that he could be very dangerous. Skip looked into his mirror. The pickup was right behind him but he couldn't see the face of the driver with his ball cap pulled way down.

Skip started to slow down. The pickup slowed down as well. Skip slowed down some more, now driving only sixty in a seventy mile per hour speed zone. The pickup stayed right behind him. Skip slowed all the way down fifty-five miles per hour. Likewise, the pickup slowed. The cars in the left lane were zipping by them at around eighty. Skip kept looking in the mirror but to no avail; he couldn't see the driver. Suddenly, the pickup exited the highway on the off ramp beside them, and, before Skip could react, the pickup was gone.

Though he would never admit it, he was a little bit shaken. How long had the driver of the pickup known Skip was following the two of them? Could it have been from the start? Was it when they were in the parking ramp in Grand Rapids? Maybe when he was parked in Pentwater? After the caution he had taken and the effort to not get too close, he had been spotted. How?

Skip thought back to the parking ramp. He didn't remember the pickup arriving while he was waiting for Allison. The truck must have been there first! That revelation sent chills through Skip's body. He must have seen him put the tracker on her car.

He decided to end the surveillance when they got back. He was going to talk to the lawyer tonight.

47

The atmosphere at the U.S. Law building was still buzzing over the news of Ken Stark's heart attack in the elevator. The police had arrived along with the E.M.T.s and had taken his body to the morgue.

Jeremiah Dean and Phillip Warner were in the conference room on the sixtieth floor of the building. It was a beautiful room dominated by a large mahogany table with gold inlayed "U.S. Law Conglomerate" down the center. It was surrounded by top of the line Herman Miller chairs. To the east was a wall of windows that provided a breathtaking view of the Chicago skyline. On the south end of the room was a gas fireplace with a couple of high backed chairs strategically placed in front of it.

In these chairs, two of the nation's richest men sat, discussing their ongoing situation. The two had been partners in business for over thirty years. Jeremiah was the CEO; he had always been the face of the company. He was the one that did all the commercials and public appearances when they were a smaller investment company. He was a handsome man who had been blessed with the gift of gab and was also a smooth salesman.

Philip Warner, on the other hand, was brash and unrefined for a person of his wealth; he would say what was on his mind, and it didn't matter what he said or who he said it to. He was also ruthless in business. The two of them together were a perfect match, a partnership built for success, and they had risen to the top quickly.

Jeremiah knew little about the illegal workings of their company, and Phil had always wanted it that way. He reasoned it would be easier for Jeremiah to fit the role of the CEO and maintain the company's image if he had a clear conscience. Though he would never admit it, and the public would never know, Phil considered Jeremiah to be his puppet. Jeremiah always did what Phil told him to do, and to his credit, he usually did it very well. However, the best thing about Jeremiah, in Phil's mind, was the fact that if the shit ever hit the fan, Jeremiah would be the one covered in it. Hopefully it would never come to that.

Phil had always been very good at taking care of any problems that would arise, but that damn lawyer from Michigan, the man whose stupid little lawsuit could have destroyed their whole company, would not go away. Phil thought he had done the work to get rid of that problem. Ken Stark had provided them the perfect opportunity, and Phil and Blaine had taken care of the rest. It hadn't been easy.

First, they needed someone expendable, someone who wouldn't talk, to carry out the plan. Jeremiah's son-in-law Simon seemed to be the perfect someone.

Simon had been desperate to get Jeremiah's approval. Jeremiah had never liked him; he didn't have the requisite pedigree to marry his only daughter. Jeremiah had been so upset about the marriage that he wouldn't even speak to Simon. When Phil found out that Simon had come to Jeremiah and confronted him about the investment fraud, Phil knew what he had to do. He sent the guys to Simon with the plan, promising him a high position at the company if it was well executed. But if it didn't go well, they couldn't risk him talking so, for insurance, Phil had his guys threaten Simon's wife's and daughter's lives should he decide to not go through with it. His guy Hawkins could be very convincing.

They made Simon think this was all coming from Jeremiah. It couldn't have gone any better, except for two things. One, the lawyer didn't die, and while it was great he had been laid up for so long, now that he was better, he'd begun snooping around. Two, that stupid Simon kid had been drinking before he did it. If not for that, it would have simply been ruled an accident and they all could have moved on. Phil would have given him a spot at the firm, and he even would have talked to Jeremiah to ease up on the kid. If only the stupid punk hadn't been so scared. He went to the bar and started drinking, foiling the plan and forcing Phil's men to continue their threats against Simon's family in case he decided to talk.

Simon wasn't a problem anymore, but the lawyer could well be. It was too bad about Stark - they may miss him a little. He was a good asset legally and he knew a lot about their business dealings, but at least the risk of him talking was gone and that significantly eased Phil's mind.

Although both Phil and Jeremiah were ready to retire, issues kept preventing them from being able to. They needed to secure their legacy and make sure the business was safe in Phil's sons' hands. Phil was terribly proud of his sons, Blaine and Darrin, and he hoped they could take the company even farther than he and Jeremiah had.

Jeremiah spoke from the chair beside him, interrupting Phil's thoughts.

"Where are your boys today? Are they coming here to discuss all the crap going on? Did you know about my ex son-in-law?"

Phil looked up from the newspaper he was barely reading. "Yes, I heard, Blaine told me. I'm terribly sorry, Jerry. How's Elizabeth doing?" Phil asked.

"Not great. She's awfully sad. We did our best to warn her about him, but she was always so stubborn. Do we know anything about Simon's death?" Jeremiah asked, even though he knew if it had been Phil's doing, Phil would never admit it.

Phil gave Jeremiah an annoyed look and shook his head.

"What the hell is going on and how is Stark's death going to affect us?" Jeremiah asked as he looked at Phil. He was looking at him the same way he had thousands of times during the building of their business empire. In the past, Phil had seen it as a look of power, of strength. This time, Jeremiah's look disgusted him. It was like the look a child would give his father when asking him why he couldn't go out and play. Phil set down the paper and sat up in his chair. If people actually knew you, he thought to himself, our company would go bankrupt.

"Well, there's no doubt we will miss his legal expertise, but we will be fine. It's not like we can't find another lawyer." Phil laughed as he said this; after all they did have access to over a thousand lawyers that worked under the corporate umbrella of U.S. Law.

"I suppose you're right. Where are your boys today?" Jeremiah repeated.

"I thought they would be here," Phil shrugged. "Blaine should be here shortly. I'm not sure about Darrin. Blaine told me he was still in Michigan and should be back soon. At the very least, I expect him at the office in Indianapolis on Monday."

Jeremiah looked at Phil. "Are they coming to the lake this weekend?"

Just as he finished speaking, Blaine Warner threw open the door and entered the room. Blaine was Phil's oldest son and presumed head of operations after Phil retired. Blaine was a stocky man like his dad, standing five-foot-eleven and weighing anywhere between 220 and 230 pounds, depending on his motivation. Unlike his brother Darrin, who stood six-foot-one and weighed around 195 pounds, Blaine had always had to fight to keep his weight down. Darrin had gotten the athletic good looks from their mother, and Blaine had gotten the drive to succeed from his father. Together, Blaine and Darrin were to take over the positions left by Jeremiah and their father. Blaine and his father watched one another as he entered, gauging each other's body language.

"What's it like out there?" Phil asked.

Blaine shrugged and answered, "The police are gone and it's calming down now. People are just getting ready to go home a little early, that's all. By Monday, it should be business as usual."

Phil nodded. Though he never said so, he was extremely proud of Blaine. He was going to do an exceptional job when he took over the company. He could think outside the box and knew how to get things done. It had been Blaine's idea to use a fire accelerant in the Deters' crash to ensure fatalities. It was exactly that kind of thinking that had helped make their company what it was today, one of the wealthiest in America.

"So, what should be our next step, Blaine? What are we doing about the lawyers from Michigan? Are we going to let them keep snooping around?" Phil asked his son.

Blaine looked at Jeremiah.

"Don't worry about him!" Phil snapped. "Answer my damn question!"

Blaine quickly looked back at his father, "We have it handled. As far as you two are concerned, the situation is settled."

Phil didn't seem convinced. "Well, it better be. I don't want to hear anything else about that fucking lawyer! You got that?"

Blaine nodded. "I'll deal with it," he said and headed to the door to leave.

"Hey! Come back here!" Phil yelled again. "You keep Darrin out of this. We need him clean; he has to keep a good reputation if he's going to be the next face of the company."

Blaine forced a smile. "Yes, sir, I'll take care of it." Blaine stood there for a minute waiting to be excused like a twelve-year-old from the dinner table.

"You can go now, son."

Blaine turned to walk out, and Phil added very calmly, "One more thing before you go."

Blaine looked back, dreading whatever was coming next.

Phil looked at him and said, "Good work, son. We'll see you at the cabin tomorrow."

Blaine nodded and left. Phil and Jeremiah watched him go, and then Jeremiah stood up and turned toward Phil. "Bright and early at the cabin tomorrow?"

Phil nodded. "Be there by seven so we can get on the lake early—we could use a break."

Jeremiah nodded, "Sounds good. We should get to the jet soon, though; I'll call the driver."

48

Allison was back in Grand Rapids now; she had looked up the location of a security dealership and was walking in with the flash drive she had found at the cottage. The place was filled with little gadgets. She saw tiny cameras, microphones, recording devices, and tracking systems, anything and everything for eavesdropping or spying on someone. It gave her the creeps as she wondered what kind of people would buy this stuff.

She walked up to the counter. There was a younger man standing behind it looking at his computer. He never looked up as she approached. He had a tee shirt on that read "If they come for your guns, give them your ammo first."

"Excuse me," Allison said trying not to sound irritated at his lack of consideration, "can you help me with something?"

The clerk looked up at her and said, "I wasn't ignoring you; I was watching you the whole time." He turned his computer screen and Allison saw herself on it. She looked around the store to see the cameras, but all she saw were the two hanging down by the doorway. This image was coming from the counter, and there were no cameras visible.

"Ok, where's it coming from?" she smiled as she asked the clerk to fess up.

The clerk smiled back. "Where do you think it's coming from?"

Allison looked at the image and then looked around at the items on the counter. There were some pens, a service bell, a bottle of water, and a couple little display racks with little clip on cameras.

"I have no idea," she said.

The clerk smiled even bigger and he grabbed the water bottle and picked it up. The picture on the computer moved simultaneously.

"Look," he said as he removed the top of the bottle, just above the label.

The top half came off, cap and all, with water still in it. He showed her the inside of the bottle. Behind the label was the camera.

"Wow," Allison said trying to show some enthusiasm. It was obviously important to the clerk that she had some. "That's really cool."

The clerk was satisfied. "What can I help you with today?" Allison reached in her pocket and pulled out the flash drive. She handed it to the clerk without saying anything. The clerk grabbed it and whistled.

"What?" Allison asked. "What is it?"

The clerk looked up at her and said, "This is expensive, that's what this is. We don't carry these. I can order them if you would like, but you need to pay upfront, of course."

Allison shook her head. "I don't want to buy one; I just want to know what it is."

The clerk handed it back to her.

"That is an ACX brand hidden audio transmitter. There are a lot of recorders on the market that look like flash drives. In fact, we sell a lot of them here. But they just record. You put them somewhere and when you're done, you plug them into your port and they play the audio it recorded. The one you have actually transmits the signal to another devise so people can hear the conversations taking place in real time. There are a just a handful of those available for sale, but even those have a battery life typically less than ten hours. The one you have has a battery life of up to two weeks, which is phenomenal. Better yet, when it's coupled with an ACX charge transmitter, you can recharge it simply by being close by, let's say within a hundred yards, so you could conceivably leave this permanently planted. Like I said, it's expensive. Don't see these around a lot. Where did you get it?"

Allison ignored his question and asked him another one instead. "Have *you* ever sold any of these?"

The clerk shook his head quickly. "I haven't. Like I said, you would have to order them, but I could ask the owner if she's sold any."

Allison smiled and said, "That would be great." She handed him her business card. "Do you sell anything that could uncover any hidden cameras or recorders?"

The clerk nodded in amusement. "Of course we do. There are some right over here. Would you like to look at some?"

"Actually, I'd like to buy one. I'd like the best one that you have that's the easiest to use."

The clerk grabbed a package off the shelf and handed it to her. "This scanner will do the trick nicely, and it's simple to use. There are eight small led lights on it. If you walk into a home and it shows any lights, there is something transmitting. The more lights that go on, the closer you're getting to the device. It will sound a small alarm when you're within a foot of the device."

Allison walked back to the counter. "I'll take it."

She purchased the device, left the store, and got back into her car. As she drove, she started thinking about what she'd recently said while at the cottage. The first night she was there, the night she met Darrin on the beach, she'd had a phone conversation with Marcus and he had said he was down south. If someone had been listening, (she shuddered at the thought of someone listening to their private conversation) they could have followed him to Simon's apartment. It was possible for someone to then go to his hotel, steal his gun out of his car, and then go back and finish the job she knew Marcus couldn't do.

Her thoughts went back to Darrin again. He was within a hundred yards! Was he the one listening? She hated to think that, but she had to assume that was the case. He was part of the family Marcus had been trying to bring down. Why else would he have been up in Pentwater?

"You idiot!" Allison yelled at herself. She was upset with herself for falling so quickly.

Agent Skip Lamont had been waiting patiently outside the little store Allison had entered. "Spywares" was the name on the sign; Skip had searched it on his computer and found out, just as he had figured, that it was a hidden surveillance shop. The FBI had gone through extensive training in the subject. And even though the majority of the world's population never thought about it, they probably should. There were a lot of sick and crazy people that love spying on innocent folks for whatever perverted or twisted reasons they had. The selling of hidden devices was a multibillion dollar industry that the FBI was very concerned with.

Now the woman he was following was inside one of these stores. Skip hadn't seen Darrin Warner's pickup since it exited the highway around Grand Haven, but he was keeping a vigilant lookout for it. He was pretty certain that it wasn't around here now, but he was being extra cautious and observant.

Allison was exiting the store now, carrying a bag. She had bought something, and Skip was curious to know what it was. She got in her car and drove off, with Skip close behind. After a fifteen-minute drive, they arrived at a house in Jenison, just west of Grand Rapids. This is a quaint little neighborhood, Skip thought. Allison walked up the sidewalk to the house. Skip could see an older woman looking out the front window at her. Allison opened the door and walked inside.

Skip quickly got on his computer and found out the home belonged to Brian and Marcia Deters, the lawyers' parents. Skip put the car in park and turned it off. "This is as good of a time as any," he said as he got out of the car. He walked up to the house and knocked on the door. Allison opened it quickly. Skip was taken aback at first; he had seen Allison from afar but hadn't noticed how beautiful she was. Standing face to face, less than two feet apart, that point was driven home.

"Yes? Can I help you?" Allison asked a little impatiently.

Skip held out his badge that identified him as an FBI agent. "Yes, ma'am, you sure can."

49

Allison's parents were sitting at the kitchen table. "Would you care to join us for coffee?" Allison asked him.

"That would be right nice of you," Skip said, entering the room past her and pulling out a chair to sit down.

Allison grabbed him a cup of coffee and asked, "Cream or sugar?"

Skip nodded. "Please, that would be great."

Allison brought him the coffee with some cream and a bowl of sugar and sat it in front of him. Allison's parents were staring intensely at Skip.

He smiled at them and said, "Thank you for allowing me into your home."

Allison sat down. "So what can I do for you, Agent Lamont?"

"Please, call me Skip" he said with a smile.

Allison smiled back but was thinking that Skip was a ridiculous nickname.

"So, what can I do for you, Skip?"

"Well, Miss Deters," Skip paused for a second, waiting for her to ask him to call her Allison, but the invitation never came. "I need to ask you a few questions about Atlanta."

"What about Atlanta?" Allison asked with genuine curiosity.

Skip looked at Allison's parents and then back to Allison.

"It's ok, they can be here. I have nothing to hide from them."

Skip nodded. "Miss Deters, this past Tuesday you met with Diane Parker at Mama's Cup O' Mud? Is that correct?"

Allison nodded; she was confused at what was happening here.

"Well, Miss Deters, according to police reports, immediately after your meeting, Diane Parker was murdered while sitting in her car a block from the restaurant."

Allison stared in disbelief. She was visibly shaken and Skip noticed it right away. It would be hard to fake that reaction, and that was all Skip needed to confirm that Allison knew nothing of the murder.

"Were you aware of this?" Skip asked her, although he already knew the answer.

Allison was stunned. "No, I had no idea. Why? Why was she killed?"

"I was hoping you could shine some light on that for me," Skip replied softly.

Allison looked at her parents who were staring blankly at the FBI agent, and then she looked back at Skip. "Was it because she talked to me?"

As the question came out of her mouth, she was horrified to learn that she knew the answer. Of course that had something to do with it! She had put Diane Parker in danger by meeting with her. Someone didn't like Diane talking to her.

"How about telling me what you talked about?" Skip fixed a stern stare at her.

Allison looked at her parents again and the concern on their faces grew. "Maybe it would be best if you went to the living room." She turned back to Skip. "Better yet, why don't we take our coffee out onto the porch."

Skip nodded, grabbed his coffee, and followed her out the sliding door and into the porch. He looked around quickly. It was a typical little three-season porch with some windows and patio furniture. Allison sat on the love seat and Skip pulled up a chair. There was a small table between them and it had a few photos on it. Skip picked up one of the pictures studied it. It was a picture taken at some sort of picnic. Allison was there, and so were her parents. There was also another couple with two boys. Skip assumed it was her brother Marcus and his family. Everyone looked so happy. Skip stared at Marcus, trying to get a read on him from his picture. He looked like a successful and happy man; he didn't look like a killer. Skip set the photo down and turned to Allison, who was quietly watching him.

"They looked happy," he said.

Allison nodded, fighting back a tear.

Skip leaned in toward her and said quietly, "How about telling me everything you know."

Allison hesitated and weighed whether or not she should tell him everything. It could only help to have the FBI on the case, she decided. She looked at Skip. "Ok. I'll tell you everything. Maybe you can help us."

Allison spent the next twenty minutes telling him everything she could think of regarding the crash and the investigation she and Marcus were doing together. Skip was very attentive. She told him about Marcus's law suit that could have shaken up the firm of Dean & Warner. Allison noticed Skip's eyes light up when she talked about the stock fraud that Dean & Warner was allegedly guilty of. After she was done telling him everything she could think of, she asked him to wait there while she got something from her purse.

Allison went and grabbed Marcus's letter that he had written and handed it to the agent. She watched him intently as he slowly read through it. At one point, he stopped and asked, "What is 'reason number 4?'" Allison explained to him the reasons that Marcus said would motivate people to commit murder, reason number 4 being greed or monetary gain. Skip nodded his understanding and continued reading.

When he finished, he said, "This last part is very interesting to me—would you mind if I read it aloud?"

Allison shrugged. "Sure, go ahead".

"*...Simon is dead. Which brings me to his murder—there is still an investigation going on into that, and I'm probably the only lead they have. I'm certain the detective in Marietta, Bruce Harper, will eventually be calling me to go back down there. I'm not ready to go back; I must get solid proof linking Jeremiah Dean and Ken Stark, and I need my freedom to do so. I know how I'm going to do it, but I can't have the police getting in my way right now. I want to connect things to the top. I want to connect them to Jeremiah Dean; I know he's involved, but I don't have enough proof yet. I want him to pay. I know they are nervous right now because people are dying - people that were connected to the crash. Someone is killing everyone who knows about their fraud. That makes me a big target. That's why I need to disappear for a while. I'll check in on you every so often, and if I think there's a chance you're in danger, I'll come back immediately; right now, I don't believe you are.*

I need to finish this, Allie. I need to settle the score."

When he finished reading, he looked at Allison. "Where is he Allison? Where's Marcus?"

Allison stared at him, "I have no clue. Like it says there, he didn't tell me."

Skip wanted to find Marcus. He no longer suspected Marcus but he wanted to find him for selfish reasons. He didn't want him out there trying to solve the case without him. This could be his homerun, the case that puts him on the Bureau map. Skip was going to make sure he would be the one to break this open.

"You haven't sent this to Detective Harper, have you?" Skip asked impatiently.

Allison shook her head.

Skip again stared at her for a bit, and then he said, "I do have a few questions for you, though. Why does Marcus assume that you're not in danger? I mean, people are dying all around; how come you wouldn't feel a little threatened?"

Allison grimaced as if his words caused her pain. "I'm not totally sure why I shouldn't feel a little threatened, but who else knows about me and what I do or do not know? Besides, I trust Marcus."

Skip shook his head. "Whoever killed Diane Parker must know about you, and if they would kill her for what she knows, I can't see any reason why they wouldn't do the same to you."

Allison glared at him. "Are you trying to scare me? Is that what you're doing? Why would you want to do that?"

Skip shook his head again. "I'm not trying to scare you. I just want to cover all the bases. We don't want you to get hurt, do we?"

Now it was Allison's turn to shake her head. "I understand what you're saying, but if Marcus feels I'm ok then I'm inclined to believe him. He would never let anyone hurt me."

Skip decided not to push it any further and changed the subject. "So, Allison," Skip paused to see if it was ok that he used her first name, and she didn't correct him. "Allison, is there any reason you can think of that Phillip Warner's son Darrin would follow you up to Pentwater today?"

Allison felt like she'd been punched in the stomach. "What?" she stammered. "Darrin was following me? That's impossible—he flew home to Indiana today."

That surprised Skip. "Yes, to be honest, we were both following you. You know him?"

Allison saw the confusion on the agent's face and she knew that this was going to be tough to explain. She decided to tell him everything about

Darrin as well—how they met up north and had spent so much time together over the past week. How he never told her who his father was, even when he knew who her brother was. She even told him about the supposed rental cottage that Darrin had been staying in.

Skip listened carefully to her story before asking, "Why did you go up there today?"

She then told him about her fear of there being recording devices in Marcus's cottage, and she wanted to check it out.

"You drove all the way up there for that? Wouldn't they have removed them by now?" Skip was a little surprised by Allison; she seemed way smarter than that.

Allison shrugged her shoulders. "I assumed they would have but I just needed to look anyway. Besides, they may have still had a use for them."

Allison then told him about what she had said inside the cottage the previous weekend and how it could tie things together. Allison reached into her purse and pulled out the fake flash drive she'd found. Skip recognized the equipment immediately; it wasn't Bureau quality, but for surveillance in the civilian world, this model was exceptional. He reached out his hand and took it from Allison.

"You found this there?" he asked.

She nodded. "It was in the pencil jar on the desk, but there's no computer up there, so I was suspicious."

Skip nodded. It was making sense. "And then you went to that store to have it checked out. Did they know what it was?"

"He knew right away. I bought a detector when I was there as well."

She went to the kitchen, grabbed the device out of the bag, and brought it over to him.

"Do you know how to work this?" she asked.

Skip smiled. "Of course I do."

"Would you mind?" Allison handed it to him, returning the smile.

She was hoping he would make the sweep for her. She didn't feel like messing with it; all she wanted to do was call Darrin. She needed to know if he'd gone back to Indiana or not. Had he lied to her again? Maybe it was a mistake. Maybe it wasn't his truck, or maybe it wasn't him driving. She had to find out.

Skip headed to the front entry of the house to search for listening devices, and Allison stepped outside to make a call. Darrin's phone only rang once before he answered.

"Allie, is everything alright?"

Allison was relieved to hear his voice regardless of what was going on, but she didn't let on to that.

"Hi, Darrin. Did you make it home safely?"

Darrin knew something was up. "I'm sorry I didn't call yet, but yes, I've been home for hours."

Allison was crushed. "Why are you lying to me? I know you were following me today!"

There was silence on the other end.

"Darrin? Darrin talk to me!"

Darrin began, very deliberately, "Is someone following you Allie? How do you know? How can you be sure? I haven't been following you; I'm in Indiana. Did you see him? Are you ok?"

"No, I didn't see anyone. The cop following me did."

"You have a cop following you? Is he a cop or a fed?"

Allison was surprised he asked for a differentiation. "He's an FBI agent from Atlanta. How did you know to ask that?"

Darrin seemed worried, "It just makes sense, that's all. You need to stay close to him, ok? You need to stay safe."

Allison had mixed emotions. She was happy to know that he cared so much and that he was concerned about her safety, but she was also troubled, concerned about his earlier lies and why he would think she could be in danger. How would he know if he wasn't involved? It was becoming obvious to her that he was, or, at the very least, that he knew more than he was letting on.

"The agent followed your truck today. He ran the plates. It was your pickup."

Darrin started to plead with her. "Please, Allie, I need you to trust me! You have to trust me! My truck is at the airport. I drove there this morning after I left your condo. Believe me—I'll never let anything happen to you."

Allison felt like crying. What was happening? She got mad at herself; she needed to be strong. "So, what are you going to do at home?" she asked feeling much calmer.

"I have to go confront my brother. He and my father are going to the fishing cabin tomorrow; I need to get there to talk to them. Try to keep the agent close to you. I'll be back soon, and when I am, I'll tell you more, I promise."

Allison was relieved. She wanted so badly to believe him, but there were some questions he would have to answer. She didn't say anything.

"Allie? Allie?" Darrin repeated her name. "Allison, I love you. Please don't forget that."

Allison was fighting back tears again. "I love you, too." And then she hung up.

50

Skip had been busy; he found two more devices in the house. The first was another "flash drive" in the office by Marcus' computer, just like the one Allison had found at the cottage. The other was an ink pen buried in the kitchen junk drawer. It was also very high quality. He showed them to Allison as he dismantled them.

"They were still operational," he said with enthusiasm. "Someone's been listening. I'm not certain, but I doubt they could hear us on the porch."

Allison looked at him intensely. "Did you check the porch?"

Skip nodded, "It was clean."

"Where are you staying tonight?" Allison asked, hoping he was staying close by.

"I'm at the Marriott downtown. Why?" he asked with the utmost curiosity.

"Since you're staying in town, would you mind taking a ride to the airport with me? I need to see if Darrin's truck is there."

"Could we stop for some food first?" Skip put his hands together as if he was begging.

Allison was relieved she could still laugh despite all the recent revelations. "Of course we can."

After a trip through the Arby's drive thru so Skip could get a sandwich and curly fries, they headed to the airport to check out the long-term parking for Darrin's pickup. As they pulled into the ramp, Skip glanced at Allison.

"You really think it's here?"

Allison shrugged. "I believe it is, don't you?"

"Only if he recently brought it back. Four hours ago, it was next to me on the highway."

They drove back and forth throughout the parking ramp. Suddenly, Skip slowed way down. On the left was a pickup with Indiana plates.

"That's the truck," Skip said solemnly. "He must have driven it back here."

Allison looked over at it. "That's definitely Darrin's truck. Maybe you were mistaken. Maybe it was a different truck?"

Skip shook his head. "I ran the plate; it was this one."

Allison jumped out of the car and walked over to the truck. Skip pulled his car over and got out as well. Allison pulled on the door handle and it was locked. She looked over at Skip and shrugged. "Who wouldn't lock their truck here?"

Skip walked over and looked inside. "Well, let's look at the parking ticket. The ticket from the gate is on the dashboard. I can't read it—can you?"

Allison leaned over and peered through the windshield. "It says Thursday, 8:45 a.m." Allison felt some justification. "See, it must have been a different car."

Skip wasn't convinced. "He could have just paid the maximum and kept his ticket. He simply put the original one back on the dash after he came back in."

Suddenly, Allison froze, turning as white as a sheet. Skip noticed right away.

"What is it? Allison! Talk to me!"

Allison pointed to the floor of truck. On the driver's side, below the seat, Allison could see the handle of a gun, barely hidden. What caught her eye were the silver letters embossed in the wood. DHD, it said. Skip looked down, then back at Allison, then down again. It was a 9mm pistol that had a customized cherry wood handle. That couldn't have been cheap, he thought, but didn't think much more of it. Skip looked back to Allison; she was still pale.

"It's a gun, that's all. It's just a gun," he said.

Allison stared into his eyes. "It's Marcus's gun."

51

Detective Bruce Harper woke up early on Friday morning. He was one of the few people that still liked to hold an actual newspaper while he read it. He walked out to his front lawn and grabbed the paper. He could never figure out why the press boy couldn't make it to his porch.

As he sat in his recliner and caught up on the news, one small headline caught his eye: "Jeremiah Dean and Phillip Warner's Personal Attorney Found Dead in Elevator." He quickly read through the article. The attorney, some guy named Ken Stark, had been on his way to meet with them. Initial cause of death was ruled as a heart attack. Bruce got up and went to his computer. He opened his email and looked again at the email he had received from Allison Deters the night before:

Dear Detective Harper,

My name is Allison Deters. I am the sister of Marcus Deters with whom I know you are very familiar. I'm sending you a letter that he wrote to me about the case we are currently working on. I am doing this because I am worried about his safety. In the letter, you will find evidence that we have discovered regarding his crash in 2013 as well as the murders of this past week. He had expressed the desire for you to have it if case I didn't hear from him. I have decided to forego his wishes and send it to you now in the hopes that it will inspire you to believe in my brother's innocence, motivate you to help bring these people to justice, and, most of all, to save Marcus from any harm. Marcus mentioned to me his confidence in you and your abilities. Please read the letter, and I trust you will do whatever you can to expedite an arrest. Any contact you would like to have with me can be sent back to this email address—it is a secure email that I set up specifically for this purpose. I will contact you immediately if needed. Thank you.

Sincerely,

Allison Deters

Bruce read through the entire email again. After reading the letter, there was no doubt in his mind he wanted to help, but how? Ken Stark was mentioned as a cog in the planning of the crash, and now he too was dead. How could Bruce help with this case that crossed over so many lines, a number of which were well outside his jurisdiction? The scenario Marcus and Allison had uncovered made so much sense, he believed it wholeheartedly. But proving it could be tough, if not impossible. The only way that he could even contact Dean & Warner would be to connect them to the Daniels murder. Trying to connect crimes to someone in the upper echelon of society could be difficult at best.

In the context of the situation, and with the circumstantial evidence Marcus had laid out, it may not be out of the question. Except most of the connections to the case, the people that could actually confirm the allegations, were being eliminated one by one. His main concern and his one responsibility to his community was the Daniels murder. It was his job to investigate all possibilities and leads, to do whatever it took to find the killer and bring him—or them—to justice. But what could he do himself? It wasn't like he could go to Indianapolis and arrest Jeremiah Dean and Phil Warner, especially with no evidence. Suddenly Bruce got a sick feeling in his gut, and then he started to get angry, really angry.

"I need to call Skip," he said aloud.

52

Forensics officers were pouring over Darrin's truck. Skip had called the Grand Rapids Police last night to have it impounded. Now, first thing in the morning, he joined them at the GRPD impound lot to see what they'd found.

The officers had bagged and tagged Marcus's gun and were bringing it to the lab. Skip wanted it crosschecked with the forensics from the Daniels and Parker murders, and he suggested they crosscheck any evidence from the Wainwright homicide to see if they matched. They were also sweeping the vehicle for fingerprints. Skip knew that it would be easy to cross-reference the Warner kid's print with the Army. He was certain they would find those, but what he was most interested in was if they would find anyone else's.

He was tired; he hadn't slept but maybe a couple hours the night before. He had dropped Allison off around 11:30 p.m. and then he had returned to the airport to wait for the GRPD to get there and secure the truck before he left for his hotel.

When he'd taken Allison to her condo, he warned her not to say anything to Darrin about the pickup and, preferably, to stay away from him completely. He could tell she was crushed. Skip felt badly for her—Darrin Warner must be a scumbag to use her like that. He was going to do everything in his power to bring the Warners down.

When he had gotten to his hotel room, he'd taken out his laptop and written a report from the day. Then he'd lain awake thinking about the case and how he was going to be talked about all over the country. Every Bureau office would be discussing it—the arrests of two of the most wealthy and influential people in the country, being pulled off by a single agent. He would be able to name his position.

However great that would be for his career, he figured he also needed to focus on Darrin's apprehension. If he could nail him, too, it would also be huge, and it made sense since that seemed to be where the evidence was leading him first. Even if he couldn't connect the top two, he would still be a big deal at the Bureau to bring in one of the sons—for serial murder, no less.

He thought through the pieces and plans he had so far. If the forensics came back with a match on the gun, which he was confident it would, he would have a murder weapon in his possession. The motive could have been to cover up the previous murders of the Deters family, which was, in turn, carried out to cover their asses on the illegal investment fraud. If he paired the weapon and the motive, his next step would be to find the Warners and arrest them. He was sure he could get a warrant if the gun matched. Then he would assemble a special team, with him taking the helm, to question them. Finally, and most significantly, he would have to place someone in Marietta at the time Marcus's gun was stolen.

Despite so many thoughts roiling through his head and keeping him up most of the night, he woke up early. He wanted to be there when they went through the truck.

When they'd removed the gun last night, they knew right away it was indeed Marcus's. It was registered under Marcus's name and Allison confirmed that Marcus's wife had given it to him as a gift when he became partner. Allison also offered that Marcus owned a number of other guns. He was sort of a collector, and he loved target shooting and hunting. As Skip was pondering the evidence, one of the officers held up a bottle.

"I found this buried in the glove compartment." He handed it to another officer who bagged and tagged it. "It has some type of pills in it, but the bottle isn't labeled."

Skip nodded his head. "Ok, get on that right away; I want the forensics done today! Not in a week!"

One of the officers started to leave with the pills. "Yes, sir, we'll get on it."

While Skip was bossing the police officers around, he got a call from another. He looked at his phone and frowned. "What does he want?" he said out loud and rolled his eyes.

"Skip Lamont," he said as he answered his phone.

"Skip, this is Bruce Harper. Good morning."

"Good morning, Bruce. What can I do for you?"

"Well, for starters, I was hoping you could update me on what's been going on up there, and also I need you to answer a few questions."

Skip was annoyed; he didn't want to take the time to talk to this small-time cop; he was busy and tired. The last thing he wanted was this yahoo worming his way into his case. He had no intentions of sharing the credit for bringing down the Warner kid with anyone else.

"What do you want to know, Bruce?" Skip asked curtly.

Bruce could hear the annoyed tone of his voice and was instantly ticked off, but he chose to ignore it and asked, "Have you contacted Allison Deters yet? And did you find out anything about her? I'm at a point where I really need to know."

Why does he really need to know? Skip thought. It's my investigation.

"Yes, I contacted her yesterday, and I've made some progress. I believe you are right about Marcus. I think he was being set up. Also, I think I know who may have killed both your victim as well as Diane Parker."

Bruce broke in. "What? Who?"

Skip was feeling good about himself now. "I can't say right yet, but you will be the first to know when I can."

He loved putting cops in their place. Bruce remained quiet for a moment. He wasn't going to give Skip the satisfaction of upsetting him.

"Ok, Skip, when you feel you can let me know, I would love to hear more. Can I ask you a question, though?"

"Sure, Bruce, go ahead, but I can't promise I'll be able to answer." Skip needed to remind him who was in charge.

Bruce knew exactly what Skip was doing; Skip was trying to pull rank. One had a federal job with jurisdiction and clearance all over the country, and the other had an office in a city in Georgia, a city that wasn't Atlanta.

It wasn't the first time in his career Bruce had dealt with a bigot either. Bruce didn't know if it was because of his job in a city department or if it was the fact that he was black—he assumed it was a little of both—but he always felt he had to prove himself to these jackasses, and he was getting sick of it. The best thing for Bruce to do now was to play along with Skip and see where everything came out in the end.

"Ok, Skip, I can appreciate that. I won't ask you anything too important. I know it wouldn't be wise to tell me significant facts about the case at this point. I just wondered—did Allison Deters show you a letter from Marcus?"

That caught Skip by surprise. How did Bruce know about the letter? He must have gotten it as well. "Of course, she did," Skip said in a condescending tone. He wanted Bruce to know there was no way that he could know something that Skip didn't. "How do you know about the letter? That's what I would like to know."

Bruce was nonchalant in his reply, "Oh, Allison emailed a copy of it, and she also wrote something to me in her introduction that I found interesting." Sometimes life brought little happy moments, and for Bruce, this proved to be one of them.

"What!" Skip demanded. He was mad. "What did she say? Was it about the case? You really should tell me."

"Well, if I decide that it's pertinent to the case, I may share it with you, but right now I need to consider it a private message intended only for me. Thanks, and good luck on the case."

Bruce hung up without letting Skip reply. He knew he struck a nerve and that gave him a lot of gratification, as unprofessional as that may have been. Bruce was smiling. He did have something he needed to do, though; he needed to email Allison back. Bruce went to his computer and opened the email from Allison. He hit the reply tab and typed:

Dear Allison,

Thank you for trusting me with this information. I knew all along that Marcus was innocent, and I would love to help in any way I can. Please keep me informed on the happenings up there. I know you have met FBI agent Skip Lamont and that he's working the case. If you could let him know that I am going to be coming up there soon, I would appreciate it. If there is any other information you would like to share with me, please do.

Please be careful,
Bruce Harper

"There," Bruce said aloud. "This will tell a story."

Now he just needed to wait for the call from Skip that may or may not come. Bruce had had a bad feeling overtake him when he read the email from Allison earlier. He knew from experience that it was something he wouldn't be able to shake until he heard from Skip.

53

It was a calm morning on the private fifteen-acre lake in the middle of the vacation property owned by Dean & Warner. The property was located just over an hour east of Carmel, Indiana. The lake was one of three spread throughout the eleven-hundred-acre piece of property. Purchased together by Phil and Jeremiah back in the late eighties, it had been a favorite spot for the two future billionaires to go to ever since. It wasn't the best financial decision to buy the land at the time, as the two were only a couple years into their investment firm. They had been seeing steady growth, but a luxury item like the vacation property wasn't something they would have recommended to any of their clients, and it certainly put a strain on their cash position. But it was a beautiful piece of property with magnificent pine and oak trees, a haven for deer and other wildlife, and a sanctuary for the men.

They built a small cabin the following year, a little 900-square-foot building with a wood stove and no running water, and, over the next thirty-some years, the two spent many weeks there together hunting and fishing.

By now, the little cabin was long gone and a 20,000-square-foot compound stood in its place. The full log home had eight bedrooms and seven bathrooms; it also had a grand seating room with a stone fireplace that rose twenty feet to the exposed logs in the ceiling. There were various deer and fish mounted on the walls, and the west exterior wall was mostly glass so they could have a nice view of the closest lake. The home sat on the east side of the lake, providing beautiful views all year long. There was also an 8,000-square-foot barn to house all the toys and equipment needed to accommodate the filthy rich and their families.

All summer and fall, the grounds were teaming with employees. Landscapers and caretakers were planting flowers, cutting lawns, spreading wood chips, planting food plots for the deer and performing other random tasks; there were cooks and wait staff, and there was a cleaning crew that cleaned a different part of the compound every day. The staff didn't arrive until May, and Jeremiah and Phil liked to get up to the lake in the spring before that to just relax and relive the old days when it was just them in a small boat talking about business and catching fish.

Jeremiah was feeling a little strange this morning. Phil had met him at the dock at 7:00 a.m. and they were out in the lake as planned. Phil had brought a couple of coffees in travel mugs for them, and they sipped on them as they fished. Jeremiah had already caught a couple pike and threw them back, but Phil had yet to get a bite. He seemed not to care, which struck Jeremiah as odd; Phil was always extremely competitive about everything, and fishing was no exception.

"Are you alright this morning?" Jeremiah asked with a little concern in his voice.

Phil looked at him somberly. "Yes, I'm ok, just a little tired, I guess."

Jeremiah nodded and began to bring in another fish. After he let it go, Phil smiled at him.

"You always were the better fisherman."

In all his life, Jeremiah had never heard any words that gave him chills like those. He knew Phil better than any other person alive, even his wife, and he knew that Phil never gave out compliments like that, especially not to him.

"Where are your boys?" Jeremiah said nervously. Phil just stared at him.

Jeremiah was starting to get dizzy. He looked down at the coffee mug as it slipped out of his hand and dropped noisily on the boat floor. His eyes were wide with fear. He tried to stand, but he couldn't; he tried to talk, but nothing came out. The last thing he saw before he passed out was his lifelong business partner and best friend looking placidly at him.

Phil stood up quickly and grabbed Jeremiah. He needed to get to him before he fell on the floor; it was going to be hard enough to throw his limp body into the water without having to pick him up and over the side. Phil grabbed him and leaned his body on the rail of the boat. Slowly, he eased Jeremiah over the edge until gravity finally took over and Jeremiah's body splashed into the water. Phil waited as the body slowly sank to the bottom forty feet below.

Phil started the boat and headed to the far side of the lake. Once he got there, he poured the remains of Jeremiah's coffee into the water and ran the boat ashore. He went about a hundred yards into the woods and buried the travel mug. Then he went back to the boat. He drove to the middle of the lake and watched as Blaine approached in the speedboat. Blaine slowed down and waited for his father to climb in. They never said a word as Phil tossed his fishing gear into the speedboat and stepped from one boat to the other. They headed back to the dock, leaving the fishing boat unattended. Phil knew it would take about an hour for the boat to drift to the southeast corner of the lake. He figured he would call the police around noon and let them know what happened. He would tell them Jeremiah had gone fishing this morning by himself, and when Phil and Blaine came up, they saw the boat adrift.

As Blaine tied up the speedboat at the dock, he felt something he'd never felt before—he felt ashamed. Jeremiah had been like an uncle to him. Blaine had either killed or had ordered someone else to kill at least a dozen people, all for the sake of business. Somehow, he could justify them all in his head, but this? Sure, it would speed up Phil's plan to have his sons take over the company, but why? They were going to do that eventually anyways.

Phil could sense what his son was thinking. "He would have talked. Eventually, he would have. Mark my words—this was the only way to guarantee he wouldn't. He was weak. Elizabeth would have confronted him about Simon's death eventually, and we couldn't risk that."

Blaine nodded at his father and realized again that he was terrified of him. Jeremiah was as much family as he was. Phil grabbed his fishing gear and brought it back to the barn. As he walked up the drive to the log home, he couldn't shake the feeling he was being watched. He stopped and looked around; when he didn't see anything, he kept walking. Still, he felt uneasy and that someone was there.

He stopped and looked around once again just before entering the main house. Nothing. He warily watched as a vehicle came up the drive. Phil recognized the car immediately and called out to Blaine.

"It's Manuel. Darrin must be here."

The car was one of Phil's. Manuel was Phil's driver when he was in town. The Cadillac pulled up to the house, and Manuel got out and opened the door for Darrin. Darrin got out and breathed it in; he loved it here. It had been way too long since he had been to the property, ten years or so he thought, since before he'd joined the Army. He walked up onto the front deck and watched as his father rushed to greet him. Phil gave Darrin a big bear hug.

"Came out to show us how to fish, did you?" Phil said with gusto as he waved goodbye to Manuel.

Blaine, who had been watching, felt a little disgusted. His father had just killed his longtime friend and business partner, and, just minutes later, he was acting like a kid at Christmas. Darrin looked over at Blaine and saw his demeanor.

"Hi, Blaine. Is everything cool?" Blaine forced a smile and nodded at Darrin, all the while receiving a strong glare from their father.

"Everything is great. Glad you made it."

Darrin looked around. "Where's Jeremiah? I saw his Lincoln out front."

Blaine looked around and was about to say something but Phil stopped him. "We just got here a few minutes ago. He may be in his suite or maybe the barn. We were about to get him to go fishing. Why don't you go to his suite and see if you can find him?"

Darrin nodded and entered the house. He walked through the great room toward the hall to the suites. He was looking forward to seeing Jeremiah; he had always referred to him as Uncle Jeremiah growing up and enjoyed being around him, much more so than his own father. He'd found it odd that his cousin Elizabeth, Jeremiah's own daughter, seemed not to like her father at all.

Phil wanted Darrin to be the next Jeremiah. He had always said that Darrin would someday be the face of the company. He had been so upset when Darrin joined the military. Darrin hated the lifestyle his father lived and wanted no part of it; joining the military was his respite from the cutthroat business world. Now it seemed there was no turning back; he was destined to work at the company and carry on his family's legacy.

Darrin reached the end of the hall and Jeremiah's suite. The door was open.

"Uncle Jeremiah?" Darrin called.

No answer. Darrin walked in and saw it undisturbed. He exited the room and rejoined his father and brother.

"He's not there."

Phil looked at Darrin and shrugged. "He's probably at the barn; we can go down and check. Are you ready to catch some fish?"

"Sure, but at some point, I need to talk to you."

Darrin looked at him in a way that let Phil know he was serious.

"Ok, we can talk on the boat, but times-a-wasting. Let's go. We'll meet up with Jeremiah at the barn."

Blaine was in awe at his father's calmness as he spoke, talking about Jeremiah, who he had just murdered, as if he was just next door. Phil and Blaine both knew they wouldn't be fishing today, and it disgusted Blaine how his father protected Darrin, "the future face of the company," as he always said.

Blaine was always the one to do the dirty work, and there was no shortage of it. The amount of different crimes he had committed for the good of the company was staggering, but up to this point had all been without consequence. Now, since Simon had gone off and gotten drunk before the crash, everything was going to shit. The lawyer was causing chaos, and now both Ken Stark and Jeremiah were also dead.

Blaine knew why they were here today. Besides getting rid of what his father had called an "unknown risk factor," they were going to discuss how to get rid of the lawyer.

But first, they had to deal with Darrin. They had not expected him to be here today, and they were fortunate he hadn't shown up an hour earlier. Blaine knew that someday, after Phil was gone, he would deal with Darrin in his own way. For now, he had to deal with him on his father's terms. He followed Darrin and Phil down to the barn and waited for the show to begin.

It was Darrin who first mentioned the boat missing from the dock. Blaine watched with disgust (or admiration, he wasn't sure) as Phil discovered the boat adrift near the southeast shore. Darrin ran ahead of the other two and waded out and grabbed the boat, which by now was only twenty feet from shore.

"His fishing gear is in here!" Darrin yelled back to shore.

54

Allison was spending Saturday morning in her office. She was reflecting on all she had been through in the last week. It had been chaotic, to say the least. Marcus had gone missing and she went up to his cottage to find him. Of course, he wasn't there; he had been in Georgia visiting Simon Daniels and the crash site. While he was there someone had followed him, stolen his gun, and killed Simon, and right now that someone looked like it was Darrin—at least, that's what the FBI agent was sure of. Except for the fact they found Marcus's gun in Darrin's truck, the idea that Darrin was the one behind Simon's murder, let alone Diane Parker's and John Wainwright's, struck Allison as ridiculous.

She thought back to the day Diane was killed and the night John Wainwright was killed. At those times, she had no idea where Darrin was, but the night Simon was killed, Darrin was with her. That was the night they spent together at his cottage, and he was there all night with her, wasn't he? Allison thought back. They had spent a great day in Ludington together and then came back to his cottage. (The cottage that his company owned but that he had said he was renting.) The thought interrupted Allison's train of thought and brought a hot flush to her face.

"Ok, Darrin, if you're not guilty, why the lies?" she said aloud.

He'd never told her that he was a real-life "Jason Bourne," and he had also neglected to mention who his father was. She focused again on that night. They had gotten back, drank some wine, talked for a while, and then they both fell asleep on the couch. She remembered that distinctly. Allison figured they were sleeping by ten and were there all night; she remembered sleeping so soundly.

"Ok, Allison," she was talking to herself again. "Let's say he did do it—how could he have pulled it off? Could he have gotten there and back without you knowing?"

Although she didn't believe it to be true, or to be honest, she didn't want it to be true, she would have to determine if Darrin could have done it himself. In order for Darrin to have killed Simon, he would have had to have left the cottage at 10:00 p.m. and been back there and on the couch with her by 7:00 a.m. at the latest, all without her waking up and seeing him gone. That gave him nine hours. The closest airport was in Muskegon, a good half hour away. If he had a private plane there waiting for him, he could possibly have been in Marietta at 12:30 or 1:00 a.m. Then, he would have had to find Marcus's car, steal his gun, go to Simon's apartment, kill him, and return to the airport by 3:00 a.m. to get back to Pentwater by 7:00. Allison shrugged; it seemed possible but not probable.

Allison looked up the number for the Muskegon airport and called it. A recorded message came on. She chose the option "Muskegon Airport Charter Service" and waited for someone to answer.

After a couple rings, a bubbly female voice came on. "Charter Service! Thank you for calling. How can I help you?"

Allison tried to match the girl's enthusiasm. "Good morning! My name is Allison Deters. I'm an attorney with Davis, Hayes, and Deters, and I am working on a case that may require your help. Would you have access to some information about your outgoing flights?"

The girl on the other end responded quickly. "Does this have anything to do with a flight on the night of April 2nd?"

Allison was surprised. "Yes, it does, how did you know that?"

"Well," the girl started off, full of energy. She was one of the fastest talkers Allison had ever heard. "A detective from Georgia already called about the same night, and I can tell you what I told him. There was a flight that left just before 11:00 p.m. and landed in Hartsfield Airport outside of Marietta at 12:18 a.m. It left Hartsfield Airport at 3:14 a.m. and arrived back here at 4:37 a.m. The flight was booked by an anonymous male and was paid for with cash upon his arrival. The reason I know he paid cash was that the detective asked for credit card information. I couldn't have given him that, you know, but I looked to see if there was one used. A lot of times our charter clients are anonymous. We afford our guests that option; it's a valuable asset to many of them. We have a lot of rich and famous clients, you know. A lot of famous people fly here and limo to Grand Rapids. We have a limo service as well! Did you know that?"

The girl was rambling on at a mile a minute, and Allison hadn't heard anything past 4:37 a.m.

"Ok, thank you." She cut the girl off and hung up the phone.

It would be an understatement to say she was crushed. Allison felt devastated, violated, and humiliated, but most of all, she was furious. Furious at herself, furious that she wasn't the person she thought she was. Was she really another female victim blinded by the looks and charm of a man? She abhorred that thought. She was smarter than that, and she knew it. Her anger grew, but the source of her rage wasn't the fact that she was taken in by Darrin but that however hard she tried, she couldn't stop feeling that Darrin couldn't be involved. After all, she still loved him.

Allison was thinking hard. "Wait a minute," she said to no one. She closed her eyes and concentrated. The detective in Marietta—what was his name? Harper, that's what it was. He was the one Marcus trusted. Somehow, he had known to check this airport as well. If he had, wouldn't he have found out who the pilot was and questioned him? Of course he would have. What did he find out? Allison wanted to know.

Her mind suddenly shifted to Marcus. Where could he be and what was he doing?

55

Skip Lamont was reading the forensics reports that had been sent over to him via email. The gun was Marcus's, that they had known, but they also confirmed it was the gun that had killed Simon Daniels, Diane Parker, and John Wainwright. The markings on the bullets were all identical, and they matched the bullets fired by the forensics team in the lab. Skip was impressed at how fast he had gotten the information on the bullets and the pills that were found in the glove compartment as well.

Those were a prescription drug called Lunesta, a very strong sedative that helps users fall and stay asleep. The pills were a surprise for Skip; he was thinking they were some type of poison or recreational drug, but sleeping pills? He was a little disappointed. They were a strong prescription pill but not that hard to get; doctors were happy to prescribe it for claims of mild insomnia. Did Darrin have a hard time sleeping? Skip couldn't blame him after killing three people; maybe his conscience was getting to him, he thought.

As Skip was going over the reports, he received a call from his home office. It was his boss, Senior Agent Andrews. Skip cleared his throat.

"Agent Lamont," Skip answered in his most professional tone.

"Hey, Skip. How's everything going up north?" He asked but didn't wait for an answer. "Haven't received a report from you yet. Wondering what you're up to."

Skip had anticipated this; he was supposed to send daily written reports to the home office for his superiors to go over, but he hadn't yet done so.

"I know, sir, and I am sorry, but I haven't had time yet. This case has me all over the place up here. I will get you a report by the end of the day."

That he'd been very busy was accurate, but the real truth was Skip didn't want to risk someone else at the Bureau trying to weasel in on his case when they heard the details.

"Don't sweat it, Skip. I'm not in the office anyway. It's Saturday." He said with a laugh. "I don't work weekends if I don't have to."

Skip knew this to be true but had completely forgotten that it was indeed Saturday.

"Besides," the agent continued, "Detective Gaines has been keeping me informed a little bit." Skip was unaware that his boss had been in contact with Joanne.

"Yes, sir," Skip replied.

Agent Andrews continued, "I just wanted to give you a call; I heard some news that may be of interest to your case. It's pretty big, and I don't think it will be long before it's all over the internet, so I wanted to give you a heads up."

"Yes, sir, what is it?" Skip sat up with anxious curiosity.

"Well, I know you're working the Parker and Daniels murders, and I was just informed that the Daniels kid's ex father-in-law, Jeremiah Dean, is missing and presumed drowned at his hunting retreat in Indiana."

Skip didn't know how to respond. He simply asked, "Really?"

"Yep, the local police were called in by his business partner, and they're going to search the lake for the body. The info came across our news wire maybe an hour ago. I'm not sure if it will affect your case at all, but I thought it was worthwhile to let you know."

"Yes, sir. Thank you for telling me, sir. I'm not sure either if that will affect my case, but I appreciate the information, that's for sure."

"Ok then, you keep up the good work and don't forget to send a report. I want one entered into the database by Monday morning."

"Of course, sir," Skip replied and heard the phone go quiet.

Skip was a little rattled but not deterred. This doesn't change anything, Skip thought. I'll go ahead with the arrest of Darrin Warner for the murder of Simon Daniels. After that, I'll try and piece together the other two murders. As for the lawyer's family—their crash being deemed murder would probably be impossible to prove, but what does that matter? I can get Darrin with what I have right now.

With any luck, Skip could march Darrin into custody before he had to submit his report. He didn't want any other agents climbing onto his ride to the top. First things first, he had to find Darrin, and the best way he could think to do that was to call Allison.

Allison was on her way home. She had had enough. She was tired, frustrated, and confused. She thought she was in love. She finally met someone that seemed to be the perfect fit, someone she could enjoy being with all the time. She had never had a man in her life that she didn't want to get away from at least once in a while, but she could see herself being with Darrin continuously—that is, if he wasn't a murderer.

Murderer. Could Darrin possibly be a murderer? Could he really be an evil person that killed the three people that could have shed light on the cause of Marcus's crash? Could he have done that just for money, aka reason number 4?

No way, not Darrin, she assured herself. But all the evidence seemed to point to him. He did have a long military background, one that demanded he be ruthless. Had he brought that ruthlessness back home with him? Could Allison have been so entirely suckered in by his handsome face and attentiveness? Absolutely not, Allison thought as she shook her head in frustration. She refused to believe it. She didn't care anymore about being weak or being just another one of those girls; she loved Darrin, and he didn't kill anyone. She knew that in her heart. She just had to figure out who did.

Agent Lamont called, making her anxious right away. She picked it up. "Hello?"

"Are you at home?" Skip asked.

Allison could hear excitement in his voice.

"No, I'm on my way, though. Why?"

"Do you know where Darrin is?" Skip asked impatiently.

Allison was flushed. She didn't want to tell him, but she knew the law, and if he was innocent, she would prove it. Not telling Skip would only make things harder for her.

"Darrin is at home in Indiana. He said something about going to meet his family at the cabin. Why?"

Skip didn't answer; he just hung up. Allison threw her phone down on the passenger's seat.

56

"Damn it! He's going to arrest him!"

Allison's mind was racing. She needed to track down the pilot of the charter and show him a picture of Darrin right away. That would prove Darrin wasn't the one. She quickly changed lanes and instead of getting off the highway, she continued toward the Muskegon Airport. She had a forty-minute drive ahead of her.

Her phone rang again, this time from an unrecognized number. She thought about ignoring it but instead picked it up.

"Hello?" she said and waited for a response.

"Hello, is this Allison Deters?" It was a man's voice on the other end, a voice Allison didn't recognize.

"Yes, this is. Can I help you?" Allison asked, a little more rudely than she should have.

"I'm sorry to bother you Mrs. Deters. This is Joey Bishop from Spywares, you asked me to call you if I found out who bought those listening devices like the one you had."

Allison was ashamed with her previous tone of voice. "Oh, yes, Joey!" she said with much more warmth. "Were you able to find something out?"

Joey started to talk to her as if they were best friends. "Well, I asked the owner to look up if we had sold any, and she actually remembered selling a few of them to someone. Like I told you before, you have to order those, so I guess that's why she remembered. Anyway, she looked up the order and showed it to me. There was a customer that bought four of the ADX devices—two of the fake pens and two of the fake flash drives."

"You know what was really weird though?" He didn't wait for Allison to respond. "He didn't order the matching listening devices along with them, so they were basically useless. You have to have the listening devices to hear what's being picked up by the microphones. After she showed me who had bought them, I really thought I should tell you right away, but she said that if news got out that we were giving away that information, our customers would go to someone else for their gear. You know, that would be bad for business."

"Oh, I can totally understand that Joey." Allison said, playing along with him.

"Yep, but I don't care. I want to tell you." Joey waited for Allison to respond.

"That's great, Joey. I really appreciate you sticking your neck out for me." Allison was half amused by the tone of Joey's voice but still terribly curious about what he was going to say.

"Yep, I really wanted you to know." Again, he waited for Allison to respond.

Allison was starting to lose her patience and fought to keep her voice calm. "Who bought them, Joey?"

Joey paused, seemingly for effect. "They were ordered and paid for by a Marcus Deters."

Allison almost dropped her phone.

"I wondered if that was someone related to you."

Allison heard Joey's voice over the phone which was barely still in her hand. She held it up and said, "Thank you, Joey," and hung up.

57

Phil Warner and his sons were at the cabin watching the police boat in the middle of the lake. Phil had told them a spot that they liked to fish. Of course, it was about eight hundred yards away from the actual spot that he had dumped Jeremiah's body. There were four police officers on the boat; two of them were divers that were suited up in their gear and ready to go. Phil had pointed them in the wrong direction as he was hoping to delay the recovery as long as possible. He doubted there would be an autopsy, but who knew? The longer the body was in the water, the harder it would be to find anything.

For a man that had just committed murder, he was very calm. No one would expect foul play; no one would suspect anything but a drowning. Jeremiah had simply slipped and fell out of the boat. The lake in the spring was still very cold and his layers of clothes would get very heavy when soaked with water. Everyone would see it as just an unfortunate accident.

Darrin was leaning against one of the porch columns while he watched the police boat on the lake; he was visibly shaken by the day's developments. Jeremiah was dead; he knew that, even without the body being found. He had talked with the police when they arrived, and they seemed unaffected by the situation. To them, it was just a typical drowning that just happened to involve one of the richest men in the country. Even a man that has anything money can buy can fall off a boat.

It had been four or five hours since Darrin had arrived, and the time had flown by. Since they'd discovered the abandoned boat and called the police, everything had been a blur. They'd notified their families about what was happening. Darrin's mother had listened silently and then had started to cry. Shaken by her sobs, Darrin assured her he would let her know the minute they knew something for sure. Both his father and Blaine had been calling business associates and family members between interviews with the police.

It was a chaotic scene, and Darrin couldn't wait for it to be over. He had spent maybe five minutes talking to the police when they arrived, detailing the finding of the boat and where exactly it was, but that was it. They had spent much more time talking to his father and Blaine.

Darrin didn't know what was being said, and he really didn't care; he just wanted to get out of there. He wanted to see Allison. Allison! He thought. He never talked to Dad about Allison. He needed to talk to him; he had to make sure that she was safe. With all the crap that was going on, he could only imagine what his family's limits were, and he needed to make sure that they left her alone. The way things looked, he wasn't going to have that conversation anytime soon.

Suddenly, there was a buzz from the driveway gate. The buzzer rang in three different places in the cabin and as well as in the barn. Darrin went to the panel inside the front door. He opened it and looked at the camera image from the gate; there was a man in a sedan sitting at the gate looking directly into the camera. Darrin asked if he could help him. The man held something up to the camera and Darrin read it. It was an FBI badge with the name *Nicholas Lamont* on it. Darrin pushed the button to let him in.

"There's a federal agent here," he called out to Blaine.

Blaine looked over at his father in the yard, still talking with a police officer; they were just bullshitting, not really talking about the drowning. Blaine looked up the drive and saw the car approaching. He walked over to his Dad and calmly announced, "There is a federal agent here. He must want to talk about Jeremiah."

Phil nodded and looked inquisitively at the officer he had been talking to.

The officer shrugged. "We didn't call the feds."

Phil left the officer and walked up toward the cabin with Blaine. Skip Lamont was pulling up. He was amazed at the size and beauty of the log home. He instantly felt more disdain for these people. "A cabin in the woods," he muttered to himself. He had made the four-hour drive from Grand Rapids in just over three, driving eighty-five miles per hour the whole way.

Adrenaline was coursing through him. He'd be making an arrest today, a big arrest, an arrest that would get the whole Bureau talking. Skip parked his car next to one of the police cruisers and got out. It was a busy scene; there were two police cruisers and one SUV that had a small boat trailer attached to it. All the vehicles had "Indiana State Police" marked on them. All eyes were on him now as he walked toward the group of men by the cabin. He nodded at the officer that was looking at him from down by the lake.

There were three men on the large porch waiting for him to approach. Skip knew which one was Darrin as he had seen pictures of him already. He figured the older man must be Philip Warner, but he had no idea who the third man was. There was something about the third man—he looked mean, real mean. Skip thought about his gun that was under his coat in an over shoulder holster. He was hoping desperately he wouldn't have to use it; in fact, if there hadn't been cops there already he would have waited and called for backup. As he looked at the three men, it suddenly didn't seem quite as important to arrest Darrin on his own.

"Hello, gentlemen. Having a tough day, I see."

The stocky, mean-looking one spoke up right away. "No shit, what was your first clue?"

Skip was sorry he had started the conversation that way. He raised his hands up as if to apologize and continued. "My name is Skip Lamont. I'm a federal agent, and I'm here to take Darrin in for questioning about the murder of Simon Daniels."

"Like hell you are!" Phil shouted so loudly the officers by the lake looked over at them.

Skip held his ground. "Relax; don't do anything you'll regret. Darrin needs to come with me."

Phil was stuck. There was no way he wanted to let Darrin go with the fed, but he had other issues to deal with now.

"Don't say anything, Darrin; we'll get K--our lawyer to you right away." Phil had started to say Ken Stark but caught himself.

"It's ok; we know I didn't do anything." Darrin spoke with confidence, but he was nervous.

Skip handed them his card and told them if they had questions they could call the office number.

"Fuck you," was all Phil said, in typical Phil Warner fashion.

Skip opened the rear passenger door and waited for Darrin to get in.

Darrin looked at him calmly. "I'll go with you, but I need to make a call first."

Skip shook his head. "I don't think that's a good idea."

"No call, and I won't go without my attorney." Darrin glared straight into Skip's eyes.

Skip turned away and looked around; everyone was watching them.

"Ok, but make it quick," Skip relented.

Skip watched intensely as Darrin walked away and made a call. He couldn't help but wonder who he was talking to. Darrin's call only lasted a few minutes, and he came back to the car and got in without saying a word. Skip waved to everyone who was still watching him and got into the car himself. He headed down the drive and out of the complex.

As they waited for the gate to open, Darrin noticed the news vans parked outside the grounds. There were four of them, all waiting to get a glimpse at what was going on inside the billionaires' compound.

"Shit," Phil said to Blaine as the car containing his son disappeared. "What now, Blaine? What's our plan now?"

Blaine just shrugged, "I think we need to deal with this first, don't you?"

Phil reluctantly nodded in agreement. Blaine was amused at the sight of his blood-and-guts father, the man that was seemingly bothered by nothing, being visibly shaken by the fact Darrin was being questioned. Blaine knew Darrin was going to get arrested though. That fed wouldn't have taken him away if he was just being questioned; he'd just wanted to avoid a scene.

"Let's concentrate at the task at hand, and then we'll go get Darrin. He's a big boy. He'll be fine."

Blaine spoke with confidence but he wasn't so sure. They must have something good on him for that fed to come here and cart him off. The guy had been cocky. He was trying to make a name for himself at Darrin's expense—that much was clear. Blaine hadn't had to eliminate a cop before, but there was always a first time for everything.

It was starting to get dark now; the Indiana sun was just visible over the western tree line, and soon it would set. The officers were starting to pack up. The divers had returned to their rescue boat and were busy bringing in their gear. Phil and Blaine didn't see the stranger advancing

189

toward them until he was only fifty feet away.

Phil looked at him and yelled, "Hey! What are you doing here?"

The man kept coming toward them and put a finger to his lips, asking them to be quiet. He was upon them now, and he looked over at the officers.

"Trust me; you don't want them coming over here," he said with a coolness that made Phil and Blaine instantly believe him.

"What do you want?" Blaine asked the new arrival.

The man never looked them directly in the eyes. He was wearing a camouflage jacket and cap and had a scruffy beard; he looked like a typical Indiana hunter.

"What are you doing on our property?" Blaine was getting impatient but spoke quietly, cautious of attracting the officers' attention.

"I want your cell number." The man was looking directly at Blaine now, and he had the feeling he had met this person before.

"Why?" Blaine was looking at Phil now.

Phil stepped into the conversation. "I don't know who you think you are, but we don't give out our numbers to just anyone."

"Well, I suggest you change your policy right now." The camo-dressed intruder had a tone to his voice that Blaine couldn't ignore.

The officers were starting up the lawn to the cabin now, and the intruder nodded toward them.

"You might want to hurry."

"Ok, it's 317-732-7664," Blaine blurted out quickly.

The intruder turned away and started down the drive. "I'll be in touch," he said as he walked off.

"Who was that?" one of the officers asked Phil as he joined them.

Phil answered quickly, "Just a local hunter wanting permission to hunt small game on our property. Happens all the time. Obviously, the gates mean nothing to them. I told him no, like always."

The officer nodded his acceptance of that explanation. "I'm sorry, but it's getting dark. We're heading out now. The dive team will be back in the morning. Will you be around?"

Phil nodded, "Of course, Officer, whatever we can do."

As the officers left, Phil and Blaine went into the cabin; once the door was shut, Phil lost it. He started ranting about the boldness of that stranger, how he was going to kill the S.O.B. if he ever heard from him again.

Blaine just stared at him. Who was this man? he thought. He had never seen his father act like this before. He was usually in control, but for some reason this incident caused him to panic and completely lose his cool.

Blaine's phone dinged to indicate he'd received a message from an unknown number.

"Well, that didn't take long," Blaine said with trepidation.

He opened the video he'd just received, pushed the play arrow, and held it out so his father could watch it with him. As soon as it began, Phil's heart stopped. He knew he was screwed.

It was taken that morning. The video showed Phil lifting Jeremiah over the side of the boat and throwing him into the water.

Then the footage skipped and started again with Blaine picking up his father in the speed boat and bringing him back to the dock. The video jumped for a second time before cutting to an image of Jeremiah's travel mug, the one that had contained the drugged coffee. It was sitting next to the shallow hole Phil had buried it in.

Blaine watched as Phil went to the table and sat down. He looked beaten. It was a look Blaine had never seen before on his father's face, and a look he hoped to never see again.

"I'll take care of it," Blaine said to his father with such blatant ferocity that Phil instantly relaxed. "This guy obviously wants something; we'll just see what it is and deal with him then. We just need to calm down and wait for him to call. We'll let him think he can call the shots, but he's a dead man, I promise you that."

In that moment, despite the stress and turmoil of the day, Phil knew that his business and his legacy were in good hands with Blaine. His boy was just like him, and he was incredibly proud. "Thank you, Blaine," he said, rising and placing a hand on his shoulder.

58

Skip had taken Darrin to the field office in Indianapolis where they were now sitting in an interrogation room. It had taken close to an hour to get there and neither person had spoken a word. Darrin was taking his father's advice, refusing to answer any questions without an attorney present. This fed seemed intent on nailing him, so he wasn't going to give him any ammunition by saying something he may regret. As Skip's gaze bore through him, Darrin wondered what he was thinking. He felt like Matt Damon in Good Will Hunting during his stare down with Robin Williams. Unlike Mr. Damon, however, Darrin wasn't going to be the one to break the silence.

Skip waited a few more minutes before he finally spoke. "Aren't you curious why you're here?"

Darrin shrugged.

Skip was a little put off by the rich kid's attitude, but he'd be lying if he said he wasn't expecting it. "I want to ask you some questions about the Simon Daniels murder."

Darrin gave Skip a blank stare and simply said, "Lawyer."

Skip was a little irritated, "Do you think you need one?"

"Don't you?" Darrin fired back, "You don't have a clue who killed Simon, and you're hoping it was me so you can make a name for yourself. I definitely want an attorney."

"I'm sure your lawyer will be here soon," Skip snapped back at him. "I bet Daddy has someone on the way even as we speak."

Darrin sneered across the table at Skip. He was right; Darrin's father most assuredly had one of his best attorneys already en route. Darrin was sure he'd be out of there within an hour, but he wanted to find out what Skip knew, so he decided to ask a few questions of his own.

"Ok," Darrin began, "I give. Why am I here? Why would you think

I know anything? Simon was married to Elizabeth Dean who was like a cousin to me. That's all I know."

Skip didn't say anything. He just looked at Darrin and then started to smile. "You didn't like him much, did you?"

Darrin was getting angry. The fed was trying to rattle him, and if not for Darrin's military training, it may have worked. He'd been effectively trained to keep calm in trying circumstances.

"Didn't know him. I was in the military the whole time they were together. I didn't even go to their wedding because I was overseas. Why on earth would you be asking me these questions? Please tell me you have something to justify bringing me here—at least then I can try to help you."

Skip eyed Darrin carefully. He didn't want to give him too much information, and yet, he sensed he was ready to talk and didn't want to lose his opportunity to hear what he had to say.

Just as Skip was deciding how to best proceed, a tall, slender gentleman in an expensive looking suit knocked and entered, leather briefcase in hand. He had jet black hair and tan skin; he looked as if he had just gotten back from a tropical vacation. Skip stood up and the man walked right past him without even a glance in his direction. He held out his hand to Darrin, and Darrin shook it.

"Hi, Darrin. My name is Victor Martin. I'll be representing you today. Have you said anything to this gentleman?"

Darrin shook his head. "Not really."

The man looked at Skip and asked, "Has this been recorded?"

Skip pointed at the two-way mirror on the wall and nodded. "Everything gets recorded; you should know that."

Victor chose to ignore the last comment and turned back to Darrin. "If the questioning continues, only answer when I say it's ok, capeesh?"

Darrin nodded and they both looked expectantly at Skip. Skip looked directly at the attorney, and with an intense glare said, "We have enough to arrest him right now. I just want to give him a chance to explain himself first. Maybe he could tell me where he was last Saturday night and early Sunday morning."

Skip knew what Darrin was going to say before he answered. Allison had told him they were together that night.

"I was in Pentwater, Michigan that night, as well as the whole week before and almost the whole week after."

Skip had his next question ready. "Do you have proof you were there Saturday evening?"

Darrin looked at the attorney who nodded his head. "Allison Deters was with me the whole night. She can verify it."

Skip wrote something down and then he looked up at Darrin with a raised eyebrow. "Are you sure about that?"

"Of course I'm sure. We were together all night." Darrin's voice elevated a little, and Victor quickly touched his arm to remind him to calm down.

"We were together all night," Darrin repeated, this time quieter.

"You didn't board a private plane in Muskegon at 10:58 p.m. and fly to Marietta?"

Darrin looked at Victor and said, "Are you going to do something?"

Victor just waved him off and pointed at Skip. "It's ok to answer the question."

Darrin turned away from Victor and looked right into Skip's eyes. For the first time, Skip saw anger in Darrin's eyes, real anger, and all he could think about was Darrin's background. He knew instantly, despite all his own FBI training, he was no match for Darrin Warner.

"Why am I here? Ask Allison—I was with her all night!" Darrin was leaning way forward in his chair. Victor grabbed Darrin's arm and lightly pulled him back.

"Call her right now! This is ridiculous!"

Skip motioned at the mirror on the wall, and instantly another agent came in and sat down beside him. Skip raised his hand and lowered it slowly.

"Settle down, Mr. Warner. We're not through."

Victor spoke up. "Actually, if you're not going to arrest him, I think we're done here. My client has been cooperative."

Skip looked at Victor. "We have the murder weapon with Darrin's prints on it, which was discovered in Darrin's vehicle. We have a motive, we have a window of opportunity for Darrin to have gotten to Marietta, and we have evidence pointing to that he was. We have a bottle containing a sleep agent found in Darrin's truck. As we speak, Allison Deters is being tested for any traces of it in her system, and I strongly feel the results will come back positive. So, yes, Mr. Martin, I think we will be arresting him today."

The other agent stood up and read Darrin his rights while Skip and Darrin just stared each other down.

Victor told Darrin, "I'll get you out of here, don't say another word."

Skip looked over at the slick attorney. "You won't find him here. He's taking a trip to Marietta. A transfer van is already waiting to take him. He will arrive there within 4 hours or so and will be staying at the local facilities for a while if you want to try and arrange bail."

59

Allison was frustrated. She had been to the forensics lab for a toxicology test for the FBI. They wouldn't tell her what they were testing for or why, but her best guess was they thought Darrin drugged her and then flew to Marietta that night.

Allison had told Skip about her conversation with the girl at the Muskegon airport, but he seemed to blow it off. Either he changed his mind or he didn't want Allison to help in his investigation. Maybe he was embarrassed he hadn't thought to look at the flights? Whatever it was, she didn't care; she was confident the report would come back negative. Darrin would never drug her. She tried to think back to that night, and she didn't remember much past 9:30 or so. She did sleep soundly that night, but that must have been from the eventful day.

She had tried to call Darrin three times in the last hour and he hadn't answered. Her thoughts kept going back to him. What did she really know about him? Really, really know? Besides the fact that he was very handsome and swept her off her feet like a silly school girl, she knew very little about him. If, in fact, she had been drugged, what she knew about Darrin would become unimportant, and the future that she thought was laid out for her would drastically change yet again.

The man at the lab had said that Skip would have the results within an hour and would contact her soon after. It was going to be hard for her to concentrate on anything else until then. It had been just over a week since she had driven up to the cottage searching for Marcus. Quite an eventful week, she thought. Meeting Darrin, going to Atlanta with Marcus, talking to both Elizabeth and Diane. Suddenly her heart skipped at the thought of Diane. She realized she couldn't account for Darrin when Diane was killed. He didn't pick her up that night from the airport, his excuse being he had to take care of "family problems".

Allison felt a little sick. "It can't be," she said aloud. "It can't be true."

But her conviction was beginning to crumble. She needed to hear from Skip; she needed to hear there were no traces of drugs in her body.

She was going home to her condo and she would spend the remainder of this Saturday night all alone. She'd spent many weekends alone and it had never bothered her before. She could always find something to do if she wanted to. Tonight was different; she was feeling lonely, terribly lonely, and very, very sad. She wanted to call Marcus but knew that was impossible. He had said he would contact her and she knew he meant it. He had his reasons, and would contact her when he needed to, but that didn't help her now. As she pulled into her parking spot in the parking garage at her condo, she received a text message. It was from Skip.

"Traces of the drug Lunesta were found in your system. It's a strong prescription sleep agent that knocks you out and keeps you sleeping for hours. It was the same drug found in Darrin's truck."

Allison was crushed—she was such a fool! She was preoccupied when she left her car and headed toward the elevator. Suddenly, she thought she heard footsteps behind her. She hadn't heard a car come in after she'd arrived. She froze for a moment, straining to listen. Footsteps. Silence. Footsteps. Then the only sound she heard was of her own pounding heartbeat as she started to run.

60

She wanted to turn around but instinctively knew she couldn't, and as she reached the elevator, she prayed it would open right away. She pressed the button, and again the footsteps stopped.

After what felt like an eternity, the doors opened. Allison jumped in quickly, her mind racing as she thought of Diane Parker and John Wainwright. Was it her turn? She whipped around expecting to see someone almost on top of her, someone with a gun or possibly a knife. No one was there.

She pushed the button for her floor. Just as it started to close, a man jumped in. Allison screamed in terror. Refusing to go out this way, trapped in an elevator and afraid, she continued to scream and started swinging her fists at the intruder. The man reached out and grabbed her arms.

"Allie! Calm down! It's me, Marcus. Calm down!"

Marcus let go of her arms and allowed her to try to calm down. She stared at him hard; it was Marcus, but it didn't look much like him anymore.

"Marcus?" she asked cautiously.

"Yes, Allie, it's me. I'm sorry I scared you; I just didn't want anyone to see me. Are you ok?"

Allison was crying now. "No, I'm not ok! You scared me half to death!"

Allison looked at Marcus through tear-filled eyes, and with trembling lips, asked, "Why do you look like that?"

Marcus grabbed her and pulled her close, and then he gave her a tight hug, a hug that said I'm sorry, I love you, and I'm here now, all at the same time. Allison was sobbing now. With her face buried in her brother's chest, all the emotions from the past week, coupled with the scare she'd just experienced, were too much. The elevator dinged, and they entered the condo together. Marcus gently pushed her away from his body so he could look her in the eyes.

"I won't let anybody hurt you, but we need to get out of here. Can you pack a bag quickly?"

Allison stopped crying, and she looked at Marcus. "Mom and Dad?"

Marcus shook his head. "They're fine. I put them up at the Amway Hotel, and you know how they love it there. They'll be safe."

Allison was focused now. "Where will we go?"

Marcus didn't answer; he just motioned for her to get moving. It only took Allison a few minutes to get her things together. She threw a bunch of clothes in a bag, grabbed her bathroom case, and threw on a jacket. Marcus waved her on as if to say, "Let's go," and he headed toward the door. Allison quickly followed and went to the elevator. Marcus pressed the button and when the door didn't open immediately, Marcus motioned to Allison.

"Let's take the stairs," he said quietly.

They swiftly walked down to the end of the hall and entered the stairwell. They descended the seven floors of steps quickly and exited into the parking garage. Marcus grabbed Allison's hand and led her around to the back row where he had a jeep waiting. They got in and Marcus told her to get down. Allison obediently crouched down in the passenger seat out of sight; she looked over at Marcus and was terrified to see that he was holding a gun. Marcus saw the look in her eyes and put his finger to his lips, mouthing the word "quiet." His head was just above the dashboard and he was looking out toward the elevators they'd just by-passed; he saw the light go on and the door slide open. He fidgeted and gripped the gun a little tighter as he watched a man exit.

The man was well built, maybe thirty or so, and he had the inescapable look of being ex-military, what with the perfect posture and quick stride. The man was looking back and forth as he walked. He was looking for something, or someone.

Marcus had to assume he was looking for Allison. In fact, it was probably a safe bet that Allison's door had been busted open and her condo quickly searched since they'd left it just minutes ago. The man was at Allison's car now; there was a sign on the wall in front of her car that read *Reserved Condo 703*. He looked inside of her car, pulled on the handles of the locked doors, and then looked around. Only one row away from them, Marcus watched as the man made a call on his cell phone, still not budging from her reserved spot. Marcus ducked down as the man turned toward his jeep. Allison's eyes were fixated on him as she pressed her body against the bottom of the dash. Marcus slowly picked his head up to see where the man had gone. He heard a car door slam shut and then its engine start. A Nissan Altima pulled out and started slowly down the drive in the section they were parked in. Marcus lowered his head again and waited for the car to pass by. When it was past, he raised his head quickly enough to read the license plate; it was an Indiana plate with the number 644LP. He said it three times to secure it in his memory and watched, relieved, as the car left the garage.

Marcus sat up in the driver's seat and nodded to Allison; she sat up as well, all the time looking at Marcus with confusion.

"What's happening, Marcus?" She felt sick to her stomach and knew she didn't want the answer. Marcus started the jeep, and they drove out of the garage.

"Turn your phone off," Marcus ordered. Allison took her phone out of her purse and shut it down.

"What's going on, Marcus? You said I wouldn't hear from you until Wednesday unless I was in danger. So, I assume I'm in danger?"

Marcus kept his eyes focused on the road; he was looking for the Altima.

"Nothing's going to happen to you. I promise. My plans have had to change, and yes, you may have been in danger, but I have you now. We just need to stay smart and everything will work out fine."

"What's with the disguise?" she asked almost with a laugh. It was the first time she had ever seen her brother in a beard, let alone such an ugly, scruffy one. She did find it remarkable how real a fake one could look.

"Well, I said I didn't think *you* would be in danger, but I'm pretty sure *I* was. What do you think?" Marcus asked, referring to the facial hair.

"It's horrible," she laughed, "and terrifying when you sneak up on your baby sister."

Marcus's smile faded and he looked at her with pain in his eyes. "I know, Allie. I'm sorry for that. I'm sorry for everything."

Allison took a moment to gather her thoughts. Marcus put his blinker on and they turned onto US 131 North. A few minutes later, they were taking the connection to Highway 96 toward Muskegon, and Allison figured they were going to Pentwater.

"Where are we going?" Allison asked anyway.

Marcus glanced over at her and smiled. "Don't worry. We're not going to the cottage. I'm smarter than that. But we are going to Pentwater; I think a little home field advantage will be good. We're going to stay at Stan's place."

Stan was an acquaintance of Marcus's. He owned a restaurant downtown, and as a regular, Marcus knew him well. Stan's restaurant didn't open until May, so he spent his winters down south. He had always said that if Marcus needed more room for family or friends, they could stay at his cottage. Marcus knew where the key was and he knew they could stay there safely.

"For how long, Marcus?" Allison was scared again. She still couldn't believe everything that was happening, especially that the man she'd fallen in love with had drugged her, she was now forced to leave her home, she had no phone for communication, and her parents had been hustled into a hotel, totally in the dark as to why.

"Hopefully not long. It all depends on how the next couple of days go, but I promise that you'll be safe."

Marcus then asked her a favor. "Can you have that federal agent trace a license plate number for me? You can use this phone." Marcus handed her a track phone. "It's untraceable."

Allison took the phone and nodded, thankful that she'd called him often enough in the last couple of days to remember his number. After she hung up with Skip, she told Marcus, "I don't know how much of that you heard, but I'm going to call him back in ten minutes. He should have the information for us by then." Then she fell quiet.

"What else is it, Allie?" Marcus could tell something was wrong.

"They arrested Darrin," she said softly.

Marcus looked at her. "I'm sorry, Allie, but that's a good thing."

Allie nodded but couldn't hide her pain. She stared at the window as they drove, wishing she could leave her heart behind them.

They were almost to the Pentwater exit now, and Allie still hadn't called Skip. It had been twenty minutes since they had spoken, Marcus reminded her. She reluctantly picked up the phone: she didn't want to hear

Skip's voice. It just made her sad. Typing his number in slowly, she called, and he answered right away.

"Allison, where are you? Are you safe?"

"Yes, we're safe," she replied.

"Who's we?" Skip asked urgently.

"Marcus and I. I'm with Marcus."

"Allison," Skip continued, "you need to be careful. The license number belongs to a Tyler Duggan. I did a search and, get this; he was in Darrin's unit in the Army. They served together for four years on the Special Forces Team. I imagine he could be very dangerous. Is he following you?"

"He was at my condo looking for me but we lost him—at least, I think we lost him." Allison looked in the side mirror; there were no headlights as far as she could see.

"Where are you?" Skip asked again.

"We're somewhere safe. That's all I can say right now. Thank you, Skip." Allison hung up before he could say anything more. Then she relayed to Marcus what he had said.

61

Detective Bruce Harper was on his way to the Marietta Police Station. He had gotten a call from Linda Conner, the nighttime clerk, informing him they had a suspect arrested for the murder of Simon Daniels, and he was arriving soon to be detained. The alleged killer was Darrin Warner. Bruce knew Skip had arrested him and was having him brought down within the hour. Bruce knew he needed to be there when they processed Darrin, even though it was almost midnight. He wanted to ask him some questions of his own. He knew it was Skip's collar, and that was fine. He had pegged Skip from the get-go; he was an egotistical bigot that had only one thing on his mind. He was so concerned with getting ahead that he didn't care that he had arrested the wrong guy.

Bruce believed that he knew who killed Simon Daniels, and it wasn't Darrin Warner. But since it was Skip's investigation, Skip had made it clear that he didn't want any help, especially from not a black, small-timer like him. Bruce could've just washed his hands of it all, except he couldn't let an innocent man suffer for the benefit of one overly ambitious federal agent.

Bruce pulled into the station and sat in his car to gather his thoughts for a minute. Specifically, he was thinking about Allison and hoping she was ok. Bruce had absolutely believed Marcus's story about the crash. What people would do for money had always astounded him, so it wasn't a stretch to believe that the owners of a highly successful company like Dean & Warner would take out a family in order to save their wealth and stay out of prison. What he didn't believe was that Darrin Warner had anything to do with it or, for that matter, with the recent murders of Simon Daniels and Diane Parker. Hopefully in an hour or so, he would find out he was right.

62

Phil Warner couldn't sleep. He was lying in his bed and his mind raced relentlessly. How was he going to get out of this mess? One of his sons had been arrested for murder, he himself had been caught on video throwing an unconscious Jeremiah into the lake, and that lawyer from Michigan was still investigating the crash from three years ago.

For the first time, he was regretting the death of Ken Stark; Victor was a good attorney, of course, but Ken had been the best. Darrin could use him right now, and so could he and Blaine, to be honest. Blaine had his two best people on the lawyer, and hopefully they would take care of that complication, but what about the video? Why was that guy out there this morning? What did he want now? If it was money, they could pay it, no problem. But then would he go away? In today's technological climate, just one click of a button and that video would be worldwide.

He needed Blaine to find that guy, kill him, and destroy all his possessions. Whatever the cost, it had to be done. Phil took solace in knowledge that Blaine could take care of it, and there was no one he'd rather have on the job. Five minutes later, Phil was sound asleep.

63

The transport van pulled into the Marietta Police station at exactly 12:35 a.m. and Bruce was waiting. He watched as the two guards brought out Darrin Warner, his hands cuffed together in front of him, which, Bruce thought, was very good. If the guards had considered him a threat, they would have cuffed his hands behind him, and that would have made for a brutal five-hour drive. In any case, Darrin must have been cooperative.

Bruce had read the file on Darrin Warner, and from what he was permitted to see, this kid was a well-trained soldier. Bruce walked out to greet Darrin and held the door open for the three men. Bruce knew the procedure; the guards must stay with him until after the check-in which included fingerprints, pictures, and the labeling of his possessions. They took Darrin's cell phone and wallet from one of the transport guards and put them in holding. After all the protocol was done, Darrin was put into a cell, the place he would call home for the next couple of days, or until his lawyer could get bail arranged.

Bruce walked the two guards back to their van and thanked them for all they'd done. After they left, he went back inside to talk to Darrin; he was hoping he would still be awake and willing to talk, especially since there would be no lawyer present. When Bruce returned to Darrin's cell, he found him sitting on the bed with his face buried in his hands. Bruce instantly felt sorry for him, and that said a lot; Bruce had always been a good judge of character, (except once) and Darrin seemed like a genuinely good guy.

The cell had no bars. Rather, it was a room with a steel door with an unbreakable plastic window in it. The room contained a small bed, toilet, sink, and a chair. Bruce rapped on the door of the cell and yelled through.

"May I come in?" He really didn't have to ask, but knew it wouldn't do any good if he just barged in.

Darrin looked up at the window and nodded. Bruce yelled to the guard that he was going in and to unlock the door and to relock it behind him. The door buzzed. Entering, Bruce grabbed the chair and sat down across from him.

"Look, Darrin—do you mind if I call you Darrin?"

Darrin nodded his approval.

"Darrin, I know you don't have an attorney present, and I'm sure you were told not to talk to anyone," Bruce paused and waited for confirmation on this, though none was given. "Anyway, let me assure you that nothing you say here will be repeated or can be used against you. I just want to hear your side. I know it's late and you're probably tired, but I believe you to be innocent and I really need a couple of answers."

Darrin perked up a bit when he heard the detective's words. "Ok, I'll try to help you; I need to get out of here."

Darrin sounded desperate to Bruce, which struck him as a bit curious. He didn't seem like the desperate type. Bruce started by asking Darrin about his involvement with Dean & Warner. Darrin confirmed what Bruce had already known—that he had been in the military for the last ten years and hadn't even started working for the company yet, although he was planning to because his father was counting on him.

Bruce nodded as he listened to Darrin's answers and then asked him, "What do you know about the crash in Atlanta three years ago?"

Darrin shrugged, "I know Simon was drunk and he clipped a vehicle and the vehicle spun and hit the wall at seventy miles per hour, killing three people and seriously injuring a fourth, who survived. Simon was convicted and served three years, I think. He was married to a close family friend. I think her of as my cousin."

"She was Jeremiah Dean's daughter, who is your father's business partner, correct?" Bruce asked, already knowing the answer. Darrin nodded. Bruce felt he could go for broke.

"Do you think Simon acted alone?" Darrin was quiet, and Bruce followed up. "I mean, do you think there was any reason he would have done that on purpose?"

Darrin, who again had his face in his hands, looked up at Bruce. He shook his head.

"I think there was more to it than an accident."

Darrin was sick of the lies his family would tell, he was sick of the deception, he was sick of the greed and the downright evil that he knew his father and brother were capable of, all in the pursuit of more money.

"From what I know, and that's not a great deal—they try to keep me in the dark when it comes to the business—I think they made Simon do it, somehow. I don't know how, but they had him convinced he had to, and now he's dead. I do know this for sure: Blaine can be very convincing."

Bruce pushed on, "So do you think it was Blaine who killed Simon?"

"Oh, I doubt he did it himself, but he might have had someone else do it." Darrin answered.

Bruce paused for a second before he continued.

"Well, I read the report and the evidence is pretty strong against you. Can you tell me how you had the murder weapon in your truck?" Darrin shook his head no.

"Can you tell me why you had prescription sleeping pills in an unmarked bottle in your glove compartment, and why the same sleeping pills were detected in Allison Deters bloodstream?"

Darrin again shook his head more vehemently this time.

"What is it, Darrin?"

He looked at Bruce with tear-filled eyes and insisted, "I wouldn't drug Allison. I wouldn't do anything to harm her. I love her."

Bruce knew he was telling the truth. In fact, he was almost one hundred percent sure that if Darrin was tested, he would come back positive for the drug as well, something Bruce intended on having done in the morning. He didn't care if it was Sunday; the lab would have to have someone get it done right away. That is, if Darrin and his lawyer would allow it.

Bruce then asked a question he dreaded the answer to. "Do you think Allison's in danger?"

Darrin nodded and looked straight at Bruce and, with determination, he said, "I can help her. You need to let me out of here."

Bruce shook his head. "You know I can't do that, but maybe I can help her. Tell me, what else do you know?"

"I don't know anything! You need to help Allison. If Blaine is after her, he'll kill her!"

Bruce was taken aback by the sudden urgency in Darrin's demeanor but adapted quickly. "Ok, calm down, Darrin. I'll do what I can.

I have a couple more questions for you. Did you know that the surveillance camera at the Muskegon airport caught video of your truck pulling into the parking lot on Saturday night and then showed footage of a man walking out of the parking lot afterwards? The image of the man wasn't clear enough to identify, but they got a good picture of your license plate. Can you explain that?"

Darrin shook his head again. "I have no idea." Darrin was visibly shaken, and Bruce felt sorry for him. The evidence seemed undeniable and he would surely get convicted if something else didn't turn up. Bruce had other information that he didn't share with Darrin quite yet, but he knew he would soon. It was what made him so sure that Darrin Warner was innocent.

Bruce stood up and said, "I'm sorry, Darrin. I will do everything I can for you. I know you're innocent, and I'm going to try my best to prove it. Get some sleep. We can go over it more tomorrow."

64

The stars were out in force in Pentwater, the lack of city lights making the stars come to life in the clear night sky. Stan's cottage was south of town. It sat on the south side of Pentwater Lake and had been owned by Stan's family for fifty-some years.

Allison was out on the deck looking at the beauty God had put in the sky for her to enjoy, and she couldn't help but wonder why, with all the beauty God can provide and all the power that God could yield, why did life have to be so crappy at times? Why did Marcus lose his family? Why was there pain and suffering? Why are there four reasons for murder? Why was it, when she finally met the person that she felt may be The One, he turned out to be, of all things, a murderer?

Allison could barely think that thought—it just seemed ridiculous to think that Darrin could have done anything like that, but the fact of the matter was that the truth often hurt.

If Darrin did it, he used Allison as an alibi. How ironic that she would be made into an alibi for the murder of the person that killed her brother's family.

So again, why would her God, the God she and Marcus had spent so many Sundays in church learning about, let them down so badly? She knew she wasn't perfect, far from it. She sinned daily, just like everyone else, she supposed, but for some reason God had chosen her family to suffer so deeply.

For the most part, Allison had become lax in her faith—although she had prayed like crazy for Marcus after the crash. But tonight, standing on the deck of Stan's cottage, looking over the calm water of Pentwater Lake and gazing up at the millions of stars, she felt the need to pray. It had probably been two years since she'd last prayed, but tonight the words just flowed.

She prayed for wisdom and for strength, she prayed for her family and her friends, and she asked for safety for all of them. She prayed for Darrin to have peace and comfort wherever he was, and she asked for forgiveness for all her wrong doings. Lastly, she prayed for Marcus. She asked God to give him peace in his life, to reduce his pain and settle his heart, and to provide him with some unseen and unimaginable happiness.

Allison felt better when she finished. She turned to go in, but then she saw him standing there. With tears flowing down into that ugly beard, Marcus had heard Allison's prayer. He moved closer and, without saying a word, hugged her. Marcus squeezed her tight, willing his eyes to dry. As he pulled away, he reached out and grabbed her hands. His face turned solemn.

"I will always love you." He said forcefully. "No matter what happens, I will always love you."

65

Phil Warner woke up early. It was Sunday, and he knew the dive team would be coming back, and today, they would find the body. In fact, Phil had decided to tell them another fishing spot to try: this time, the right spot. He needed them to find the body and get out of there so he could move on to the pressing issues at hand. He was going to have his hands full for a while with the visitation and funeral, not to mention the press crap. But that stuff seemed like small potatoes compared to the footage their local videographer had captured, the trespasser who thought he'd get rich off him.

Phil walked into the great room of the cabin and saw Blaine on the phone. He had an aggravated look on his face, a look that Phil had seen many times before. It was a look that typically preceded someone dying.

He walked over to hear Blaine ask, "When?"

Blaine listened for a moment longer and then hung up. Phil looked at Blaine; he had turned a little bit white, so Phil knew who it was on the other end of the conversation.

"What did he say?"

"Fifty million." Blaine waited for the swearing, but it didn't come.

Phil simply said, "How do we get it to him and how do we know it's over if we do?"

"He wants it transferred to an account overseas and then he'll delete all the videos."

"How do we know he will do that?" Phil wasn't buying it.

"He has agreed to meet. I told him that we need to meet in person so we know who he is. Otherwise, no money. We can't have someone running around with that kind of information after we pay him off if we don't have some sort of recourse if he goes back on his word."

Phil nodded "Smart, and he agreed, huh?"

Blaine nodded, "I told him that was his only option. We will pay him a one-time fee of fifty million, and get to know who he is, or no deal, period. I also told him we could transfer money today but will not release it until we meet. His only stipulation was that you and I both go."

Phil frowned at that. "Why both of us?"

Blaine shook his head. "I don't know, but we should make it happen and put this behind us. He's just some dumb hick; we can pay him and never hear from him again. If he doesn't stay away, he and his family will lose their lives, I guarantee it."

Phil nodded his agreement. "Can you get the money today?"

Blaine shrugged, "I have the account number and I can get it transferred. It may be a little harder on a Sunday, but we can get it initiated at least. He told me to meet him in Michigan at 7:30 tonight; he'll call with an address later. He just told me northwest Michigan for now. We'll need to leave by 3:00 to give us plenty of time, and we'll need to rent a car anonymously. No private jets today."

"Ok," Phil said, "just bring a gun."

Blaine gave him the 'do you think I'm an idiot?' look. The same look every son gives his father at one time or another.

"I'm going to go and take care of the money; you still need to deal with the police here. I'll be in touch." Blaine waited for a response but all Phil did was wave him off.

Blaine left the log cabin and got in his car. He had made it sound so easy to his father, but he knew better. He knew they weren't dealing with a dumb hick. He had recognized the man at the cabin. Not at first, but it came to him later. The "dumb hick" was that lawyer from Michigan, the one that almost single-handedly ruined their empire three years ago. Blaine planned on transferring the money to the account, but the lawyer would never be able to spend any of it. He would make sure of that.

He started to smirk as he thought of his father, the man who never seemed satisfied with anything Blaine did, the man that wanted Darrin to take over the helm of the family business. Darrin—the guy who didn't care at all about the company. Blaine would show his father tonight that he was the better choice because he was so much more like him.

The lawyer's death was long overdue. He had escaped it once

before, and Blaine had always known they should have finished the job in the hospital, but his father had said no. His father thought it would bring more unwanted attention either to the case the lawyer had been working on or to the crash itself. It was critical the crash be considered an accident. He said to let him live out his life in misery; he was no longer a threat.

"How about now, Dad? What do you think now?" Blaine said aloud to no one in particular. He was getting angry thinking about it. He should have killed the lawyer a long time ago. He wouldn't make the same mistake again.

And speaking of mistakes, Simon should not have been the one to carry out the plan; they should have had some of Blaine's muscle take care of it, but, again, dad had other ideas.

Simon wanted into the family's good graces and into the business. He had wanted so badly to earn favor with Jeremiah, he was willing to do anything. So, it was simple to get him to cause a wreck. Blaine actually thought he seemed eager to do it, but he was apparently mistaken as the dumb shit went drinking beforehand. Blaine assumed now it was because he was weak and needed some liquid courage. It was terrible judgment on his father's part, to let Simon take part in the side of the family business that should have been left to Blaine and his guys, and it was biting them in the ass now.

Blaine was looking forward to tonight. Blaine had his two best guys on Marcus and although they'd recently lost his trail, they were still in Michigan and may prove to come in handy.

66

"Get down!" Darrin shouted, trying to be heard over the sounds of machine gunfire.

Darrin's squad of Army Rangers was pinned down.

"How many are there, Tyler?" Darrin called out on his radio.

"There are between twenty and thirty, sir." Tyler's voice could be heard clearly in squad leader Darrin Warner's headset. "I figure there are eight or ten in each building!"

Darrin's squad had been "sweeping" the air bombed street, looking for any al-Qaeda still wanting to stay in the fight. It had gone smoothly until now. Intelligence had labeled the area as non-threatening. This group of enemy soldiers had been waiting, undetected, in three separate block buildings that were not much more than rubble now. The shots rang out from the structures as Darrin's Ranger team prepared to enter two other buildings across the road. They had scattered into the doorways when Darrin shouted his command to get down.

"Is Mason still with you, Tyler?" Darrin asked

"Yes, sir!" Tyler yelled into his headset. "Vinny and Jay are in here, too."

"Roger that. I have no visual. Can you still see them?" Darrin asked.

"They're staying close to the structure. I can't see them all, but quite a few are in the street next to the rubble—maybe twelve. There are more inside." Tyler peeked out the doorway as bullets ripped into the stone only feet away from him.

"You guys, hold them off! Sam's calling for support. We need to hold them off for fifteen minutes until we can get a Black Hawk in here."

Darrin was lying flat on his back behind a two-foot-tall pile of cinder blocks. One of his men, Sam Kingman, was lying next to him talking on the radio in an attempt to get support. And lying next to him was Sam's partner, Carter Flynn.

Machine gun bullets were flying everywhere. Darrin needed to do something.

"Sam," Darrin said, "you stay down and keep trying for air support. Carter, you watch Sam's back. I'm going to try and get us out of here."

"Tyler, can you see us?" Darrin asked his close friend over the radio.

"Yeah, I can see you, sir. You guys need to stay down. Mason is moving into position to the east, and we're going to start throwing lead everywhere."

"Ok, Tyler, when you start shooting, I'm going to head to the next building west and we can all have a part," Darrin said.

"Darrin, you have to stay down! You'll get killed!" Tyler yelled into his headset.

"I'm all set. Are you ready, Tyler?" Mason asked over the radio.

"Darrin, are you going to stay put?" Tyler yelled.

"Not a chance. I'm getting in the fight. Carter and Sam will stay here for a bit. You four give them hell on three, two, one!"

The four Rangers all fired at once. Tyler, Vinny, and Jay fired straight into the buildings across the street while Mason fired from his position that was higher and to the east. When Darrin heard the Rangers' machine guns, he jumped up and headed to the doorway immediately to the west. It was about thirty feet away.

The al-Qaeda soldiers fired frantically at the soldier that ran out in the open, but no bullet found its mark. Darrin made it to the doorway and dove inside. He crawled past the window and then headed to the back of the building. He found a side door and ran behind the next building and then around it to the front corner. From there he had a good view of the firefight. The al-Qaeda were scurrying around inside the buildings and firing constantly. He could see some of them lying in the street either injured or dead. The four members of Darrin's team that had been shooting were now firing only sporadically, saving ammunition.

Darrin clutched his machine gun. He also had four grenades, and he knew what he needed to do. He looked over at Sam and Carter who were still pinned down. Darrin couldn't wait for the Black Hawk; his men were running low on ammunition, and who knew when support would arrive?

Darrin aimed at the closest building occupied by the enemy and started to run across the street toward it. He needed to get close enough and to the side of it so he could reach them with a grenade. With any luck, they'd be distracted away from him by their ensuing gunfight.

Darrin could hear the al-Qaeda soldiers yelling, and then he saw one turn his weapon toward him. With a quick burst of his gun, Darrin ended the man's life. He was now beside the building; the open windows and doorway were only fifteen feet away. He pulled a grenade from his vest and threw it into the building. Dust and rubble fell as the grenade violently exploded, killing everyone in the small shelter.

Darrin ran to what was left of the blown out building, smoke still trickling into the afternoon sky. He fired some shots before he ducked through the doorway. He fired a few more shots to ensure there were no survivors inside. He was huddled next to the middle building now, and shots were still being fired back and forth across the street.

Darrin looked to where Carter and Sam were lying. He couldn't see them but he knew they still had to be there. The enemy knew it as well, and some of them were firing continuously at the cement stones that were shielding the two men from death. The small wall was slowly giving way. Darrin pulled another grenade.

"Sam and Carter, you need to get out of there! I have you covered! On one!" Darrin threw the grenade. "Three, two, one!"

The grenade blew up in front of the middle building, temporarily shielding Sam and Carter as they got up and ran toward the same doorway Darrin had found safety in just moments before. Although Carter made it to the doorway, Darrin was horrified to see Sam struck by a bullet and fall to the ground. He was struggling to make it to the doorway. Carter ran back to help his fallen friend and was immediately cut down by enemy fire.

67

Darrin opened his eyes. He had been sleeping so soundly, it took him a moment to figure out where he was. The reality hit him like a ton of bricks. He thought immediately of Allison. He hoped desperately that she was ok. Even though he was never told the specifics of what his brother did, he thought he knew him well enough to know what he was capable of.

He knew, too, that he himself hadn't killed Simon; he was with Allison that entire night. That was their first day together, and he hoped to remember it forever. But the fact remained that Simon was dead, and here he was, arrested for murdering him.

He surmised his brother must know more about the murder. So why would he allow Darrin to be framed for it? Did Blaine want him to go to prison for the murder so he could run the company by himself? Darrin wouldn't put that past him. Darrin was positive that Blaine had been responsible for the deaths of Allison's family and was covering his tracks by wiping out everyone associated with it. Darrin knew how vicious Blaine was, and had always been.

Darrin recalled the phone conversation he'd had with Blaine a week ago. Blaine had been worried about Darrin's relationship with Allison, thinking it was a threat to the family. Darrin said he was going to continue seeing Allison and come back when he wanted to, and there was nothing Blaine could do about it. After all Blaine should have known there was a chance he would meet Allison at the rental, it was Blaine that told him about it in the first place when Darrin had said that he wanted to get away.

But what was it Blaine had said? "There's always a way?" So, could this be Blaine's way? Framing him for murder? Darrin didn't want to believe his own brother would do something like that, but he knew that the truth was that Blaine could do it without losing a second of sleep over it.

As Darrin was pondering his situation, there was a knock on the door. The buzzer went off, and with a click, the cell door opened. Detective Harper motioned for Darrin to follow him and said, "Come on, let's get some breakfast. I want to talk to you again." Darrin stood up and went to the door. He held out his wrist for the cuffs but Bruce shook his head.

"No handcuffs," he said, "coffee and breakfast. I just want to talk."

Darrin followed Bruce into the police lounge where there was a covered plate sitting on the table. Bruce pulled out a chair for Darrin. Darrin cautiously looked at the detective and wondered what his angle was? Why was he allowed to eat in here eating instead of in his cell like the other inmates?

Bruce seemed to read his mind. "I thought we would come in here to talk. We don't generally have many inmates come here, maybe a drunk here or there every so often, so we don't even have a cafeteria. I brought you this from the diner down the block—the food's great, but it's even better when you can't see the inside of the restaurant while you're eating it," he said with a big grin.

Getting right to business, he continued, "You're a special case, a federal case. You probably won't be transferred until tomorrow since the judge isn't around on Sunday. I'm sure your lawyer will be here soon, so we need to talk now. But go ahead and eat first. It's a pork omelet with cheese and a side of grits—I hope you like grits."

Darrin started in greedily on his omelet. Bruce was right; the food was great. Darrin ate every bite, including the grits, and Bruce just sat back and sipped his own coffee.

When Darrin finished, Bruce smiled. "Pretty good, right?"

Darrin nodded. "Very good, thank you."

Darrin gave Bruce a puzzled look.

"I know," Bruce said, "you're wondering why you should talk to me now, especially without your lawyer. Am I right?"

Darrin nodded.

Bruce's smile faded and his face became stone cold. "Because I'm the only one that knows you're innocent, and I want to help you and get the real killer at the same time."

"How do you know I'm innocent?"

Bruce answered him with conviction in his voice, "Because I know who the real killer is. I know it and believe it so strongly, I'm willing to risk my career on it, but I need your help."

Darrin studied Bruce's face. He was serious, as serious as any man he had ever met, but did he know the killer? And if so, why would he need his help?

Darrin admitted the obvious. "From where I sit, I feel I have no choice. I need someone to prove my innocence. But how can I help you?"

Bruce leaned in close to Darrin. "You can get me close to the killer." Bruce paused for emphasis. "And you can help me protect Allison."

Darrin's eyes opened wide and he quickly shot back, "What do you need? I'll do anything to protect Allison."

Bruce could tell he had hit a hot button for Darrin; he was in love with her.

"Well, I'm going to need you to take me somewhere. I'm going to get you out of here, and we're going to take a drive north. I think Allison's in trouble, and we need to get to her before it's too late."

68

As she looked out the large window on the north side of the cottage, Allison took a drink of her morning coffee and smiled. She couldn't believe it was ten already; she had slept so soundly. The sun was shining on the water of Pentwater Lake, and there was a stiff breeze tossing small waves against the shore, unlike the eerily calm water from last night.

Marcus wasn't around; the jeep was gone, so he may have gone for groceries or something. If that was the case, he probably would have gone up to Ludington, so he could be gone for a while yet.

Allison decided to go for a walk. Just south of the lake cottage, there were some woods with trails that she had hiked before with Marcus and the boys, another lifetime ago. She was going to take advantage of this time alone and enjoy the crisp fresh air of a beautiful northern Michigan spring day. With no internet or cable T.V., it'd be a perfect morning to walk, and then curl up with a good book.

Allison got dressed and ready to go. She'd grabbed some tennis shoes from the condo that would have to do as her hiking boots were still at home. She jotted down a quick note for Marcus, *On a walk, be back soon,* and headed out. As she walked up the road toward the woods, her mind began to wander.

She started to think about Sheila and the boys, and as the tears once again welled up in her eyes, she started to run. She had to sort some things out, and the running would help. Her mind was pouring over the facts as her feet alternately hit the path.

There were a couple things that were bothering her. First off, and most important, was that she still believed Darrin was innocent. Although the evidence didn't support it and Skip was positive of Darrin's guilt, she just didn't buy it. Maybe it was because she still loved him, but she didn't think that was all of it. Things just didn't add up.

Take the gun, for one. Why would Darrin leave the gun in his truck at the airport? He was smarter than that, and with everything riding on its discovery, you would think he would've gotten rid of it.

Then there were the drugs. Again, if he had drugged her, he would've tossed what was left, not kept them in the same place as the gun. Additionally, when would he have drugged her? She was with him that entire day, she had poured the wine, and if he had put it into the open bottle, they both would have had it. Everything lined up so perfectly for Skip to arrest Darrin, it just didn't feel right.

A final item that troubled her was why *Marcus* had bought the listening devices. What purpose did they serve? What made sense to her was that he planted them for her to find, but why would he do that? With all the excitement at the condo last night, she'd forgotten to ask him about it. She would do that tonight. She remembered she still needed to talk to the pilot of the private jet from that Saturday night, wishing she had done it before. He should be able to recognize who was on the flight. But, again, Skip must have done that already prior to arresting Darrin, right?

Allison looped around and headed back to the cottage. Maybe Marcus was back and they could talk. As she neared the cottage, she could see that the jeep was still gone. "Weird," she said aloud as she walked up to the door. Allison decided she would just take a shower and curl up on the couch with a book. She had noticed a bunch on a shelf under the coffee table; hopefully she could find something good. She found it strange that she felt so calm at a time when her whole world seemed to be falling apart around her.

69

"What do you mean he's gone? Where the hell is he?"

Skip was furious. He was on the phone with Selma from the Marietta Police Department, and she had just told him that Darrin Warner, his meal ticket, the arrest that was going to put his face on every news channel, was no longer there.

"I'll give you five seconds to tell me where he is, or I'm going to have your job!"

Selma was at a loss. "I'm sorry, sir, I don't know where he is. I just know he's not here."

"Well, are there transfer papers?" Skip asked impatiently.

Selma, who was more than competent in her job and had endured the wrath of many angry callers, was stammering a bit. "I have arrival documents from last night along with pictures and prints, but his belongings aren't here nor were they checked out. Can I have Detective Harper call you?"

Selma was anxious to end this call as soon as possible.

"I'll call him right now!"

Skip hung up and was seething. What was going on? This was his big break, and he had already told the guys at his office in Atlanta, including his boss. He'd called them special just to rub it in. He'd never live it down if he lost this arrest.

Skip was still in Indianapolis. He had gotten a hotel room after the transport left to take Darrin to Marietta; he'd been too tired to make the drive last night. Now he wished he had. How do those stupid bumpkins lose a prisoner like that?

He ran through the possibilities. Had his boss asked to have Darrin transferred? That didn't make sense. The primary evidence was for the murder in Marietta. Detective Gaines wouldn't have had him moved to

Atlanta, would she? The murder weapon was the same for the Parker murder, but she didn't have the authority.

He called Bruce to chew his ass out and get to the bottom of this.

Bruce looked at the name on his phone. "Well, here we go," he said to Darrin.

Darrin was driving Bruce's car. He'd asked if he could, and Bruce was more than happy to stretch out in the passenger seat for the long haul. Bruce was reluctant to answer the call; he was anticipating a very heated conversation. He didn't care that Skip was probably angry, he didn't like Skip anyway, but he didn't want that poor excuse for a detective interfering with him today.

Bruce answered his phone. "Detective Harper."

"Where's my suspect?" Skip's voice was clearly audible to Darrin in the driver's seat. He couldn't help but laugh and Bruce quickly shushed him with his hand.

"How the hell did you lose my suspect?" Skip was yelling, obviously irate.

"What do you mean?" Bruce asked.

"Don't give me that. I know you know where he is. Are you trying to get the credit for the arrest? Don't try, because you can't—it's already on record with the FBI, and if I find out you have something to do with him missing, you can believe me, you will be in the unemployment line so fast!"

Bruce looked over at Darrin and smiled. "Calm down, Skip. I don't know what you're talking about; he was at the station last night. I know because I talked to him. Maybe his lawyer got him out; you know how rich people are. Did you call Selma?"

"You know darn well that I did! How else would I know he wasn't there?" Skip was practically screaming as his blood pressure rose.

"Ok, Skip, let me check on it and get back to you."

"You better!" Skip yelled and hung up.

"Well, that was fun," Bruce said jokingly. "I'm glad that's over. I hope my career isn't as well."

Darrin glanced over at Bruce as the car headed north on I-65.

"So why are you doing this? Why are you risking your career? And what do you think I can do to help?"

Bruce remained silent for a moment as he decided how to explain. Finally, Bruce said, "I'm taking a big leap of faith in you. I believe that despite who your father is, you are a decent, respectable person and are not capable of committing the murders Skip has pegged you for.

One reason is my gut instinct about you; the other more important reason is that the evidence they have, while strong, has flaws if you look closely enough. Those shortcomings don't seem to bother the federal agent. He's only interested in advancing his career, while I'm interested in actually finding Simon Daniels' killer. I believe that you can help me do that."

Darrin liked the detective, he liked him very much. Bruce was a straight shooter. But he was still puzzled. "But how can I help you?" he asked.

"Well, first, you're already helping by driving," Bruce said with a laugh.

Darrin couldn't help but laugh as Bruce's personality came shining through. Bruce was a big guy with an even bigger soul.

"Seriously, though, how am I going to help? I'm not a cop," Darrin asked, his laughter fading quickly.

Bruce was also serious now. "Ok, I'll tell you everything I know."

"I've seen the evidence that Skip has on you, and on the surface, it's tight. The problem with Skip's case is he didn't go deep enough.

First off, for you to have committed the murder, you would have had to have been in Marietta, which you weren't. How do I know that? Simple. While Skip checked the flight schedule to Marietta and found there was a flight that could put you at the scene, he failed to talk to the pilot or check surveillance cameras at the airport, something that astounded me. I was able to view the video of the arrival and departure of the flight in question, and in both cases I knew it wasn't you getting off and on the plane."

Darrin started to speak but Bruce held up his hand.

"I also talked to the pilot, and his description confirmed it wasn't you. It was someone trying to look like you. The pilot told me that the passenger never said a word, and he found that to be a little strange, but not unheard of. The passenger had a hooded sweatshirt and ball cap on and was purposely keeping his face hidden; the pilot said that wasn't altogether uncommon either, as sometimes they fly famous people that want to be discreet. But what caught him by surprise, and what I noticed as well, was the passenger's walk."

"You see, the person that walked on and off the plane that night was a woman. It was a woman trying to look like a man, but the way she walked was a dead giveaway. Even if it had been a man, the body type wasn't the same as yours, thinner than you and not as tall. It didn't take great police work to figure that out. So, the next question was, who was it that got on and off the plane that night? At first I thought it may have been Allison."

Darrin turned toward him quickly, but before he could say a word, Bruce stopped him again.

"At *first,* I thought it was Allison, but that didn't fit either. I had received an email from her and it included a copy of a letter her brother had written to her detailing everything that was going on. Something about the email struck me as strange, so I replied to it and specifically asked her to tell Skip I was coming up to Michigan. Well, there's no way that Skip wouldn't have put a stop to that in an instant. He would've been furious if he thought I was going up there to interfere with his case."

"So, when Skip didn't call me, I knew Allison hadn't been the one to send it to me in the first place. Someone else wanted me to have the information about Jeremiah's connections to all the crimes, and they wanted me to think it came from Allison."

"You think Jeremiah had something to do with it?" Darrin asked, surprised. "I guarantee Jeremiah didn't have any involvement in murder. He wasn't included in that side of the business."

Bruce looked at Darrin and saw that he was serious, serious and unhappy.

"That's my father and brother's area," he continued softly.

Bruce watched Darrin for a moment. He was obviously telling the truth. He was also welling up with tears.

"On that note," Bruce shifted gears, "how well do you really know your brother?"

70

At 12:30 p.m. Phil Warner and his eldest son Blaine got in their rented Cadillac SUV and started on their way up to Michigan. They had rented the car under a false name as they wanted no attention drawn to their whereabouts. The divers were out near the area that Jeremiah had been dumped into the water, and Phil figured it wouldn't be long until they found the body. He had stressed to the officer on sight, "Please call me if you find or hear anything." He had also told the officer that he had pressing business that he must attend to. It was not a lie.

They were on US 31 now nearing Holland, Michigan, about thirty-five minutes or so south of Muskegon, and they still hadn't heard from their stranger. Blaine was driving, and for the first time in his entire life spent working with his father, he felt like he was the one in control.

It was odd to have his father ask him questions without already knowing the answers. Typically, whenever he asked Blaine a question, he just wanted to test Blaine, and more often than not, Blaine felt he'd failed. Phil would quickly let him know if it wasn't the answer he had been looking for. He was always testing him.

But today Blaine was in charge, and they both knew it. As they were passing through Holland, Blaine received notification that there was fifty million dollars ready to be transferred upon Blaine's final authorization.

Blaine set down his phone and, without looking at his father, he said, "Money is set to go. We have it ready to enter his account from ours in the Caymans. The bank will await my confirmation. That's our only leverage, and we can't cave until we get everything we need. It will show up as a 'pending transaction' on his account so he can see that it's there."

Phil looked at Blaine angrily, although he wasn't actually angry with Blaine; on the contrary, he had never been more proud of him. He knew Blaine was finally ready to take over the empire he had built.

No, Phil was angry that this stranger would dare threaten his legacy.

He was angry because the feds had arrested Darrin, a war hero and patriot that was to be the shining star of the company. It was no secret he had hated the idea of Darrin joining the military after college, but now he would use it to his advantage.

He was also angry because this was happening right when his two boys should be making Dean & Warner the biggest company in the world. It wasn't just about money anymore; it was the legacy, the pride, the power, the fame; he wanted it all for his family.

Actually, he thought, it was time for the 'Warner' name to be synonymous with all those things. They could now do that without the 'Dean' name in front of it or Jeremiah's face pictured whenever the company was mentioned. He had used Jeremiah and brought him along for forty years, but now it was his boys' turn to thrive. And this arrogant twosome, the federal agent and the blackmailing drifter, were trying to screw it all up. He wouldn't let it happen.

"You *are* going to kill him?" he said without wavering.

Blaine looked straight ahead at the highway. "Of course I am."

71

Allison had found a book. It was a murder mystery, ironically. She'd always enjoyed reading a good who-done-it-and-why. She was only a hundred pages in and thought she had it solved, but deep down she wanted to be wrong. It was almost always better to be surprised.

There was still no sign of Marcus, and she desperately wanted to call him. She put the book down and went to the room Marcus had slept in to see if his phone was even there or if he had taken it with him. He had made her turn hers off yesterday, but she was considering using it for just one call as she was getting so worried. She opened the bag on the dresser, looking. Just some clothing and a dopp kit, but no phone. She then opened a side compartment and was stunned, suddenly overwhelmed by both fear and confusion.

Allison could feel herself flush. She knew what was happening; she was having a panic attack. She had suffered with anxiety in college but had overcome it with self-determination, a lot of self-awareness, and more willpower than she knew she had. Once diagnosed, she simply refused to let the anxiety take over; the power of the mind is amazing when singularly focused.

Unlike back in college, however, she couldn't stop this one. She reached into the pocket of Marcus's bag and pulled out a key fob. It had a Ford logo on it with an Army strap attached to it. Allison stumbled out of the room and went to get her phone. She found her purse and started frantically digging through it, fumbling as she pulled out her iPhone and turned it on. She was gasping for air as her anxiety reached unchartered heights.

"Hello, Allie," came the voice from behind her.

Allison whirled around to see her brother watching her curiously. He was filthy, covered in dirt from head to toe, dirt that had been muddied with streams of sweat. His fake beard was matted against his cheeks and chin. Marcus was taken aback by what he saw when he looked at Allison's face; she was obviously panicking. Allison had dropped her phone in her surprise but she still held the fob. Marcus spotted it and his curiosity disappeared.

"Are you alright, Allie?" he asked as he took a step toward her.

"Stay away!" Allison stammered, pulling herself together just enough that she could yell at him. She was frozen in place and was struggling to comprehend what was happening.

"Allie, listen to me, please."

Marcus tried to calm his sister as he came closer. Allison raised her hands up as she fell to her knees; she was unable to move away. As he reached for her, she passed out and crumpled to the floor.

72

"Yeah?" Blaine answered the call he had been waiting on.

"Take 31 to the Monroe Road exit toward Pentwater. Go to the state park, and then call this number." The caller abruptly hung up.

"We got our orders."

Blaine looked over at his father, and Phil nodded. They had been informed fifteen minutes earlier that Jeremiah's body had been found. The officer on sight had called Phil personally to offer his condolences. Although Phil already knew, hearing the news from the officer saddened him and, for a moment, he grieved the loss of his friend before reminding himself that business was business.

Blaine made a call and Phil heard him say, "You're still in Grand Rapids? Well, get up to Pentwater, and call me when you do!"

73

Allison awoke and waited while her vision cleared. She looked around to get her bearings, and she didn't see Marcus. She struggled to move but couldn't. She'd been bound to a wooden chair! Her hands and feet were tied to the four legs. Her mind was racing. Where was Marcus? What was he doing? Had he finally snapped? She felt the anxiety returning but refused to be overwhelmed.

"Stay calm," she told herself sternly, which seemed to help a bit. Marcus came into her sight. "Why, Marcus?" she said with quivering lips. "How can you do this to me?"

Marcus came close to her and knelt by her, putting his hands on her knees. "Because I love you. I'm sorry, Allie, but you'll be safe here."

Allison shook her head. "I don't understand—safe from whom?"

"Safe from them," Marcus replied with a cold stare. "The ones that killed my Sheila, the ones that killed my boys. You will be safe from them."

"Who's going to protect me from you?" Allison yelled at Marcus. "You tied me up!"

"Only until I get back. It will be over soon, and then you can go. I just can't risk you interfering."

Marcus replied so calmly that it chilled Allison to the bone. He's insane, she thought as she looked into his eyes.

"Where are you going?" she asked through unwelcome tears.

"I have a score to settle." Marcus was talking with such an absolute lack of emotion, Allison didn't recognize him at all.

"With who?" Allison tried again, trembling. "Marcus?"

"Come on, Allie, think! You must know! As smart as you are, I know you know."

She did know. It was Jeremiah Dean and Phil Warner. It had to be.

"Dean and Warner" she said quietly. You're going to kill them, aren't you?"

"That's my Allie! Of course, you're only half right because Mr. Warner already saved me the trouble of killing Mr. Dean."

Allison looked at him and the confusion on her face made Marcus smile. It was not the smile that Allison had seen so often before the crash; it was an eerie smile, a smile that scared her.

"That's right. Phil Warner killed Jeremiah Dean. I followed them to their cabin retreat. I was going to kill them there, but Phil Warner changed my plans. I saw them out in their boat and I saw Warner drop Dean in the water after he had passed out. Warner had drugged him. I filmed it, and I have the evidence of the drugs and the film, so the game changed.

In fact, he's given me a way to win the lawsuit after all. I can get my client his fifty million dollar settlement, and our firm can get paid what we're owed." Allison couldn't believe what she was hearing.

"You're blackmailing them?" she asked incredulously. "How is that going to work? You'll have to explain where you got the funds, you know that."

Marcus shook his head, "Nothing will get reported. I found a way."

Allison was flabbergasted. "So you're going to kill Phil Warner? How? Where? When?"

"I'm going to kill both Phil *and* Blaine Warner, to be exact. They're coming up here to meet me. They think they're getting the video evidence in exchange for the funds. I'm sure they mean to kill me as well, but I don't think I'll allow them the satisfaction."

He was smiling again, and it was making Allison's skin crawl.

"Why do you have Darrin's key? Why involve him? He didn't do anything."

"Really, Allie? He's a Warner. Even if he hasn't done anything yet, he will. They're corrupt, they're killers, and they murdered my family! I won't kill Darrin, but I figured he might as well take the fall; he can do prison time to atone for his family. It was so easy, Allie. He's in jail right now for Simon's murder, and the evidence is there. He's going away for a long time. You couldn't possibly think I would allow him to continue seeing you."

At that, Allison turned cold. "Tell me everything right now, Marcus. Did you kill Simon?"

Marcus laughed. "You know I did, and you know I killed Diane Parker and John Wainwright. You just wouldn't allow yourself to believe it. I also killed that sleaze ball lawyer that got John involved.

Think about it, Allie. I know how smart you are. In fact, why don't you tell me how it happened? If you can't, well, then I guess I overestimated you."

Allison studied Marcus's face. He had lost all sanity and he needed help, the reality of which was breaking her heart.

She began, "You knew that Elizabeth Dean was in Simon's apartment, and that's why you didn't kill him the first time you were there. You either saw her go in while you were waiting or heard her once you got there. Suddenly, you had an alibi to convince them you weren't a killer. After sitting at the bar until closing and, likely pretending to be more drunk than you were, you drove over, shot him, and went back to the hotel. The only reason you made your little list was to distract my focus. You needed me to believe your theory so I would divert attention away from you."

Allison could see she was right as he looked at her proudly.

"You went to the detective in Marietta to tell your story and to convince him you weren't guilty while I went to talk to Elizabeth and Diane. You didn't care what Elizabeth had to say as long as I got Diane Parker's name from her and could then bring her out in the open so you could kill her. She knew about the Dean & Warner fraud, and you knew it; you've held her accountable all these years for not saying anything then that could have prevented the accident in the first place."

"That's why you were late getting to the airport, and that's why you had a checked bag, the bag you hadn't told me about. You needed the bag to transport your gun. Your gun, the one that you said was stolen and that you planted in Darrin's car. Tell me, Marcus, how did you get Darrin's key? That's one thing I can't figure out."

Marcus was enjoying this. He was proud of his work and even more proud of his little sister; she was smarter than the detective in Marietta and way smarter than that federal agent.

"It was easier than you think, but it happened by accident. I hadn't planned on putting the gun in his car until Jessica followed you the day you went to Ludington. If you hadn't noticed, Darrin kept the fob in his truck; unlocking it with the code on the door. She was right next to him when he got in his car, and she memorized the code. That was it; nothing else to it.

That, in fact, turned out to be a big break as it helped convince the fed he was guilty, especially after he thought he saw Darrin follow you to Pentwater."

Marcus almost chuckled at the memory.

"Oh, Marcus!" Allison said sadly. "Why include Jessica? How could you?"

"Come on, Allie." Marcus's smile was gone now. "You know how much she loved Sheila and the boys. She was my right hand on that lawsuit, so she knew what was going on, and she came to me. She was a huge help."

"Ok, so it was you in Darrin's truck and you stashed the gun, but what about the flight? Who was on the charter flight out of Muskegon? I know it wasn't you because you were already in Marietta. So who was it?"

Marcus didn't say anything. He just gave her the look, the look that said, "Come on, Allison, you know this." Allison thought for a minute before she figured it out.

"Jessica," she said, not as a question but as an answer.

She knew it was Jessica. Marcus was practically beaming, and it sickened Allison to see him do it.

"And she drugged me that night." Allison again was not asking.

Marcus nodded. "She drugged you both. She put the pills in a bottle of wine and left in on the counter, and then we just had to hope you both drank it. You didn't disappoint. After that she got on the plane, dressed as a man. When she got there, she went to a diner for a few hours and then flew back. Simple."

Allison was dumbfounded; it was simple when you put it all together—simple but terrifying. How could this be her brother? That was simple, too; he wasn't. This person, who committed those murders and was using his own sister to help cover it up, who had her drugged and even tied her up? This was not her brother, not really.

"So, the surveillance devices I found at the cottage and the house?" Allison asked.

Marcus shrugged. "I'm sure Dean & Warner had planted some there during the lawsuit, but they'd probably been removed, so I just staged some of my own in order to add more credibility to my innocence. Again, you were the only one to research that. Well done."

Marcus glanced at his watch. "I'm sorry about everything, Allie, but it's almost over. It seems so obvious when you already know someone is guilty. That's why I had to have you with me; you would never believe I could do all this, so you single-handedly convinced the fed of my innocence. Soon you can go about your life again."

"But what about you?" Allison cried out. "You're going to go to jail for the rest of your life!"

Marcus laughed. "Come on, Allie. Simon killed three people and spent less than three years in minimum security. Why should I serve any longer? But, don't worry. I won't be going to jail. This will all just be a bad memory, and then we can start healing from the pain we both feel. Now I have to go."

Marcus started toward the door.

"Marcus!" she screamed, and then he was gone.

74

Bruce and Darrin were in Michigan now. They had switched places when they had gotten gas an hour before, and Bruce was driving. Darrin stared out the window in silence. He was thinking about the dream he had had last night.

It was a dream he had quite often. Actually, it was a nightmare, although based on a true memory, where a decision he made had killed two of his men. It was the worst experience of his years in service, even though he was given a medal of honor for that day. He had not so much as looked at that medal since the day he'd received it.

After Sam and Carter were gunned down, Darrin attacked the remaining al-Qaeda. He stormed the last shelter and killed all seven men that were still inside. The last was done with his bare hands since his ammunition was gone.

Darrin's squad had killed twenty-two men and had lost two; the Army deemed the skirmish a success. But Darrin wished with all his heart they had been sent to a different location that day. Then his men may still be alive. On the night Allison wanted to be picked up from the airport he had gone to visit Sam's family. Sam was from Lansing Michigan and Darrin took advantage of the proximity to see his wife and kids. It was a painful night but he was glad that he had gone. Unfortunately he had no alibi for the Wainright murder as he was driving back to Grand Rapids at the time of the shooting.

Every day since Sam and Carters deaths, Darrin lived with the questions: Should he have waited with his team for air support? Was he trying to be a hero? If faced with that situation again, would he act or wait for backup? He didn't know the answers to any of them.

When he left the Army, he tried to forget everything he had seen and done. He didn't want to be that person. The one that could hurt and kill, and he certainly didn't want that person around his family.

He was worried about what today would bring; he was especially worried about Allison. One thing he knew for sure. If saving Allison from harm meant hurting someone else, well, he wouldn't want to be that someone else.

Bruce looked over at Darrin.

"Don't fall asleep on me," he said lightly.

Darrin turned and looked back at Bruce and shook his head. "I won't."

Darrin tried to call Allison again. He had called her many times during the drive so far, but each one went straight to her voicemail. This time he was excited that the call went through, but after several rings it also went to her voicemail.

"Still voicemail, but her phone must at least be on now. It rang first this time."

Bruce frowned when he heard the update. They needed to find her before it was too late.

"We should start at her condo and see where that leads us." Bruce was grasping for straws. He knew he was foolish for taking a prisoner out of lockup, let alone along on what could be a wild goose chase. If nothing good came from it, he would have a lot of explaining to do, and his explanation, at the very least, could find him unemployed.

"No," Darrin said with conviction, "we need to go to Pentwater. Allison is there."

Darrin was looking at his phone as he spoke.

"Why?" Bruce's voice immediately changed as a he felt a spark hope.

Darrin looked over at the detective. He had a lot of respect for this man, a man willing to risk so much for someone he didn't know. Darrin wasn't going to let him down.

"There's activity at their cottage. Someone came and went a few times today. It's a bearded man in a jeep."

Bruce was confused. "How do you know that?" he asked. There was no mistaking the optimism in his voice.

Darrin paused. "When the fed came to arrest me, I called a friend. I served with him in the Army, and I trust him with my life. I asked him to find and protect Allison. I told him about the three places that I knew about: her work, her condo, and her brother's cottage. He just messaged me; he hasn't found her yet, but he told me there was activity at the cottage. Allison is up there. I know it."

Bruce nodded. "Ok, Pentwater it is then."

Darrin replied to Tyler to let him know he was coming up. "Tyler is at a little place called The Antler. It's a bar-slash-restaurant in downtown Pentwater. I'll let him know we'll pick him up when we get there."

75

Marcus was waiting; he was excited that his plan was finally coming to fruition. There were a lot of things that could go wrong, but he had spent countless hours planning, and the end was in sight. He was sitting high above the state park on Old Baldy.

Old Baldy was a large sand dune, the top of which afforded guests a beautiful view of the beach and the channel that connected Pentwater Lake to Lake Michigan. He had climbed the dune many times as a child, huffing and puffing all the way up the 300-foot hill. When he was young, he didn't notice the view. Instead he would make it to the top, turn around, and head right back down running.

He would start out running slowly but his legs would pick up speed. Soon they would be propelling him down too fast for his body and he would fall in a heap, covering himself in sand and rolling the rest of the way, laughing the whole time.

His boys had run down the dune in the same fashion probably hundreds of times over the years. Now when he looked at the dune, all it did was bring sadness; it brought back memories that were no longer fond, but painful reminders not only of the loss of his two laughing boys, but reminders of a life he used to enjoy.

Over the years, the Parks Department had built a wide stairway that wound through the woods to the north of the dune, close to the top, making Old Baldy accessible for more than just the young and fit. There were even benches to rest on every so often. Once you had ascended the staircase, there was a final, short, walking path through some woods to the very top.

It was on this path, near the top of the dune, where his plan would unfold. The dune was deserted until June, making it the perfect spot. He just had to make the call.

76

Blaine parked the car in the parking lot at the state park, and he and his father stared at the water in silence. The sun was setting, and the beauty of it was amazing. Blaine couldn't have cared less. He was anxious for the call that was supposed to come. He was burning to put this guy down and the blackmail scheme he brought with him. It may cost them fifty million dollars, but at this point, that seemed a small price. He would pay it, but he would ensure the scum bag would never be able to spend it.

When the phone finally rang, Blaine could feel his adrenaline spike. He was excited.

"Yes?" Blaine answered.

"On the north side of the campground, there's a stairway up the dune. It's an easy climb, so Phil can handle it. Follow the path at the top of the stairs to the top of the dune. I'm waiting here." Marcus hung up.

"We have to go," Blaine said to his father.

"Where?" Phil asked sternly.

"We have to take a hike. Just stay close to me."

Blaine's guys were still over an hour away, so they would have to do this on their own. They found the opening between the campsites where the stairway started. The sun was low, but there was still light pouring up from the horizon beyond the water. The stairway through the woods, however, was already dark. They made their way up carefully as their eyes adjusted to the dusk. Soon, they could see well enough to navigate the stairs, the breaks in the trees allowing some much-welcomed light. As they reached the top of the stairs, there was a lookout point to the right. Phil sat down on the bench and gazed across at the lake. He held a finger up to Blaine.

"I need just a minute."

Blaine looked around; he could see the pathway through the trees that led to their rendezvous location. "Ok, but just a minute," he said, not caring that his father was tired.

Marcus couldn't see them but he knew right where they were. He sat near the top of Old Baldy, waiting patiently. He was sitting on a tree limb that had fallen from an old oak tree. Under the circumstances, one might've expected him to be nervous, but he wasn't. In fact, he was excited and, strangely enough, happy. Tonight, he was either going to destroy the men that destroyed his life or see his own pain come to an end. He was doing what should be done. What needed to be done.

In the darkness, Marcus saw the men in the shadows and heard their footsteps as they drew closer. Marcus moved into position.

77

Allison struggled to get free. She needed to get out and call the police. Marcus needed to be stopped before he did anything else. Her brother needed help, and she needed to get it for him. She was gaining some slack and was able to stretch and loosen one of the shoe strings her brother had used to tie her up. After over an hour of struggling, her right hand was almost free. With all her strength, she pulled her right arm up. The pain of the string digging into her skin was intense, but she continued. She squeezed her hand together and pulled again. Her hand slowly worked out of the string and suddenly, it was free.

She quickly untied herself, got up, and looked for her phone. Where was it? She had it when Marcus had come in. She remembered dropping it by the couch. She crouched down and found it underneath. She picked it up quickly, and checked the missed calls.

"Darrin?" she said aloud. Darrin had called seven times. She knew she needed to call the police, but instead, she dialed Darrin first. She was trembling now.

"Allison!" Darrin's voice on the other end of the phone was an immense comfort, but even so, she started to cry.

"Allie, where are you?"

Allison knew she had to pull herself together. "I'm in Pentwater, but not at Marcus's cottage. I'm at a cottage on the south side of Pentwater Lake."

Darrin was relieved beyond belief to hear her voice. "I'm with a detective and we're almost there. Send me your address, and we'll be there in less than twenty minutes!"

Allison was shocked. "How did you—"

"Never mind that," Darrin interrupted her. "Just send me the address. We'll be there shortly. Are you alone?"

"Yes, I'm alone right now."
"Ok. Stay calm. We'll be right there"

78

"That's close enough." Marcus's voice was clearly audible to the two Warner men.

"What now?" Phil shouted back, aimed in the direction of the hidden man's voice. "We did what you asked, the money is transferred, and it's just waiting on confirmation. That's fifty million dollars! It will be yours with one push of a button from our phone. Now, delete the video."

"Throw your guns forward!"

The command came from in front of them. They could make out the silhouettes of trees straight ahead and to the left. To the right there was a wide opening that led to the top of the dune. It was eerily light on the dune from the moon and stars. There was about twenty-five feet of the six-foot-wide path before they would reach the opening.

"I don't have a gun!" Phil shouted back.

Blaine grabbed Phil's gun and threw it forward. "There, that's mine. Now what?"

The gun landed in the opening at the end of the path. The moonlight that was shining through the opening looked almost like a spotlight. Blaine continued, "We don't want any trouble. We just want to settle up and leave."

"Ok, come to the opening," said the voice from the woods.

Phil and Blaine were eager to get to the light of the dune and out of the suffocating darkness of the path so they quickly obeyed. The two were so transfixed on the opening, they never saw the fruits of Marcus's day of labor.

If they'd have been there earlier that morning, they would have seen Marcus with his shovel and a ladder. He used the shovel to dig a six-foot-deep by five-foot-wide hole. The ladder was to help him climb out when he was finished. The digging had been relatively easy in the light sand, but it had taken Marcus five hours.

Marcus had then loosely covered the hole with light sticks that would serve two purposes. The first was the obvious: camouflaging the hole. The second was to aid in the death of two of the most evil men he had ever met.

It would have been hard for Phil and Blaine to see the hole in the darkness, and their haste to get into the light made it impossible. Blaine had been leading the way and went crashing through, landing with a thud. Phil had been a touch slower and managed to stop in his tracks, but a well-thought-out plan had accounted for this, and a timely push from behind sent Phil in to join his son, crumpled in a heap on a pile of broken sticks. The two men had no sooner hit the bottom of the pit, when they were doused with two buckets of gasoline.

Blaine yelled. "Wait! Wait! What about the money? You can't do this!"

"Throw out your gun," Marcus yelled from the side of the hole, out of view from the men.

"Ok, ok." Blaine was in a panic now and threw out another gun.

Marcus lit a Zippo lighter and walked to the side of the hole.

"Now your keys."

Blaine grabbed the rental key from his pocket and threw it out.

"If I see you have another weapon, you better believe me, I *will* drop this lighter."

"We have nothing else!" Blaine cried out.

Marcus slowly got to the edge of the hole. The flame cast a light that lit up the whole area out of the sheer darkness. The two Warner men were bleeding from the fall on the sticks and were soaked with gasoline. Phil sat still on the bottom but Blaine had stood up, the top of his head just below ground level.

"Push your button," Marcus said. "Confirm the transaction."

Blaine scrambled for his phone as Marcus held the lighter above him. Blaine dutifully found it and sent the confirmation. Marcus took out his phone and checked the account; it was there.

"Thank you," he said to them politely.

"Great, can we go now?" Blaine stammered. He didn't care about the video anymore.

"Do you know who I am?" Marcus moved in closer and held the

lighter up. He no longer was wearing the beard or the camouflaged clothing. There was instant gratification for Marcus as he could see in the eyes of the men that they indeed recognize who he was.

"Why did you kill my family?" Marcus asked with an eerie calmness that revealed to Blaine just how crazy he was. The person holding that lighter over Blaine's gas-soaked body was without a doubt planning on dropping it. How could Blaine save his own life? What could he say that would stop this person from inflicting on him the most gruesome death he could imagine? Blaine was terrified.

"Please," he begged, "we had no idea Simon was going to kill them. We told him to scare you, that's all! Please, you have to believe me!"

Blaine was sobbing now. Phil just sat there not saying a word; Marcus turned his questioning to him.

"What about you? What do you say?" Phil looked up at him and his broken spirit was visible in his eyes. He was going to die, right here and right now. He knew it and had accepted it. It pissed him off that this slick lawyer was the end of him, but he took solace in the fact that he knew he had it coming. "Fuck you!" Phil spat up at him from the bottom of his tomb. He sat there, a crumpled old man, broken and cut up waiting for the end. Blaine looked at his father in horror; it was as if Phil wanted to die.

"Do you have any idea the torment I feel wondering if my family was still alive when the fire started? Did they burn to death? I try to convince myself that they were dead from the impact. Can you imagine that conflict going on in my head?"

At that moment both men knew what was about to happen and they looked at each other. Phil lowered his head but Blaine looked up at Marcus just in time to see Marcus drop the lighter. The flames flew up high as the heat and their screams filled the night sky. Marcus sat on the ground and started to cry. Jessica stepped out of the darkness and laid a hand on Marcus's shoulder, one of the hands she had used to push Phil Warner into the pit to his painful death.

"It's all over," she said. The screams were gone now and the fire was just smoldering. Jessica helped Marcus stand, and they both grabbed shovels from behind the oak and started filling in the hole.

"We will never speak of this again," she said as they continued to hide the evidence of what had just happened, one shovelful after another until the hole and everything onside it was gone. Marcus picked up the weapons and the rental car key and they headed down the dune. They reached the car and drove to the cottage where Jessica got out and got into the jeep. She then followed Marcus to a secluded spot on the lake where Marcus knew they could dump the car. Marcus stopped the Cadillac at the top of the hill facing the water, put the guns in the glove box, and stepped out. He put the car in drive, and they watched it plummet down the one-hundred-foot hill into the deep water below.

79

When Bruce and Darrin arrived at the lake cottage, Allison ran out to meet them. She threw herself into Darrin's arms and he hugged her tight.

"It's ok, I'm here now," he said to her as he held her close.

Allison wanted to stay there in his arms forever. Bruce waited a few moments for the two to reunite before he interrupted.

"Where's Marcus?" Allison and Darrin separated and she looked at the stranger that had asked the question.

"Detective Harper?" she asked.

"Yes, ma'am, please call me Bruce." His voice was soft and gentle for such a large man.

Allison held out her hand. "Bruce, I'm Allison Deters."

Bruce reached out and shook her hand and smiled.

"Where's Marcus, Allison?" Bruce asked her again.

"I don't know, he may be at his cottage but I'm not sure, he left a while ago. Please, we need to find him, he's not well and I think he's in trouble."

Bruce opened the back door for her. "Ok, let's go find him."

"Let's start at his cottage," Darrin demanded.

Bruce looked over at Darrin. "We can pick up Tyler on the way."

Darrin nodded his head. "I will call him right now."

Allison was watching the detective from the back seat. She was trying to get a read on him and figure out what kind of person he was. Her first impression had been positive. He seemed friendly, smart, and caring, but why was he here? She knew who he was; he was the detective from Marietta that Marcus had told her to send the letter to if she didn't hear from him, but why was he here now?

She cut to the chase. "Why are you here, Detective?" she asked bluntly.

The detective turned slightly and caught a glimpse of Allison.

"Because Marcus took me for a fool and then I acted like one. Because I believed his lies from day one, and now I need to make it right."

Allison looked at his face in the mirror; it was illuminated by the street lights as they drove through the small town of Pentwater. He was a good man, Allison could tell. And she couldn't lose any respect for someone that had believed her brother. She knew Marcus better than anyone else and had fallen victim to his ruse as well, but what impressed her most was the detective's ability to see past the tricks and not jump in head first like she and Skip had.

"How did you know?" she asked the detective. "How did you know it was Marcus?"

Bruce looked at Allison in the mirror and could see the pain in her eyes.

"It was the letter from you. Or, I should say, supposedly from you. I received an email signed from you that had the details of the case written out perfectly for me. Details that only proved Marcus was innocent. After reading it I decided there were two possibilities. One, you wrote it and everything you said was true, or two, Marcus wrote it and he was trying to look innocent."

"So, I answered it with a test, a test that only you could have passed. I told you to tell Skip I was coming to Michigan to help in the investigation. There is no way that Skip wouldn't have called me and cussed me up and down for even suggesting that I would do that. When he didn't call, I knew it wasn't you that sent it. Was It?"

Allison shook her head.

"So, it must have been Marcus, and I'd already let him walk right out of my station. I'm not too happy about that. That's why I asked Darrin to help me find you and Marcus. In doing so, I'm risking my career, but I have to find your brother before he kills anyone else."

Allison remained quiet as she took in what the detective had said. It all made sense. The truth was always right in front of you; choosing to believe it was often the trickiest part. It was once impossible for her to believe that Marcus had killed anyone, but once she accepted it to be true, everything else logically fell into place.

Bruce continued, "I do have a question for you, though."

Allison's eyes met his in the mirror again. "Yes, what is it?" She replied softly, curious where this was going.

"Do you know any female that would have helped him?"

80

Marcus and Jessica had made it back to the cottage. They put the shovels back in the shed and Marcus locked it up. The jeep Marcus was driving was parked a couple of cottages down; he didn't want anyone to see it up front, and he had his pick of empty cottages to park it at. They went inside to wash up but kept the lights off. Marcus grabbed Jessica by the arm and pulled her down. There was a car coming. He could see the lights penetrating the darkness. Marcus watched as the car turned down the road toward his place and passed by right in front of it; it was the same car he had seen at his office a few days before. There were two men in it.

It was moving slowly by his cottage and he could see them looking in his direction. The car continued on and parked at the Dean & Warner-owned cottage at the end of the street. He watched as the two men got out and walked up to the rental property, and he immediately knew who they were. They worked for the Warners, and Marcus started to wonder if they, too, had been involved with his crash three years ago.

Marcus turned to Jessica and said, "Stay put. I'm going to check that out."

Jessica's eyes opened wide and she shook her head vehemently, showing her concern. "No way, Marcus. You can't go over there."

Marcus raised his gun so she could see it. "I'll be fine, just stay put and keep down."

Marcus left his cottage by the back door and walked quickly to the rental at the end of the road. He made sure he wasn't spotted by walking behind the cottages and staying away from the light being cast down by the two nearby streetlights. When he got to the rear of the cottage, he peeked in the windows.

The two men looked to be right at home as the lights were on and they were walking around the cottage freely. Marcus could see that the taller one was listening on his cell phone, not talking. He set his phone down. He must have tried to call one of the Warners. Good luck getting a hold of them, Marcus thought.

Marcus went to the far side of the rental and made his way to the porch. It was the same porch that Allison and Darrin had connected so well on over coffee the week before. He quietly opened the door and stepped inside, all the while keeping his eyes fixed on the pair inside the kitchen. Marcus could see that one of the men had set a gun down on the counter; the other, the taller man, had one visible in a holster.

The man with the holster was talking, and Marcus was close enough to hear him.

"I don't know, what do you think we should do? Blaine won't answer his phone."

The other man opened the refrigerator and looked inside; he frowned at what he saw.

"No beer," he said ignoring the question.

"Come on, Hawkins. Quit screwing around. What should we do?"

Hawkins looked over at the taller man with the holstered gun.

"We wait here until the boss calls," he answered as he pulled out some juice from the fridge. He untwisted the lid and sniffed the carton, tilting his head back and forth while weighing the risk of taking a drink.

Marcus was well inside the cottage now; his gun was pointed at the man with the holster, and he walked slowly toward him. He was only a few feet away when the man noticed him. Hawkins had his back to Marcus as he was pulling out a glass from the cupboard. Marcus kept the gun pointed directly into the taller man's face.

"Hawkins," the man with the holstered gun said as he raised both his arms.

Hawkins turned around and immediately saw Marcus standing there with a gun two feet from his partners' face.

Marcus looked at him and said quietly, "Get on your knees, both of you."

The two men slowly bent down and rested on their knees. Marcus went to the man with the holstered gun and took his weapon, keeping his gun pointed directly at his face. He then tucked the newly acquired weapon in his pants and proceeded to the gun on the counter. He picked it up and unloaded it as the two gunmen sat on the ground and watched.

Hawkins knew exactly who they were dealing with. He and Alex had been hiding out in this very cottage some three years ago keeping surveillance on this man; they had watched him and his family for months, listening to countless conversations with hidden devices. He had also stayed in a house behind this man's home in Grand Rapids.

Hawkins had been the main relay of information on Marcus Deters to the Warners. He had also been the one that threatened Simon and his family and then rigged Marcus's van so it would burst into flames. Hawkins was the Warners' go-to.

"Hello, Marcus," he said calmly.

81

Bruce Harper's car pulled to the curb in front of The Antler. There was a man standing outside, and Allison was shocked to recognize him as the man that was at her condo the day before. Darrin got out and gave him a quick embrace. Allison couldn't help but smile as she became aware of the bond between them. She didn't know it then, but it was a bond that was more than just friendship, a bond built by years of living together under extreme conditions and putting their lives on the line together. Darrin and Tyler were more than brothers and more than friends. They had a relationship that only people who had survived combat could understand.

They both got into the car, and Darrin introduced Tyler to Allison and Bruce.

"Glad to meet you, sir," he said to the detective.

Bruce nodded. "Same here."

Then Tyler turned to Allison and reached his hand out to her. She took it and gave it a shake.

"And you as well," he said with a genuine smile.

Allison smiled back. "Thank you for your help."

Tyler turned back around. "Turn left here," he said to Bruce. "Beach Street is about a half mile up on the right. We should start there."

As they turned onto Beach Street, Allison yelled out, "There's the jeep he was driving."

They all looked simultaneously at the jeep parked up the road. They drove past the jeep and went to Marcus's cottage. There were no lights on as they pulled up to it. They stopped on the street in front.

Bruce said, "Maybe I should check it out. You guys stay with Allison."

Tyler looked at Darrin. "I'll go with him."

Darrin nodded and the two men got out of the car. He didn't want to ask anyone to go with him, but Bruce was glad to have Tyler backing him up. They quickly walked up to the cottage. Bruce had his gun drawn and was ready for anything. In all his years on the force, he had never fired his weapon, and he was desperately hoping that this wouldn't be the first.

They reached the front door and gingerly peered inside. It seemed there was nothing to see. Bruce shone his flashlight through the window. Tyler and Bruce immediately looked at each other. There were footprints on the tile floor, sandy dirty footprints, and they were easily visible when the beam of light hit them. Furthermore, there were two different sizes.

Bruce checked the door; it was locked. He motioned for Tyler to back up, and then Bruce gave the door a hard kick. The door flung open. They both carefully entered the dark cottage. They heard a startled scream when they entered, and Bruce rapidly moved toward the sound he'd just heard. The bathroom door was closed, so he put his hand on the knob and when he tried to turn it, he found it locked.

"Police, open up!" Bruce yelled through the closed door.

Bruce and Tyler could hear someone behind the door, and Bruce yelled again.

"Police, open up or we will bust the door down."

They heard footsteps and then the lock was unlatched. Bruce stepped back with his gun drawn as Jessica opened the door.

82

"You know me?" Marcus asked. He was curious but not surprised.

The two men were both kneeling before him and he had a gun pointed directly at them.

"How do you know me?" Marcus knew the answer but he needed to hear it from them. The one named Hawkins just smiled at him and the other stared with terror in his eyes.

"Tell me who you are and how you know me." he repeated. Hawkins just kept smiling, infuriating Marcus to no end. Being more nervous, the taller one started to talk.

"I don't know you," he lied. "This is the first time I've ever seen you."

Marcus pressed the gun against the man's head.

"What did you say?" he asked the trembling man.

"Please," the man begged, "please, I don't know who you are."

Hawkins was looking at the trembling man with disgust.

"Come on, Alex. Don't you remember the guy we came here to kill?" he asked his partner.

Alex stared back at Hawkins with disbelief in his eyes. Marcus looked at Alex who was trying so hard not to show his fear but was failing miserably. Marcus wondered how many times Alex had been the one holding the gun? How many people had he scared or killed for the Warners?

"Tell me what I need to know, Alex." Marcus said.

Alex just shook his head. "I don't know anything."

Marcus turned his eyes on Hawkins. He had already admitted that he knew him; the question now was how much did he know? Marcus assumed he knew a lot. Hawkins was looking back at him with such a calm, cocky look, it gave Marcus some pause. Hawkins was not afraid. In that instant, Marcus pulled the trigger and ended Alex's life. His body slumped to the ground, and blood poured out over the kitchen floor. Marcus turned to Hawkins and pointed the gun in his face.

"Now, how do you know me?" Marcus scowled.

Hawkins smirked as he looked at his dead partner.

"I know you because we were sent here to help the boss kill you. I'm guessing we're too late to help him. I assume you took care of him already?"

Marcus didn't say a word; he just kept staring.

Hawkins shrugged. "Anyway, I know a lot more about you than that. I was there when your family died in that crash. I know everything about it."

Marcus was desperate to hear more. "Like what?"

Hawkins again calmly shrugged, "The way I see it, my information is the only leverage I got. If I tell you now, I'm a dead man."

Marcus hated the fact that this man was right. He wouldn't kill him until he heard everything. The knowledge this man had wouldn't bring his family back, it may even make it more painful, but he had to know. He had to know everything.

Hawkins continued, "I know about the lawsuit and the fraud. I know who, what, where, why, and how. I know it all, and the only way I tell you anything is if you let me walk out of here."

Marcus was tormented. As far as he was concerned, this was his last piece of the puzzle. If he killed Hawkins, there would be nothing left to do. When the police came, he would simply start acting out his alibi. In a few years, he would most certainly be free. Nobody would blame him for going insane after what he'd been though. It would be easy.

He held the gun closer to Hawkins' head. The steel barrel was grazing his temple; he leaned down so their faces were just inches apart.

"Do you have kids?" Marcus asked softly.

Hawkins looked up at Marcus, and as he did, Marcus made up his mind.

"No!" Hawkins yelled in his face, swiping at Marcus's gun as he did. Shortly thereafter, a shot rang out as the gun discharged.

83

Darrin and Allison were watching closely from the car. They watched as the detective kicked in the door and the two men slowly entered the cottage, weapons drawn. It was then that Allison noticed something odd. There was a small amount of light coming from the cottage on the end of the street; it was the cottage that Darrin had been at. She nudged Darrin and pointed. Darrin looked and saw the light as well.

"It looks like there's a light on in the kitchen."

The kitchen was at the back of the cottage so the light was just a faint glow, barely visible from where they were parked.

"Marcus?" Allison asked.

Darrin shrugged. "Who knows? I don't think I left any lights on."

Suddenly they heard a shot coming from that direction. They both jumped out of the car and ran up to Marcus's cottage. They met Bruce, Tyler, and Jessica at the front door.

"Did you hear that?" Darrin asked Bruce.

"I heard it. Where did it come from?" Bruce was still holding on to Jessica's arm.

"I think it came from the cottage on the end of the street," Darrin told him.

"Marcus is there!" Jessica burst out. "You need to help him!"

Bruce and Darrin ran in the direction of the rental cottage.

Bruce yelled to Tyler, "Get those girls out of here!"

Tyler grabbed Allison and Jessica and headed toward the car.

"Darrin!" Allison shrieked as he disappeared between the cottages.

84

Marcus looked out the window and saw three people walking the other way down the street. He knew who the two women were; it was Allison and Jessica. But there was also a third person, a man that he didn't know that was leading them away.

Marcus had crawled over to the window and was bleeding badly from a blow to his head, a blow delivered by the man who was about to lose his life. Marcus had made up his mind he was going to kill Hawkins even without learning the horrible details he might reveal. In a split second, Marcus had decided he didn't need to know, or even want to know anymore; he just wanted this whole thing to be over.

But before he pulled the trigger, Hawkins had knocked Marcus's arm back with his left hand, grabbed the coffee pot off the counter with his right and hit Marcus as hard as he could in the forehead. As Hawkins ran off, Marcus was able to fire one shot that struck him in the back shoulder. Hawkins had made it out the side door anyway.

Now, after crawling to the front window, Marcus was watching the three people walking away. The street lights cast just enough light to make them identifiable. Allie! he thought, but how? Marcus held out his hand and rested it on the window glass. He grabbed hold of the window sill and pulled himself up. Where had Hawkins gone?

Detective Harper stayed close to the cottage. He wanted to make sure that no one could see him coming if they were looking through the picture window. He quickly made his way to the front door and grabbed hold of the knob. To his surprise, it turned. Suddenly, Bruce was in the cottage. Marcus hadn't seen him coming as he was focused on Allison and Jessica, so he was startled when he saw the detective from Marietta in the living room pointing his gun at him.

"Marcus, it's Detective Harper. Drop the gun."

Marcus had almost forgotten he was holding a gun. He looked at the detective and threw the gun down toward the kitchen. All he could think of was how he had obviously underestimated the detective. Bruce looked in the direction of the gun, and just past it he could see the feet of someone lying down in the kitchen, blood pooling around them.

"Who else is…"

Before Bruce could finish his question, he was falling forward from the impact of a bullet in his back. It was Hawkins. He had retrieved another gun from his vehicle, saw the detective go into the cottage, and followed. Hawkins turned the gun on Marcus.

"Where is Blaine Warner?!" he shouted.

Marcus could only manage a blank stare.

"Where is he?!" Hawkins repeated. Marcus backed against the wall and slumped to the ground. The blow to his head was getting to him, and he was dizzy and exhausted. Hawkins walked up to him and kicked him. Marcus just kept staring up at him. Hawkins sneered.

"Let me tell you something before you die. It *was* Alex and I who killed your family. Or at least we helped. We put an accelerant by your gas tank and all it needed was a spark. It worked perfectly, except for the fact that you survived, but if you don't tell me where Blaine is, I'll change that right now."

Marcus stared at Hawkins with pure hatred. His heart broke again at hearing about the intentionality of the fire in the accident. Maybe they had survived the impact. It probably was the fire that killed them. He shuddered as the thought of it came back to him.

Bruce had fallen into the opening between the living room and the kitchen. He was conscious but he was not able to move. He heard everything the intruder had said to Marcus. The body that belonged to the feet he had seen earlier was now right in front of him. The man was dead, and Bruce feared he would be too if he didn't do something soon. He knew Darrin had gone around the back, but where was he? Just then, he got his answer. Darrin was tiptoeing through the side door from the porch. He nodded to Bruce as if to tell him he would be fine, and he quietly continued toward the living room.

"If you don't tell me where he is, you're dead!"

Hawkins was getting irritated with Marcus. He needed to find his boss. Not only was Blaine the reason he was so financially well off, but Blaine was also his friend.

"I'll count to three; then I'm going to shoot you in the knee. Then I'll count to three again, and if you still don't tell me, I'll shoot you again, but in won't be in the knee."

Hawkins took his gun and pointed it between Marcus's legs.

"Tell me where he is."

"Hawkins!" Darrin yelled from the kitchen.

Hawkins spun toward the voice calling his name. He recognized Darrin at once. Now he pointed the gun at Darrin; he knew Darrin was not to be messed with.

"I'm looking for Blaine and your father; they came up here to meet with him," Hawkins said as he pointed at Marcus, "and I haven't heard from them."

Darrin kept walking slowly toward Hawkins with his hands raised in the air. Marcus, though wounded and dizzy, watched the unarmed Darrin as he approached the two of them. He was amazed at how calm he was, even as he stepped over the detective's bleeding body, the detective who obviously had just been shot by the man he was confronting.

"I don't think they're here," Darrin said.

"I know that!" Hawkins spat back at Darrin. "But he knows. He knows where they are, he's just not telling me."

Darrin lowered his right hand slowly and pointed it at Marcus.

"Do you know where they are?" he asked Marcus.

Marcus shook his head as he looked at him. Darrin knew that his father and brother probably weren't coming back, but he never faltered.

"He says he doesn't know."

"Come on Darrin." Hawkins said. "You know he knows where they are, and if he doesn't tell me, I'm gonna blow his damn head off."

Darrin again looked at Marcus.

"Tell me where they are!" he suddenly yelled at him.

Marcus again, shook his head. "I don't know," he said quietly.

Darrin stepped closer to him. "Tell me where they are!" Darrin repeated.

Hawkins watched anxiously as Darrin closed in on Marcus. He was getting more and more curious. What was Darrin going to do? Was he going to beat the information out of him? Would he kill him if he didn't talk? He hadn't been in a situation with Darrin before, and he wondered if he could be as vicious as Blaine.

Marcus was in pain and his head was bleeding as he sat on the floor with his back against the wall. He warily watched Darrin as he approached. Darrin took another step, and now he was standing directly over Marcus and next to Hawkins. Hawkins watched with excitement, assuming Blaine's little brother was about to tear this lawyer apart.

"Tell me where…"

Before he finished his sentence, Darrin grabbed the gun in Hawkins hand and twisted. Hawkins was able to get off one shot before his wrist broke. The bullet struck the wall harmlessly, and Darrin quickly had Hawkins on the ground with his wrist painfully pressed against his own back. Darrin picked up the gun that Hawkins had dropped and pointed it at him while he stood him up.

"Are you ok?" he asked Marcus.

Marcus nodded and pointed to Bruce who was still lying on the floor but seemed to be conscious. "What about him? He needs help."

Darrin looked over at Bruce. "You both need help. I'll call the police and tell them we need two ambulances."

Marcus stood up and walked over to Bruce. "Detective Harper?" Marcus said. "Are you ok?"

Bruce was conscious and aware of everything that was going on around him.

"Where are they Marcus? Where are the Warners?"

Marcus stared right into the detective's eyes and smiled. "I don't know."

Darrin looked on with mixed emotions. If they were dead, they deserved it, of that he was sure. But they were still his family and their loss would be hard. Darrin grabbed his phone and called 911, and then he called Allison to tell her they were all safe.

Darrin took Detective Harper's handcuffs and secured Hawkins to the front porch railing. He didn't want to hold onto him until the police arrived. He and Marcus were able to roll Bruce over and get him comfortable while they waited for the ambulances. Allison arrived with Jessica and Tyler, and she ran up to Marcus. She threw her arms around him, and both of them started to cry.

"What were you thinking?" she asked him.

Marcus shook his head. "I'm sorry, Allie. I'm sorry you had to go through all this."

Marcus then put his lips to Allison's ear. "I never saw the Warners," he whispered.

She turned and saw Darrin watching them quietly with Tyler and Jessica. Allison went to Darrin and fell into his arms.

"I love you, Allie," Darrin said as he squeezed her tight.

The police and the ambulances arrived at about the same time. First, they put Bruce on a stretcher and into an ambulance headed for the hospital. Then they covered Alex's body and placed him in a second ambulance headed for the coroner. The police then started questioning the rest of them.

Marcus watched as one of the officer's unlocked Hawkins from the railing and started walking him toward a police car. Without detection, Marcus grabbed the gun that was on the floor, put it in his belt, and ran down to Hawkins and the officer that was leading him.

"Wait a minute!" Marcus yelled to the officer.

The officer turned with Hawkins and watched Marcus approach. Hawkins smiled haughtily at Marcus when he saw him coming.

"I need to ask him something," Marcus said to the officer.

The officer looked at him with confusion as he held Hawkins tight.

"Real quick," Marcus said to the officer.

The officer nodded as Marcus approached Hawkins and stood with him face to face.

"Why did you kill my family?" Marcus asked softly.

Hawkins grinned. "It was just business," he laughed.

Marcus pulled the gun quickly and fired three shots into Hawkins' chest.

Allison screamed as she watched her brother commit another murder. Marcus threw the gun down and his hands up in surrender even before Hawkins flopped to the ground. Two officers jumped on Marcus, pinning him down.

85

Tuesday, October 11, 2016. Allison was at her desk. Her work schedule was heavy and hectic, but that suited her just fine. She was in the middle of another securities fraud case, a type that had become somewhat of a passion for her. She hated to see hard working people get their money swindled away by greedy investors. While she was working, she received an email from a bank in Switzerland:

Dear Ms. Deters,

We are writing to inform you that an account on which you were listed as the secondary party has come to meet the terms set by its originator. After six months of no activity, all funds are to be made available to you. This time has elapsed, and we are notifying you of the funds since you have now become the primary holder of this account. We appreciate the opportunity to continue to service any financial needs you may have in the future. Please use this link to access your account statements at any time. Any withdrawals from this account must be accompanied by the secure password provided by the originator. If such a password is unknown, this must be addressed in person. Thank you in advance for your continued patronage.

Stephen Voltz
President
Stockholm Bank and Trust

When Allison finished reading, she sat back in her chair and thought for a moment. What account? From whom?

"Marcus?" she asked aloud.

She stared at it and pondered what to do. Finally, she sat up straight and clicked on the link. A greeting came up and asked for the account number which she entered on her screen. A second screen popped up asking for the password. What could it be? she wondered. She knew nothing about this account; how would she know the password? She thought about it hard for a bit, thinking of the possibilities: Sheila? The kids' names or birthdays?

No, that wouldn't be it; those were too simple. It would be something only she would know. Allison put the cursor on the password bar and began to type. *Reason number 4.* After a brief lull, the account activity and balance displayed, and Allison's jaw dropped. Balance: fifty million, one hundred and thirteen thousand, two hundred seventy-seven dollars, and forty-five cents.

As Allison looked at the figure in disbelief, her email notification chimed with another message from the bank, so she opened it.

Dear Allison,

This is a secure email that was instructed to be sent to you in the event that the Swiss account was ever opened. If you're reading this, I may be dead, and I'm truly sorry for that as I can only imagine how hard that is on you. The money you see in the account is from the Warners. It was a payout meant to keep me quiet, and maybe they chose to keep me quiet permanently and that's why you're reading this now. Whatever the case, you know what the money is for, and I hope you can transfer it accordingly. I'm sorry about all you have been through, and I hope you are able to live a happy life. Thank you for all you did during those weeks preceding my death. I know it was wrong of me to use you like that, but I could see no other way to accomplish all I needed to accomplish. Of course, if you were able to open the account, you remembered our talk about murder and the reasons for it. I must confess that I left out one reason; I left out reason number five. Why I did will be obvious to you. Reason number five, of course, is REVENGE. I always loved you, Allison, and I always will.

Your loving brother,

Marcus

P.S. If by some luck I'm not dead, will you visit me today and let me know you received this?

"No way," Allison said, wiping the tears from her eyes as she finished reading. She thought back to that night just six months ago.

She remembered how scared she had been. Not for herself, so much, but for Marcus, and for as sad and lonely as he was, she couldn't bear the thought of being without him.

Bruce had been in the hospital in Grand Rapids for more than three weeks before he could travel home. He was reprimanded but permitted to keep his job, despite the protestations of Agent Lamont. Good old Skip was going to have to keep looking for his breakthrough case as the misjudgments he made on this one damaged his career more than it helped it.

Allison smiled as she recalled how Agent Lamont had gotten chewed out for arresting the wrong suspect and failing to follow through on some simple leads. She'd thought he would have tried to track down Phil and Blaine Warner; that would have made the news. They had been missing ever since that early spring day. It was widely presumed they had fled the country with fifty million dollars after the video of them killing Jeremiah Dean hit the internet the same day they and the money from their account disappeared. Everyone assumed they were in hiding.

Now with the email from the overseas bank, Allison knew that Skip would never find the Warners, at least not alive.

Jessica only had to spend a few days in jail. Allison's firm had fast-tracked her trial, and the case against her was thrown out over lack of evidence. It was impossible to prove intent on her part for taking a plane ride her boss had told her to, and no even suspected she'd been the one to put the sleeping pills in the wine bottle.

Marcus was at a mental hospital under confinement. Despite the objections of Detective Harper, he was ruled mentally incapable of standing trial and was receiving treatments. Dr. Bryant devoted nearly all her time since to helping him recover. She remained hopeful that with enough therapy and care, Marcus would return fully to his previous self.

That thought brought Allison back to Marcus's last line of the email. *"If I'm not dead, will you visit me today?"* Allison and Darrin were already planning on seeing him tonight. Visiting hours were on Tuesdays and Thursdays, and Allison never missed. Marcus would just stare into space most of the time, but there were moments when he looked like his old self. Allison would swear she would see him looking at her with the same fondness of old.

"If I'm not dead, will you visit me today?" Allison said it out loud this time so she could hear the words. She shook her head in disbelief. "Unreal," she spoke again.

86

Darrin picked her up right at 4:00 p.m. They could visit from 5-6 p.m., and Allison always wanted to be there right at five. Darrin would go with her sometimes, when he could. It was always nice to have him along.

He had quit the family business before he even started, and in the wake of last April's events, he'd left Indiana entirely and took a job selling commercial real estate in Grand Rapids. He enjoyed it, and it gave him some flexibility to follow other pursuits as well. Allison's firm had used him a few times for surveillance on some cases they were working, and with his military training, he was very skilled at it and hoped to do more. He bought a little condo up the road from Allison's, and shortly thereafter, bought her a ring; their wedding was scheduled for the following May.

They entered the facility to see Marcus, passing quickly through the usual security checkpoints. After six months, they knew the routine well. As they walked down the hallway to the visitation room, they ran into Dr. Bryant.

"How's he doing today?" Allison asked the doctor.

Dr. Bryant smiled at Allison, nodded, and said, "Pretty well today. Sometimes, I swear he's right there, he's this close."

The doctor held her finger and thumb an inch apart for emphasis.

"That's great to hear. Thanks for all your hard work." Allison smiled at her and then continued down the bright hallway. Before they entered his room, they peered through the window and saw Marcus in his hospital clothes sitting in a chair just staring at the wall. As often as she had seen him like this, Allison couldn't get used it. The guard opened the door and let them in.

"Hi, Marcus," she said enthusiastically with a big smile.

Marcus just kept staring at the wall. Allison and Darrin both sat in chairs opposite Marcus. Allison had her usual one-sided conversation with him. She told him about everything going on at the firm, how their mom and dad were doing, the usual things. Marcus seemed to listen but showed no signs of understanding or caring. Finally, Allison brought up the bank account.

"I got an email from a Swiss bank today," she said to him, all the while watching closely for some sign of reaction. There was nothing. "It looks like we've got quite a pile of money in there, and I'm supposed to divvy it up between your old client and the firm. I guess I can get that done somehow."

Still there was no reaction.

"Well, you must have had a great plan, because here I am." Marcus's head turned slightly and he looked her in the eyes. His lips turned up slightly into a small smile, and in that moment, Allison could see the old light in Marcus's eyes. His smile got larger and he raised a finger to his lips.

"Shhh."

The End

Thank you to all my friends and family that have been so supportive over the last few years. Most of all, thank you to my amazing wife Michelle; I wish everyone could see the incredible strength and courage you have shown in dealing with both the loss of our daughter and in raising our granddaughter. Without you, I never would have been able to finish this book which was an overwhelming commitment that I made to Courtney, and one that I just had to fulfill. And to our son Jarod, who still gives us a reason to smile and to be so terribly proud.

Thank you to Heather Bulliss and Jackie Selvius for helping with the editing of this book.

Made in the USA
Lexington, KY
07 July 2017